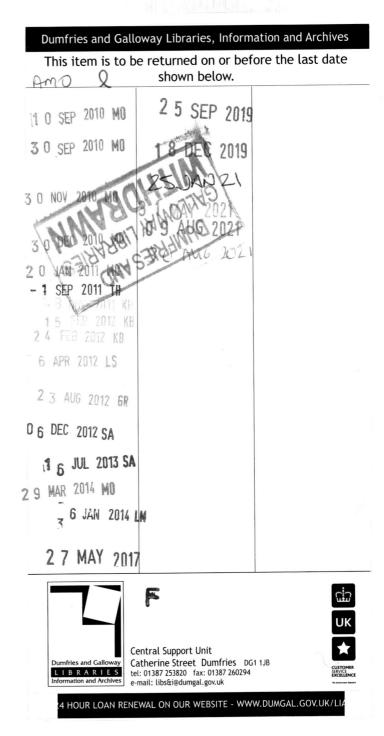

A CAUTIOUS APPROACH

A CAUTIOUS APPROACH

Stanley Middleton

HUTCHINSON
London

Published by Hutchinson 2010

2 4 6 8 10 9 7 5 3 1

First published in Great Britain in 2010 by
Hutchinson
Random House, 20 Vauxhall Bridge Road,
London SW1V 2SA

www.rbooks.co.uk

Addresses for companies within The Random House Group Limited can be found
at: www.randomhouse.co.uk/offices.htm

The Random House Group Limited Reg. No. 954009

A CIP catalogue record for this book
is available from the British Library

ISBN 9780091936952

The Random House Group Limited supports The Forest Stewardship
Council (FSC), the leading international forest certification organisation.
All our titles that are printed on Greenpeace approved FSC certified paper
carry the FSC logo. Our paper procurement policy can be found at:
www.rbooks.co.uk/environment

Typeset in Times by Palimpsest Book Production Limited,
Falkirk, Stirlingshire

Printed and bound in Great Britain by
CPI Mackays, Chatham ME5 8TD

I

Grey cloud darkened the sky this December morning though the weather was warm for the time of year. The man walking quickly through the gate of the public park looked upwards hoping to discern signs of a brighter future, but in vain. It had rained sharply less than an hour ago, and drops still hung if thinly on the hedgerows. The place seemed deserted.

The man, Norman George Taylor, glanced at his wristwatch. Half-past nine on this Christmas morning. Taylor pulled his mouth into a grimace of distaste.

Back in the streets he had met an old woman, dangling a paper carrier bag from her fingers, who made no reply to his cheerful greeting, and almost immediately afterwards a middle-aged adult male, holding tightly on to the back of the seat of a child's fairy-cycle, keeping the boy rider, son or grandson, upright. From time to time the man loosened his hold on the machine, but almost at once had to return it with his steadying strength. Both boy and man appeared stressed, without signs of success, expecting an accident any minute.

'Good morning,' Taylor called. 'And a Merry Christmas.'

'And to you,' the man muttered.

'A Christmas present?' Taylor asked, pointing at the bicycle.

'Yes,' the answer came grudging. 'Thank God it's not an aeroplane.'

Once inside the park Taylor slowed his pace and looked round. He found nothing to cheer him; wet grass and black trees might have a beauty of their own, but did little for his mood. Passing the cricket field he sang to himself as he stepped out smartly again. In honour of the day he sang a carol, 'While Shepherds Watched', not to the usual tune, 'Winchester Old', but to a Yorkshire version, 'Lyngham', that his father used to favour.

His dad had been in a church choir at one time in his youth, and he occasionally sang old hymns or chants at home. This

1

was a speciality of his because the last line of each verse was opened by the basses alone with: 'And glory shone around' or the generous words 'To you and all mankind'. The old man was in no way religious by that time, never frequented a place of worship within his son's recollection, but his face lit up, his head was thrown back, as he sang his piece from his youth. Not that his dad's voice was anything to shout home about, a decent choir man's baritone, but his expression brightened and his head shook as if he directed the Berlin Philharmonic.

Once he'd commented on it to his son: 'Me and the chap next to me, by name Harold Hooks, used to give it some stick, I can tell you. We made the rest of the choir when they came in sound, well, what they were, ladylike.' He'd scrub his stubbly chin. 'I don't know why his parents gave him that name, I'm sure. It was bad enough in these parts if your surname began with an aitch. But to saddle you with one on your first was beyond reason. Neither got sounded.'

'In for a penny, in for a pound,' George said.

'I'll say,' his father agreed.

'Had he a good voice?' the son asked.

'Yes. Well, better than mine, but we could make a joyful noise between us.'

Taylor, as he walked, imitated his father even to the shake of his head, but the effort did little for his spirits. There was no one about to hear him; only his legs kept time with the old tune. As he broke off he tried to recall the name of the composer of 'Lyngham'. He'd looked it up at least twice before but he could not remember it now, nor even the poet who wrote the words. As he slowed down he seemed to think that he was a well-known writer, responsible for other beauties besides this Christmas verse.

He had not travelled above a hundred yards when he saw in the distance another pedestrian approaching him. Even at a distance the newcomer gave the impression of energy, his elbows working strongly in rhythm with his legs. The vigorous figure was accompanied by no dog. By the time he was ten yards away, Taylor had prepared his greeting.

'Good morning and a happy Christmas,' he called out.

The figure, now clearly seen as a man roughly of Taylor's age, bundled up in an overcoat of golfer's tweed and a thick scarf, jerked to a standstill.

2

'Thank you, and the same to you.' The voice was low, cultured, not unfriendly.

'Not very promising,' Taylor improvised. 'Still, it's December and not cold.'

'Exactly.'

They stood, two men apparently in their early-forties, summing themselves up. Both were hatless, but Taylor's thick head of hair straight – he often used the phrase learned from his father and his grandfather – as a 'yard of pump water', contrasted with the springy growth of the newcomer's crop, greying vigorously round a circle of baldness on the crown.

'Couldn't you sleep, then?' the stranger enquired.

'No. I was in bed early last night. Nothing to stay up for.'

'But up with the lark this morning?'

'Much as usual. And breakfast doesn't occupy me long. Cereal, coffee, toast with cheese.' He didn't know why he offered this information. It kept the conversation alive, he supposed.

'Diet and exercise keep me alive,' the stranger offered.

'You look well on it.'

'Oh, thank you.'

The other man stood, wrinkling his brow as if trying to think of a suitable topic to keep this staccato conversation alive. Finally, he threw his shoulders back, with almost military smartness, as if he had solved the problem.

'Are you going anywhere particularly?' he asked. 'Would you mind if I walked along with you for a little while? I don't seem this morning to be very fond of my own company.'

'I was making for the far end of the park, when I'll turn back.'

'May I accompany you?'

'Yes. It seems a shame to be alone on Christmas morning.'

They set off stride for stride together, but did not speak. It appeared sufficient to both to be in the other's company. Their pace was easy; there was no competition. After a while the stranger said, 'My name is Andrew Barron.'

'And mine's George Taylor.'

They shook hands, briefly halting the progress of their walk.

'I'm heterosexual.'

That surprised Taylor. This information should not have been necessary to excuse a loneliness or boredom on Christmas Day.

'Oh, so am I,' he replied.

3

This time they did not shake hands. The far gates of the park came into view by the side of a small wood.

'I live just beyond the gates,' Barron said. 'I wonder if you'd like to come in for a cup of coffee or tea. Even for something stronger in view of the Day.' He pointed in rather a self-deprecating way at a row of large Victorian villas behind the trees on the other side of the avenue.

'Not much traffic about,' Taylor said as they went over the road by a pedestrian crossing.

'No. Some mornings it's horrendous. I feel quite terrified.'

'They're all in bed.'

The two men pushed through an elaborate iron gate, and up three steps to a wide, stained-glass, front door. Barron fiddled with his keys before he let himself through into a spacious hall.

'Hang your coat up,' Barron invited his guest, 'and sit down in there.' He indicated a white door. 'What is it you drink?'

'Coffee, please. Milk. No sugar.'

Taylor took off his heavy coat and scarf which he handed over to his host.

'Sit yourself down. In there.'

The guest obeyed, pushing open the white door, and after his host had pointed out an armchair, settled heavily down on it.

'Beautifully warm in here,' he said.

'I don't begrudge money I spend on heat.'

'Do you occupy the whole house, then?' Taylor asked. He had imagined that Barron lived squashed in a flat, tucked away on the third storey.

'I'm afraid so. It's a bit wasteful. Too large a house for one man. These things happen.' He hurried away with Taylor's outdoor clothes. The guest stared round.

He sat in a large room, lighted by a huge bay window which occupied most of one wall. The ceiling delicately plastered was painted the same colour as the walls, a kind of off-white, magnolia perhaps. A gold-framed mirror hung over the marble mantel-piece, and four oil paintings dominated the room. One was of a boy, hunting-dogs at his feet, standing under a massive oak tree. He was dressed in eighteenth-century style, with a cocked hat. His expression seemed cheerful, even mischievous, as if he had committed some minor offence of which his elders and betters would not approve but would never be able to accuse him of perpetrating. The others, darker, were Victorian landscapes with

4

叶脉

书签

叶脉，是采用天然的植物叶片，经过十几道工序纯手工制作而成，叶脉薄如蝉翼，透明如纱。

『叶脉书签』经传统工艺与现在技术完美结合，把丰富多彩的画面和谐的与树叶自然完美融为一体，给人美丽的享受。每片叶脉书签又向人诉说着一个传说、一个故事，阐述着一种历史文化。

叶脉书签 *(Veins bookmarks)*

天然叶脉
book mark

woods and distant hills, and in one men and women harvesters, carrying bundles, staggered smiling under their burdens, but did nothing to lighten the grimness of brush-work.

A massive settee, darkish red with three vast armchairs loomed over the old-fashioned expensive wall-to-wall carpets, baring wide spaces. The window curtains, drawn back now, were red velvet, not exactly the colour of the furniture, but somehow matching, adding to the out-dated grandeur of the room. The walls had been recently painted but oddly did not clash with the rest. A large table, highly polished held a small tumble of books and two large photographs, while a greyly ornamented tuffet had been tucked away in a corner by the window. Electric illumination was provided by a chandelier, rather ugly and outsized. How efficient this was Taylor could not guess. He disliked it; fumbled in his mind for a suitable adjective, deciding finally on 'gruesome'. Would that word be easily applicable to the rest of the room? He decided not. What saved the place was its warmth; not the dryness of the hospital or chain-store, but an all-embracing soft, comfortable, welcoming, friendly heat that appealed strongly to him as he leaned back into the depths of his chair.

Barron came in carrying a silver tray with coffee-percolator, milk and cups, all huge, and a small plate of chocolate biscuits, some wrapped in sparkling paper. He laid these rather noisily, on the table, spoiling any effect at symmetry. Perched back in his seat, he sat with fingers rather vulgarly round his cup.

'This is the life,' Barron said.

'Very good,' Taylor answered. He felt comfortable and grateful to be so.

'Do you walk in the park often? I've seen you there before, and thought to myself, he looks an interesting chap. I wonder what he's got to say for himself.'

'Not much. You can only have seen me at weekends.'

'That's so.'

'How can you tell that a person's interesting just by looking at him?'

'There are usually clues. The face rather than the clothes. Mind you, I'm often wrong.'

'Do you always try to find out?'

'Certainly not. A good many interesting people would tell me to clear off and mind my own business. I like to cross-question folks. They don't seem to care, well, some.'

'What do you want to know about me?'

'Oh, everything. Or what you are prepared to tell me.'

'My name is George . . . Norman George Taylor. Until recently I was a teacher, but I was advised by my doctors that I needed a few months in the fresh air. So I resigned, or rather the Education Authority allowed me to stand down for a year. I have worked as a postman here since October last.'

'And it has done the trick?'

'Well, I'm still alive.'

'Your illness was as bad as all that, was it?'

'I was anaemic, lacking energy, never really well.'

'Did you enjoy teaching?'

'I often asked myself that.'

'And answered it how?'

'Ah, you have me there. I suspect that was at least half the trouble. Sometimes, when I felt well, it was great. I taught history and literature. But the amount of marking I had to do made me question my vocation. When I read the dull, brutish accounts of historical events which they turned in for marking, I despaired. It made me think I was wasting time teaching them about King John or Queen Elizabeth or George the Third. What connection had these figures with their lives and interests, with their futures?'

'And that was at the bottom of your disenchantment with history?'

'Disenchantment? I don't think so. I didn't think their essays were connected with my illness. Often I gave quite lively descriptions or explanations at what had gone on in the past. No. I hadn't sorted that out for myself. But I hoped that tramping the streets with nothing more interesting to read than the addresses on envelopes would set me right.'

'And has it?'

'Not so far.'

'But you don't earn as much as a postman as a teacher?'

'No, but I'm unmarried, without family responsibilities. So I bought a flat in Beechnall and moved into it. I let out my house in Mansfield, where I taught, and that easily made enough to pay my mortgage.'

'So you're content?'

'No.'

They both indulged themselves in speechless drinking of coffee, which Taylor judged delicious. It was Barron who eventually broke the silence.

'I suppose that I ought now to give some account of myself,' he said.

'Not if you don't want to.'

'There's nothing I like better than talking about myself.'

A minute or two of awkward silence as Taylor made no comment at this point.

'I'm like you, so far as one thing is concerned. I haven't made up my mind what I want to work at. I shall be forty-five at my next birthday, and it's ridiculous that I haven't really ever found a suitable career for myself.'

'And you can't account for it?'

'I don't know about that. I've been left enough by my late grandparents and other relatives to live quite comfortably without working five days a week. At Cambridge I read English in the first part of the Tripos, and law in the second. I then went to Nottingham Trent and studied for my Law Society Examinations.'

'Which you passed?'

'It was an excellent course, and I enjoyed it. Perhaps more than anything else I've done in my life. After that I worked in the offices of cousins of my father's. They were decent old boys, but didn't in any way extend themselves. They were conscientious, but didn't wish to tackle difficult or challenging cases. After about a year they passed them on to me.'

'You could handle them without difficulty?'

'I wouldn't say that. But I was prepared to read hard. And they were perfectly satisfied that I should spend time with law books. It meant that the firm got something of a reputation for handling tricky cases.'

'I'd have thought,' Taylor said, 'that was a good reason to stay with these cousins rather than dropping the law.'

'I didn't altogether drop it. If they had something they didn't want to deal with, they'd hand it over to me. They kept my name on their notepaper. Moreover, no sooner had I agreed to this than Trent offered me a part-time lectureship – two lectures and a tutorial a week. It took up all the spare time I thought I was making for myself for a start keeping up with the work. I didn't mind, though, because I was still interested in the law and Bart and Dennis, the cousins, had an excellent law library as did the Trent, and I used them both.'

'Do you still do that?'

'No. I decided against it more than ten years ago. The university was always pressing me to do a PhD, but that held no attraction. I wanted cases that were actually bothering people now.'

'And thus you had spare time? But what about money?'

'It was just about this period that relatives died conveniently and kept me solvent. And after my grandfather passed away, I not only had this barn of a place, but enough money to pay the council tax and keep it in good order. That's only three years ago, and ever since I've thought about letting out rooms which'd bring me in a nice little sum, but I've done nothing about it.'

'Wouldn't it cost you a packet with new bathrooms, showers and sinks?'

'I'd have to shell out, but my grandfather had already done a great deal of the extra work himself. He was the sort of man who thought to the future, and he was very good at DIY. He never learned the art of sitting down to idle in an armchair. He was only happy when he had a job on hand.'

'Unlike his grandson?' Taylor said.

'I don't know. I'm getting rather tired of retirement at my age. I shall change my ways. Already the young men who have taken over at Bart and Dennis's are pressing me to come back for a day or two each week. The new men are a lively pair, and are out to make money. Old Tom Dennis died last Christmas and left me his share in the business, and so they think it might be a financial advantage to have me back in the firm, toiling to add my bit of the profits.'

'And will you join them?'

'I've already done so. But only for two days a week.'

'And the rest of the week?'

'Ah, that's it. Once I've been back a month or two and got used to it, I shall have to think seriously about how I'm going to fill in the other five days.'

'Are you a sporting man? How about golf, or tennis, or cricket?'

'No, thanks. Jogging provides me with physical fitness.'

'Would it have to be some outdoor procedure?'

'By no means. I have considered writing?'

'What? Poetry? Novels? Journalism?'

'I wouldn't mind that.'

'You're not thinking of starting a pop-band?'

'I'm not interested in that sort of stuff.'

'As a classical musician then? Accompanying singers?'

'I'm nowhere near good enough. I know my limitations. But I'll find something if it's only robbing banks. Not that that's at all likely. I've been brought up to look at any sort of illegality as being outside my sphere of interest. But I don't despair. There are all sorts of advertisements that keep my spirits up and rising. Old gents wanting companions on a world-wide trip. Ladies wanting their wayward husbands taken in hand by a man of ideas. You'd be surprised.'

'I can see you're able to fill in your free time with planning the future.'

'Come, now. Don't be so cynical.'

'Well, I wonder if you're serious.'

At this moment the front-door bell pealed long and harshly.

'I wonder who that is,' Barron said, raising his eyes. 'I'm not expecting anybody.'

The bell sounded again. The caller had little patience, it seemed.

'I'm coming,' Barron murmured, and made a shambling exit in the direction of the front door.

Inside a few minutes he was back, ushering a young woman, maybe in her thirties, into the room. Taylor glanced in her direction and stood up.

'Let me make introductions,' Barron said. 'George Taylor. Mrs Mirabel Lockwood.'

Taylor held out a hand which she barely touched in return.

'I'm sorry if I'm interrupting something,' she said. 'I thought I'd have to haul Andrew out of bed.'

She pulled off her coat and draped it over the back of the settee. Underneath she was revealed as wearing a dress of a shining material that outlined a strikingly lissom figure. Her nipples rose tantalisingly under the summery cloth. Round her neck she wore a necklace of rectangular beads in black, which enhanced yet challenged the beauty of her dress. She moved with speed, but silently.

'I'll get you a cup of coffee. Freshly prepared,' Barron said, and left the room.

Mirabel draped herself in an armchair, hitching up her dress.

'Are you an old friend of Andy's?' she asked, smoothing the material over her thighs.

9

'No. I met him for the first time less than an hour ago.'

'Typical. Perhaps your face interested him.'

'I doubt it.'

She breathed deeply, in and out.

'He's not so far off fifty and he's never come to terms with his place in the universe.

'Meaning what?'

'He doesn't know what job to do.'

'That's not surprising. Many people these days change career more than once. And he must have enough money to live on.'

'That's a big part of the trouble. He's never been short. He's had too many elderly relatives who've died and left him, well, considerable sums.'

'And he's thrown those inheritances away?'

'No. But, as I don't know the exact details, I'm not sure he's got enough to live on for the rest of his life. And that might not suit. Imagine he let his grandfather's house out he wouldn't like it. Lodgers are a pain. They'd either be reckless and damage his property or agèd and incapable of looking after it. It would drive him mad. He should have stuck by his legal career. I worry about him.'

At that moment Barron reappeared with her coffee. He seemed pleased.

'There should be some biscuits, if my friend here hasn't eaten them all,' he said. 'Or was he so dazzled by your appearance and conversation that he's sat there incapable of raiding a small tin?'

'Another remark like that,' she said, 'and he won't be your friend much longer.'

'What did she tell you about me?' Barron asked Taylor, jovially.

'All pretty complimentary.' George Taylor spoke diplomatically.

'Did she not mention that I couldn't decide how to choose a suitable job and keep it or how to spend my spare time?'

'Well,' Taylor said. 'Well, now.'

'It's nothing to boast about. You've just been lucky. Most of us have to work for a living,' Mirabel answered.

'You don't.'

'I don't work then?'

'You have no need to do so.'

The faces of the two grew serious now, almost stiffening

with anger. This was clearly a long-standing matter of controversy between them.

'May I remind you,' Taylor said, 'that it's Christmas Day. Peace on earth and goodwill to all men. And women. If you must argue then I'll take my scarf and coat and clear off, so you can have the whole house to fight in, and no spectators.'

The other two stared at him as if he'd spoken in some language unknown to them. After a while Mirabel, recovering first, murmured sweetly, 'You mustn't mind us. We're very old friends.'

'Tell you what,' Barron said, 'I invite you both to lunch today.'

'What's on the menu?' Mirabel asked.

'Fish pie, rice and broad beans. Not very seasonal. But Christmas pudding for the second course.'

'Made by you?' she pressed.

'No. Straight from Tesco.'

'What do you say?' she asked Taylor. 'Are you otherwise engaged? Or dieting? I warn you that Andy serves large helpings.'

George Taylor did not answer immediately. Events were moving too quickly. He pulled himself together.

'That's most kind of you,' he said, 'but I'd be in the way. You and Miss Lockwood . . .'

'Mrs,' Barron corrected him.

'Mrs Lockwood would do better to have lunch together, quarelling, as you seem to do usually, for pleasure. If I stay you'll have to be on your best behaviour, and the occasion will be dullness personified, if that's the word. You know what I mean. I'm not exactly the life and soul of any party.'

'That's to be seen,' she said. 'Andrew chose you to drink coffee with him, so he must have seen something in you.'

'I was like him . . . a lonely man, passing the day by walking in the park. We were similar. Or so he found out. I might have been the father of six, driven outdoors by the shouting and quarelling over their presents.'

'That's not the impression I get,' she said.

'Have you been married?' Barron seemed suddenly to wake up.

'No. One serious girlfriend. It came to nothing,' said George.

'You see what sort of entertainment you'll find, or suffer, here. A lawyer's cross-examination.'

'But I'm not on oath. I can answer with any old rubbish. Oddly enough, I ran across the ex-girlfriend only last week in

11

Sainsbury's. I would have guessed she would have walked straight past me. It didn't end well, the relationship. But, no, she stopped, all charm. It surprised me. We must have spent ten minutes together at least, all very pleasant, civilised.'

'But with no result?' asked Mirabel.

'No. We parted and that was that.'

'No suggestion of a further meeting?'

'Not a word.'

'And did that disappoint you?' Barron asked.

'No. I was surprised we talked so pleasurably. I didn't expect it.'

'Did she look any different?'

'Not that I noticed, though it must be ten years since . . . She looked a bit tired, I thought, but she was not wearing make-up, or very little. She dressed well, but with not quite the smartness I remembered. But there, she was just out for a quick transaction in Sainsbury's.'

'It's ten years since you parted. How many times have you met her since then?'

George Taylor screwed up his face in thought.

'Half a dozen, locally. And she was very hoity-toity each time. That's what was so surprising about this meeting.'

'And did she give any hint why she was so pleased to see you? He shook his head.

'No. I would guess it was nothing to do with what I did and said.'

'What was it, then?' asked Mirabel.

'No idea. She'd perhaps had some good news: a win on the Lottery, a friend's recovery from illness, the booking of a holiday.'

'And it rubbed off on you?'

They quizzed him for a short time before Barron refilled their coffee cups and marched smartly out to make a start on the lunch. 'I don't need any help, thank you. It's all very straight-forward.' He seemed pleased with himself.

The guests said little for the first few minutes. George stood and carried the biscuit plate over to Mirabel. She cast a wary eye over the delicacies, then chose one and seemed to spend long minutes removing the silver paper from it and folding it with infinite pains into a perfect square which she handled, not knowing how to dispose of it, as if it would explode. Finally it was parked on the arm of her chair.

She then looked over at Taylor. She smiled, and said, 'I remember when I was engaged to Andrew, and later Charles . . .' She stopped. Barron had called her Mrs Lockwood, though she wore nothing on her ring finger.

'And?' he asked.

She stared hard at her naked finger, and then gently massaged it.

'You were engaged to Andrew?'

Taylor waited for her to add to her snippets of information.

'We broke it off,' she said.

'He or you?' he asked, more rudely than he meant.

'It was mutual. Reciprocal. Andrew isn't the marrying sort, but he proposed. He had the ring all ready, and a huge bunch of flowers he had hidden in his kitchen.'

'And he went down on his knee?'

'Not quite . . . It wasn't on.' She moved lithely in her chair. 'But we remained friends. He attended my wedding to Charles Lockwood, and made a witty and entertaining speech, though in what capacity I couldn't make out. Perhaps Charlie had asked him. But he did it well. He does most things well, does our Andrew, if he sets out to do so.'

'People are odd,' he said.

She spoke for a short breathless period about her present friendship with Barron. It had been gradual, after the breaking of her engagement. Andrew had been most helpful. That was some years ago. 'It's a good job I didn't marry Andy. I don't think it would have lasted long. Now, when we don't see each other for weeks on end, he does all sorts of little jobs for me, and often gives me sensible, sound advice.'

'How did you first meet your husband?'

'I went to Charles's law lectures at the university. He impressed me, and gave me good marks for the two or three essays I wrote for him. At the end of the year he asked me out for a meal, and it went on from there. We didn't hang about and were engaged soon after he moved to London.'

'And all went well at first?'

'Very well. I was working in a solicitor's office and studying for my exams. I thought I worked hard until I saw the time and effort he spent on preparing his lectures. You know, in many ways he reminded me of my father.'

'Was your father a lawyer, then?'

13

'No, he was a headmaster, but I always thought it was his job to educate the whole world, not just the eight hundred boys he was responsible for.'

'You didn't go to his school then?'

'No. It was a boys' public school. He used to thank the Director of Education for making his work so much easier by shunting all state-educated people into comprehensive schools. And he tried his hardest to educate me. I was unfortunately his only child.'

'Why unfortunately?'

'My father was interested in all sorts of subjects, branches of the arts. And he tried to catch my interest.'

'With no success?'

'No, not really. I did take up some of the things he brought to my notice.'

'Things? What things?'

'Classical music. I learned the piano. We played duets together. I liked that because I was a better player than he was. But I had to like what he considered good, and despise that which he found poor. In literature too.'

George Taylor enjoyed these continuing reminiscences, for she told them with zest. Whatever the subject matter she had some view to promote, and that with vigour. When he asked her if she wasn't like her father in this, she agreed with him.

They talked on, with scattered pauses, for a time until she quite naturally, giving no offence, took up with a book. He asked its title. '*The Penguin Book of French Verse to the Fifteenth Century.*'

'Who's the first and who's the last?' he asked.

'The first's anonymous. "The Life of Saint Alexis." The last,' she flicked over the title pages, "Popular Songs" by François Villon. You'll have heard of him. 1431–63. There's some of his "Last Will and Testament".'

'Is it in the original French?'

'Yes.'

'And you can read it?'

'The editor provides a translation.'

'Oh,' he said in disappointment.

'I read it when I come here. Andy always leaves it out for me to pick up.'

'And is it worth reading?'

14

'That's difficult to answer. I don't know the original language well enough. But now and then a line strikes a chord. For instance, *"Mais où sont les neiges d'antan"* has become quotable by English writers.'

'What's it mean?'

'"But where are the snows of yesteryear?"'

'And what's the whole poem about?'

'The transience of beauty. How lovely and famous women have gone forever.'

'Is the rest of the poem memorable?'

'Yes. He makes use of names of the great ladies who are no longer with us, are mere historical memories.

> *"La royne Blanche comme lis*
> *Qui chantoit à voix de seraine,*
> *Berte au grand pié, Beatris, Alis,*
> *Haremburgis qui tint le Maine*
> *Et Jehanne la bonne Lorraine*
> *Qu' Anglois brulerent à Rouain."'*

Her voice held him, wheeled him into a quiet trance so that he no longer sat in this modern, middle-class parlour. So taken was he with the angelic tone that he did not even ask for a translation as he sat transfixed. She provided it.

'"The queen, Blanche, who was white as a lily, who used to sing with a siren's voice; Berte with the big foot, Beatrix, Alice, Haremburgis who ruled in Maine; and Joan, the good maid of Lorraine, whom the English burned at Rouen." Don't ask me who they were. The only one I could say anything about is Joan of Arc, and that would be little enough.'

'What about the big foot?' he asked. 'Surely that was no sign of a beauty.'

'I don't know. I ought to find out, to have found out, but I never did.'

They fell into silence again, he with eyes down to his book. He'd picked it up at random from the top of a line of books: *Collected Poems* by Thomas Hardy. By coincidence he had been reading 'Former Beauties' from *At Casterbridge Fair*.

> These market-dames, mid-aged, with lips thin-drawn
>   And tissues sere,

> Are they the ones we loved in years a-gone
>   And courted here?

He smiled, and compared Hardy with Villon. Both men had said something important to him that morning. Finger in at page 223, he allowed his eyes to flicker along the titles on the shelf at eye-level nearby. With a leap of the brain he noticed *The Oxford Companion to French Literature*. He closed Hardy; extracted the *Companion* with a clumsy delicacy from its place; looked without much expectation for Berthe, the lady with the big foot. *Berthe aux grands pieds*, the page announced, a title in blacker type than the rest. He could translate that. Both the lady's feet were large.

He cleared his throat, importantly. Mirabel looked up.

'I know who Berthe was,' he announced.

'Oh, yes.' She waited, a superior smile on her face. 'Go on, then.'

He made her wait.

'The wife of Pépin le Bref and mother of Charlemagne.'

'And?' Her question sounded faintly ironic.

'She had trouble over the marriage ceremony. On the night of her wedding to Pépin, some enemies snatched her away from her bed and replaced her with another woman, who presumbly turned up for the ceremony and married the king in Berthe's place.'

'When did all this take place?'

George fumbled in his book, and had to seek a further reference.

'In the seven fifties.' Now she was nodding vigorously and smiling at his discovery. 'You're just like my father too. If you told him something he didn't know, he'd ferret about with his book and wouldn't be satisfied until he'd brought you some further snippet of information on the subject.'

'Isn't that good?' he asked naively.

'He didn't like to be shown up in ignorance.'

Taylor nodded. 'But I wonder why she was considered among the beauties if her most striking characteristic was large feet?'

'I don't know. It might tell you in the *chanson de geste* they mention here. We'd have to read that. It might be the result of her wandering in the forest after her enemies had married the false Berthe to Pépin. Or it may be that when she became queen she wore very highly decorated, elaborate shoes which drew attention to themselves by their size.'

'I never thought of that.'

'No. And I don't know what the truth is.'

At this moment Andrew Barron poked his head round the door.

'Are you all right, folks?' he asked in some sort of comical accent. They said they were. 'Lunch is well on the way. We'll have a glass of sherry before we eat. I'm sure George here always whets his appetite before dinner. Don't you?'

'Never.'

'You disappoint me. But you'll join us today, at Christmas, won't you? Sweet, amontillado or dry?'

'Sweet, if you please.'

'Sweet to the sweet.' With that Barron closed the door.

The guests returned to their books.

Lunch quickly followed the sherry, and was excellent. Andrew served substantial plateful, to which they did justice. George insisted on washing up, and Mirabel dried. 'I know where to put the pots away,' she said. 'I know what it's like to let strangers loose in the kitchen. You can't find anything for a week.' They had finished one bottle of white wine between them, George refusing a second glass, and afterwards sat sleepily in the drawing-room, hardly mentioning more than a couple of sentences at a time until twenty past three when George insisted he should leave. They did not argue with him, and he completed the morning's walk, pleased with life.

II

George Taylor wrote a tasteful card to Barron, thanking him and Mirabel for their hospitality. He hoped to return the kindness shortly if they'd let him know a convenient day for a shared meal.

He heard nothing, and wondered if Andrew Barron was away, or if he, George, had failed some unannounced test, and had been put aside as uninteresting. Back at work he trudged the streets in the wet cold of January and found February equally unaccommodating. At first he cast round in his mind for suitable topics to entertain his guests, if they bothered to accept his invitation. There had been four break-ins in the street, and he had chatted to a policeman about the excitement. The constable looked young, fresh-faced and innocent, but strong enough to push him straight through a brick wall without unduly exerting himself.

'Cheeky-daft they are. They broke into the house while the people were in the back rooms.'

'Did they get away with much?'

'A bagful of ornaments, trinkets, bits of bric-à-brac which were on the mantel-piece and window sills and tabletops. Some of them were really valuable.'

'So they wouldn't get anything like the amount they were worth?'

'No. We think they were youngsters. Professional thieves might know where to get a decent price.'

'You think you know who did it?'

'There are three or four little gangs. We'll question them all. You'd be surprised what you can get out of them. Some of them will brazen it out, won't say a word, act innocent as babies. But some of them aren't very well supplied up top, and will let slip some crucial bit of evidence that'll land somebody up in jug.'

George thought he could impress guests with such inside

knowledge of the criminal life, but he got no chance, only silence from the Barron end.

Two days later as he drew the curtains of his bedroom in the flat he noticed that fire blazed fiercely in an upstairs window of the large house opposite. He rang 999 and they thanked him, but said they had already received calls, and the fire engine should soon be there. Even as they spoke he heard the sirens. The firemen ran round the back, put up their ladders with lightning speed and were flooding the burning room with their hosepipe. He was surprised at the speed and efficiency with which they worked. They moved rapidly, seemingly knowing exactly where to direct their efforts, and yet worked without rush or panic, and had the flames quickly under control. When they were on top of the fire, George, bursting with curiosity, put on a scarf, hat and anorak, and walked, in the night air, the not inconsiderable distance to the next street. The fire engine stood exactly where he'd expected it. A crowd of dark-clothed spectators hovered about, seeing little of the action. The fire had been confined to the back of the house.

George attached himself to the local know-all, a man in his sixties who had lived in the street all his life. The house belonged, the wiseacre informed his three or four listeners, to an elderly couple who were fortunately away just now, but who had carefully left the upstairs bedroom doors firmly closed so that the fire, fierce as it had been, was confined to one room only.

'The damage was not as large as it might have been,' he pronounced.

'They don't keep valuables, then, in the bedroom?' someone enquired.

'I don't know. I don't go round people's bedrooms. But they're not without a bob or two, and I'd guess the furniture was both old and valuable. And,' he concluded, 'it will be well covered by insurance.'

'How did it start?'

'They won't know that until the fire's completely out, and the experts have a look.'

'Have the people who live here been told?' a man asked.

'I expect so. They're not far away. Lincoln or Newark.'

'How do you know that?'

'The old lady next-door told me. I'd called in on her when all the kerfuffle started. I do the odd job, and I call in of an evening to see if she wants anything doing, any shopping, gardening, that sort of thing. She said they were away.'

'Who lives there then?' a woman enquirer this time.

'People called Lockwood. He owns a factory in the Lace Market.'

'Are they relatives of Charles Lockwood?' George asked, surprising himself.

'Do you know him?'

'I know of him. I was talking quite recently to his ex-wife.'

'That would be their son. Lives in London now. Solicitor to, and on the board of, some big insurance company. I don't think from what their neighbour says that he comes back home much. He's just got married again, hasn't he?'

'I don't know,' George answered. 'I've never met him.'

The know-all, taking a breather now the fire was over, asked a fireman if there was much damage.

'Room's pretty well burned out. It flamed hellish while it was gooin'. And there'll be smoke damage about the place, if I'm any judge.'

The know-all continued with his catalogue of catastrophe, but ended by saying again that the owners weren't short, could easily replace the burned objects even if they hadn't insured them against fire, which he would give a pound to a penny they had. 'They're the sort who don't throw their money away.'

'Misers, you mean?' some other bystander.

'I don't mean anything like that. In my experience people who are used to having money, don't throw it away.'

'What did his factory produce?' another asked.

'Clothes for places like Marks and Sparks, John Lewis. Big shops. In the war they were commandeered to produce military uniforms and so on, and they made a packet. His dad was in charge then.'

Taylor broke away and made his way back to his flat. He looked out of his window to discover that the firemen were still at work in the back garden, their ladders up to the windows.

On the next day, when he returned from his round and before he began to prepare his main meal, he walked round to Myrtle Avenue again. He slowed his pace by the house where they had watched the fire, and finally stopped by the fence, a work of well-painted iron, its shape complicated, even artistic. He expected no signs of the last night's trouble, and so was surprised to see the remnants of the furniture, burned black and shapeless, though he did not know whether that was wholly on account of the flames or of some helpers' handling of the ruined bed, wardrobe, dressing table and chair. They were parked haphazardly on a huge rectangle of canvas on the front lawn.

An elderly man appeared from the back of the house and stood glaring at Taylor who stared at the ruins of the furniture.

'Doesn't do much for the garden design,' Taylor said cheerfully.

'No. They must have burned pretty fiercely to get into that state.'

'They must have been very dry.'

'Well, yes. When you get old you don't fancy living in damp houses. And though we were away, we always leave the central heating on.'

'An electrical fault?' Taylor queried.

'That's what the fireman decided. I wasn't sure. We had the whole house rewired only about six months ago. And there was a small window smashed in.'

'Big enough for an arsonist to squeeze through?'

'Oh, no. But big enough to set light to this pile.'

'I live just over the back, in the flats on Marlborough Road. I saw the fire blazing when I came in and rang for the fire brigade. They told me an engine was already on the way.'

'And was it?'

'Yes, within two or three minutes. Someone else must have beaten me to it.'

'Well, thank you for trying.'

'You think it was some yob? An arsonist who set out to cause a blaze?'

'What else can I think? Especially with the window smashed in.'

'Why do you imagine your fire-raiser started the blaze upstairs?'

'I don't know. Perhaps he thought we were at home, at the front of the house. I must say, the police didn't seem very impressed with the idea of an intruder. I suggested they were here to burgle the place, but found it difficult, and set light to it in frustration.'

'They'd find the big plate-glass window difficult to handle, wouldn't they? Or at least to handle quietly.'

'Yes, though hereabouts you could let a bomb off and nobody would turn a hair.'

'And you've no idea who'll be responsible? You've no sworn enemies that you know of?'

21

'No. Of course, if you're an employer you might well upset someone with something you've said or done. Or, if not me, one of my under-managers or foremen. We employ mostly women, and I can't see them creeping round the back of houses with ladders and torches.'

'No.' George Taylor noticed that the old man was staring intently at him. After an interval the man drew in a noisy breath.

'Excuse my asking,' the man said, 'but are you connected with the police or the insurance company?'

'No. Just a curious neighbour. I'm a postman by trade.'

'You're very well spoken for a postman.'

'Kind of you to say so. I was a teacher, but my health broke down and I was advised by my doctor to take an outdoor job.'

'Was it the stress? They tell me teaching is a difficult profession these days.'

'That may have added to it, I admit, though I quite like instructing people. I take a WEA class in Mansfield on English Literature.'

'Are you a university graduate?'

'Yes, I am.'

'In English Literature?'

'And Language. Also some History. At Leeds.'

'And you live hereabouts? In the flats over our backs, in Marlborough Road?'

'That's so.'

'And, if you don't mind my asking, are you satisfied with the job? Will you stay at it or go back to more academic pursuits?'

'I don't know. My health has improved tremendously. You'd be surprised what a difference it makes to your outlook on life when you can breathe properly. I own a house in Mansfield which I let out and it keeps my mortgage at bay.'

'Good.' The old man laughed, a throaty gargle. 'You restore my faith in the human race.'

'I'm not so sure that I'm a fair representative of the rest of mankind.'

'May I ask what in particular you lecture on for the WEA?'

'The English Novel from Dickens to Conrad.'

'Would you mind if I asked a really amateurish question?'

Taylor laughed, wondering what it would be.

'Who's your favourite? Of all those outstanding writers?'

'Dickens, he's so big. And skilful in so many quarters. And he's emotionally so powerful.'

'You prefer him to George Eliot?'

'Yes. If I had to choose, though she's closer to me than Dickens. A lot cleverer, of course.'

'And?'

'And what? There's Joseph Conrad. He's later. I really admire his *Heart of Darkness*. It starts all over the place. You don't know where you're going to finish up. And when you get to the end you see that all that staggering about at the beginning of the book is absolutely necessary.'

'I've never read any Conrad.'

'Start now. And English was his fourth or fifth language.'

The old man turned on his heel, and looked up at the first-floor windows.

'Would you like to come in and . . .' at this point he paused and coughed '. . . have a squint at my books?'

'I would, but I mustn't be too long over it. I've not had my lunch yet.'

'We'll leave it for another day, then. You know where I live. And my name is Lockwood.'

'I met a Mrs Lockwood some weeks back. On Christmas Day.'

'Where was that?'

'At the house of a man called Andrew Barron.'

'The lady would be Mirabel. My son and she were married at one time. They're divorced now, and Charles, my son, has married again. I was very fond of Mirabel; she was far too good for him. I tell you what, I have a picture of her in the hall. Come in and look at it. It will only take two minutes.'

With a sharp clatter he opened the iron gates, and led George up the drive. The path was wide, and lit from above. The dimensions loomed large, more suitable to a small chapel than a domestic residence. Mr Lockwood led him inside towards a biggish framed pencil drawing. It had a bar-light above it which he snapped on.

'Good, isn't it?'

'It's an excellent likeness. Who did it?'

'A man called Gerard Fisher, a very good draughtsman. He taught art at Goldsmith's College.'

'It's very life-like. You'd almost expect her to move or speak.'

'He was a talented man, but he died before he reached forty.'

'Was he an invalid?'

'Of sorts. He was of an extremely nervous temperament. Life seemed to stack the odds against him. He was never very robust and seemed to run into more and more serious health problems as he got older, plus other obstacles.

'When Mirabel and Charles were first engaged, she used to call round often to see us. Charles by this time had joined an office in London. She had met him at the university, Trent, in the law department. She did her degree there and he did his at Oxford, and his Law Society exams at Trent.'

A woman had joined them, almost noiselessly. She was small, and utterly neat, but gave the impression of suppressed energy. Lockwood looked up as if surprised to see her there.

'Oh,' he said, 'may I introduce my wife, Joan?' She advanced with her tiny right hand outstretched towards the visitor. 'I'm afraid I don't know your name.' Lockwood sounded abashed.

'George Taylor.' He spoke out boldly. They shook hands.

'Mr Taylor lives in one of the flats in Marlborough Road. He saw our . . . our . . .' Lockwood hesitated over the noun '. . . conflagration the other night and called the fire brigade.'

'Oh, thank you,' she said. 'They were here pretty promptly and so the damage was confined to one small bedroom. It could have been much worse.'

'I was too late. Somebody else had already rung.'

Mrs Lockwood now appeared genuinely pleased.

'That's good. Not that you were late, but that our neighbours are so careful of our affairs. It's a comfort to elderly people like ourselves.'

'Mr Taylor also met our former daughter-in-law recently.'

'Mirabel?' Her voice trilled upwards.

'Who else?' Her husband spoke gruffly.

'Is she well?' Joan Lockwood now stood close to George. 'We rarely see her. Does she still live in these parts?'

'I don't know. That was my impression. It was at the house of a man called Barron, Andrew Barron.'

'We know of him. He was a part-time law tutor at Trent University when our son Charles was there, as I said. It had a very good reputation. Concentrated entirely on preparing students for the Law Society's test. At Oxford, or at least according to Charles, they made law a kind of further step in your education.

Or so they claimed. For instance, he took Roman law. That was useless as far as his work in England was concerned.'

'It might have raised some interesting points about our own practices,' Lockwood suggested.

'Pigs might fly.' She grimaced. 'My husband would make excuses for everybody.'

'Does that include the arsonists?'

'I haven't said as much. Or not yet.'

They giggled together. Taylor was reminded of very small children laughing in delight over some toy that had caught their fancy. He remembered a colleague at his last school saying it was the most beautiful sound he would hear in the whole of his life. He had answered by asking if Mozart had wasted his time when millions of babies would be laughing out loud all over the world. His colleague had answered at once, if obliquely, that George obviously had never caught on to the infinite variety of the world. At the time he had not followed his friend's reasoning, but thought now he could begin to understand what had been said.

'She was a very beautiful girl.' Mrs Lockwood changed course. 'Or still is.'

'Oh, yes.'

'She was far too good for our Charles.'

'She reminded me of you in your youth,' her husband said.

'Rubbish. She had a lot more about her than ever I had.'

'I beg, there, to differ.'

His voice was steely, and his wife giggled, not displeased.

'It was a great pity,' she said, 'that the marriage did not last. Charles was clever enough, but only somebody like Mirabel might have made a human being of him. He did not treat her as well as he might, but I think that was because he was afraid of her.' Mrs Lockwood shook her head. 'She could answer him back as strongly as he gave. You know, Mr Taylor, I blame ourselves for the majority of his troubles. We gave in too easily to him. He was a good-looking child, and very intelligent, always top of his class. And we were so pleased with him. And he could be so charming. So he was given everything he asked for. That spoiled him. Of course, if we'd have refused him what he wanted, put obstacles in his way, the result might have been just as bad, if not worse. Charles was selfish and had a very quick temper which he'd use to get his own way.'

25

'We hoped when he married Mirabel that he wouldn't always have his own way. He didn't, but it didn't cure him. He was too far gone.' Lockwood spoke with regret.

Mrs Lockwood seemed to brace herself, drag her wits together.

'If you see Mirabel again, would you tell her that we've been enquiring after her?'

'Would you ask her if she'll come round to see us?' her husband added.

'I doubt if she'd want anything to do with us. She'll be glad to have washed her hands of our family altogether.'

Taylor looked hard at the drawing on the wall, but with little optimism. He had heard nothing from Andrew Barron or Mirabel Lockwood. Barron had picked him out at random, and they had judged him as uninteresting, too dull to waste their valuable time on, a ship that had passed, without cargo of any importance, without the outward appearance to attract even the slightest notice.

He made his way through the Lockwoods' garden, and as he opened the impressive iron gates turned to look back. The old people stood at the door still, staring out. He felt sorry for them, but knew it would not be long before they had completely forgotten him.

He pressed heavily up the street.

III

One afternoon a day or two later George Taylor dozed in his chair by the hissing gas-fire. This was his usual way of passing the time after his working day. At lunch-time, the exact minute varied, he'd return from work, prepare and eat his main meal of the day, clear the table top, wash and put away the dishes, drink a cup of milky coffee, and then cover the table with the velvety tablecloth, loosen the laces of his boots and sink into the round-backed wooden chair and, much at his ease, fall asleep. The length of these post-prandial naps varied in a manner that he could not easily predict, on some occasions they would last ten minutes, on others an hour, though never more. He took this after-dinner pleasure on each weekday, but never on Saturday or Sunday, and his working days seemed incomplete without this break. He had never enjoyed this period of rest as a teacher.

Today he was perhaps a quarter of an hour into his siesta when he was woken by the shrilling of his doorbell.

He jumped up, examined his face for signs of somnolence, bent quickly to fasten his shoe-laces and straighten his clothes before making into the hall for the front door. Through the large glazed panel he could make out that his visitor was a woman, though he had no idea who she was. She wore a cheeky hat, something like a witch's, but with some inches sheared off from the formerly pointed top. He fiddled with the lock, and the door opened with a squeak as if it had been shut for a week.

George stepped back in surprise. Mirabel Lockwood smiled at him. She spoke her name.

'You didn't expect to see me,' she said sweetly. He stepped back and she followed him indoors. 'I'm afraid we, that's Andy Barron and I, are much at fault.'

He made no answer.

'You wrote to us, inviting us over to a meal with you.'

'Yes.'

'And received no answer.' He nodded in reply. 'To what did you attribute our rudeness?'

He considered the question, with its formal awkwardness.

'I took it,' he said, 'that you didn't consider me interesting enough to continue with my acquaintance.' That matched her.

'Yes. I would have thought the same, but it's nowhere near the truth.'

He signalled her forward. Not until they were behind the closed doors of his flat did she speak again.

'It was nothing like that at all. Your invitation arrived a day or two after Christmas when we were both away. I was in Paris, visiting, again very belatedly, an old friend. And Andy was in London. His firm had put him on to a really interesting case, and it had taken his fancy and he had spent some days on it and other matters at the Law Society's library. No sooner had he, not without difficulty, sorted this out for them than they had set him on another tricky pile of work which involved two visits to Scotland and a further trip to London.

'He revelled in the work. I've never seen him so caught up or happy. The cases didn't seem very attractive to me, but they involved some out-of-the-way law which needed searching out. Andy loved it. This pleased me because I always thought the law was where he should have settled. He was just as good at it as Charlie, my ex-husband, or so I thought, though Andy denies it, and it would have meant he had a real place in life, a real job. A solicitor's work is often very dull, but as long as one's careful, the odd fascinating case comes up to catch the interest of a really knowledgeable practitioner.' She stopped. 'This is a long preamble to a tale,' she said.

'But it's why you didn't immediately write to me. I understand your excuse. And you'd have to consult each other, I take it.'

'And that wasn't easy. The two or three times we did come across each other, your invitation was never foremost in our minds. We both, however, remembered it last Saturday, and I said I'd make an appearance to apologise. That would carry more weight than a card or a letter.'

'Oh, I don't know.'

'It would in my case. I'm sure of that.'

'I'm delighted to see you in person. By a happy coincidence, I was talking about you to your ex-parents-in-law.'

'I didn't know you knew them.'

28

'I didn't. But they live in the next street to me. And they had a fire in one of their bedrooms.'

'Did it do much damage?'

'Only to the furniture in a smallish room, covered by insurance. I rang the fire brigade.'

'They'd be grateful for that.'

'I wasn't the first. But I saw the burned furniture when I walked past next day and spoke to Mr Lockwood. I mentioned you, and his face lit up. He took me inside to see your picture which hung in their hall. He introduced me to his wife.'

'They're a lovely pair.'

'Yes. They praised you up to the skies. Said that they had hoped their son's marriage to you would sort him out, but it hadn't. They were far from complimentary about him.'

'I think they blame themselves for the way Charles turned out. He's married again, quite recently. Did you know?'

'Yes. They didn't say anything about his new wife. I don't even know if they were invited to or attended the ceremony. But I tell you what they did say.'

'Yes?'

'They said that if I knew you, would I invite you round.'

'And you said?'

'What could I? I didn't expect to see you again.'

She laughed, into his face.

'And what will you do now you have met me?'

'I'll ring them this very minute. You may not need me as an escort, but if you thought it worthwhile and preferred it you could go on your own.' He looked hard at her. She seemed to be enjoying his slight embarrassment. 'Do you want me to ring them?'

'If you'll go with me.'

'That's not altogether necessary,' he said. 'There's no reason for your politeness to me.'

He stood, waiting for a further word from her.

'Go on,' she said, rather irritably, he thought.

George walked out to the telephone, which was in his kitchen. She made herself comfortable, and so remained for the next five or six minutes until he pushed the door open and signalled her wordlessly into the kitchen. There he pointed to the phone. Within a minute Mirabel was deep in warm conversation with Mrs Lockwood. They enquired of each other about health, recent excursions, the fire, but not a word about Charles. This exchange lasted a long ten minutes, so that George began to edge towards the door, only to be stopped by a wave from Mirabel.

'Mrs Lockwood wonders when you'd be kind enough to take me round there to see them. Have you a diary handy?' He picked it up from the kitchen table and waved it at her. 'Right,' she continued, 'what time of the day or night or time of the week is best for you?'

'Early-evening, but not Tuesdays,' he said, 'or any time on Sunday.'

Mirabel conveyed this to Mrs Lockwood, consulted her diary, made an entry.

'Next Wednesday,' she said to George. 'Six-thirty.' She waited as he stood dumb, spell-bound. 'Is that all right?' He nodded. She confirmed the date with Mrs Lockwood, and purred what pleasure their little talk had given her. Mrs Lockwood then obviously said, though George did not hear it, how sorry her husband would be to have missed the call. Mirabel rather hastily put down the receiver and brushed her hands together.

'Next Wednesday, here. Six-fifteen. Best bib and tucker.'

'I'll get you a cup of coffee now,' he said.

'No, thanks. I've wasted enough of your time. I'll speak to Andy and we'll make arrangements for a meeting of the three of us when I see you on Wednesday. I'm sorry that we've been so slapdash about answering your kind invitation. But it's had a happy consequence, so . . .'

'All's well that ends well.' He paused, then off-handedly questioned her.

'Aren't you at work?'

'Yes. I usually take an hour at this time to get my shopping done.' She marched out into the kitchen, and regally wrote her number on the pad by his telephone. 'In case anything goes awry with our arrangements. I'm not in the book.'

'Didn't the old folks have your number?' he asked.

'Yes. But they'd think that I'd want nothing further to do with them after Charles and I had divorced. They're old-fashioned.'

'Why didn't you get in touch with them?'

'I supposed they'd written me off, blamed me for the divorce.'

'You didn't obviously know them very well.'

'No. Perhaps you're right.'

30

She made for the door, not looking back.

George breathed deeply, uncertain of himself.

Mirabel turned up in good time on the appointed Wednesday. She had dressed beautifully but without ostentation. She had, George noticed, kept on her white motoring gloves, but wore no hat. After cursory if friendly greetings she asked, 'How long will it take to walk to the Lockwoods'?'

'Five minutes at the outside.'

She consulted her small gold wristlet watch.

'We needn't start just yet in that case,' she said. 'Are you ready?'

'Give but the word,' he said.

Mirabel walked to the window to look out over the darkened garden.

'Can we see their house from here?' she asked.

He pointed it out, with emphasis on the window of the burned-out bedroom. It seemed no different from the rest. Whether they had had it repainted and repaired he could not say.

'These are fine big houses,' she said. 'And at the time they were built people would have been able to see more of the stars than we can.'

'Light pollution,' said George. It sounded daft even to himself.

'The houses make magnificent shapes against the sky even now. Is it noisy here?'

'No. To say we're so near the centre of the city, it's surprisingly quiet.'

She continued her scrutiny for a moment or two, then wheeled on him to order, 'Get your coat on.'

'It'll be about half-past when we arrive.' He went to the next room and returned wearing his overcoat. She looked him over, made no comment but muttered, 'I feel ambivalent about this visit. As if I'd been tricked into it.'

'You'll soon find out,' he said, ungraciously.

'I'm not troubled or afraid for myself. It's the old people I worry about. Since Charles and I split they've seen nothing of me, and I fear they may have built up a picture of me that bears no resemblance to reality, made a plaster saint of me.'

They walked out together in silence, and hardly exchanged a word in the five minutes it took to travel the length of the two streets. Mirabel made some remark about the houses, the villas in the Lockwoods' street, praising their size, their solidity, even their handsome appearance.

'They're a bit large for modern families,' he said.

'Especially with no servants.'

'Times have changed,' he said, as they turned into the Lockwoods' drive. The air, as they stood outside the front door, seemed colder, thinner. They waited quite a time before the door was opened and the master of the house stood staring out, as if he did not know what to expect. He invited them in, and stepped back.

As soon as the girl drew level with him, he threw his arms about her, with a kind of jerky, mechanical motion.

'Mirabel,' he said, almost choking, 'you don't know how glad we are to see you here again.' He loosened his hold and his wife tripped forward. She seemed very small, almost like a child, as she threw herself into Mirabel's embrace. They seemed beyond speech, and swaying made sounds of pleasure. Lockwood shook hands now with George.

'I'm glad you've been able to arrange this, Mr Taylor.'

'It was no trouble.'

The visitors removed their outdoor clothes. How Mirabel managed this while remaining so close to her hostess seemed a miracle. Lockwood led George into a large sitting-room, while Mirabel accompanied her hostess to the kitchen.

'She'll carry the coffee in for Joan, who's not always very steady on her feet these days.'

The coffee arrived in delicate china cups together with a large plate of beautifully arranged biscuits. Lockwood, now sprightly, showed Mirabel to her place and supplied her and George with coffee.

'You don't know what pleasure this visit gives to us,' Mrs Lockwood began in a strong voice. Her husband, who had begun to say much the same again, allowed himself to be shouted down.

'You're both looking very well,' Mirabel said, all smiles. 'Are you healthy?'

The talk of health was almost hilarious. Now Lockwood had turned eighty his rheumatism had begun to ache without fail, but he got about. The doctor could not do anything for him, but supplied him with pain-killers.

'Do they do the trick?' Mirabel asked.

'They make him constipated.'

Joan Lockwood now began on her illness. She had had a successful operation against cancer. She had to visit the doctor every three months, but there had been no recurrence of the disease. The experts were a cautious lot and promised nothing spectacular. It might be a period of remission, but it might not. This made Lockwood angry, he said, but his wife defended the oncologists, they wanted her always on the look-out so that if the cancer returned she would warn them early and give herself a chance. She ran her fingers through her thick hair, pushing it upwards. 'Its all grown again,' she crowed. 'I did look a sight without it, I can tell you.'

They both added their commentaries in cheerful voices, even occasionally contradicting the other, as if it were important that Mirabel had an exact knowledge of the case. They did not speak directly to George Taylor, but looked at him straight in the eye as if to be sure that he followed their conversation. Mrs Lockwood said that the cancer was not her chief worry, but her fits of dizziness. The doctor had prescribed some tablets, which were only partially successful.

'I daren't stand on a chair to change a light-bulb these days,' she confessed. 'And if I stand up in a hurry or turn round quickly I feel dizzy. It's a nuisance. If I'm just walking steadily I suddenly stagger.'

'I expect any day now to hear a knock on the door and find the police returning her home under suspicion of drunkenness,' said Lockwood.

'Don't be so vulgar,' his wife snapped at him. From his expression Taylor could see that Lockwood's little joke had been ill-received and that he regretted it.

They plied Taylor with chocolate biscuits as Mirabel asked after Charles, her first husband.

'As always,' his father said. 'Unsatisfactory.'

'We don't hear much from him,' Joan said. 'As far as we can make out he's doing very well financially with these insurance companies. But we expect that. He's a clever boy, and always has been. And it appears that the actual law he has to deal with, interests him. I think his father would have liked him to be an academic lawyer once he was clear that Charles had no intention of joining him in any shape or form at the factories.'

'Do you still go down there?' Mirabel asked.

'Perhaps once or twice a week. I've two good men in charge

now, and they're doing well. One is my brother's boy, and the other has worked most of his time with me. I'm still on the board of directors.'

'And they still listen to him,' Joan said, almost fervently.

'There's little need of my interventions,' Lockwood said. 'But they put up with my suggestions.'

'And your son has no connection with the company?' asked George.

'Not he,' Joan.

'Doesn't he phone you?'

'Not unless he wants something from us. And that's never more than twice a year. When he was married to Mirabel she kept in touch by phone every week, and even visited us a few times.'

'Not so with his present wife?'

'No. We weren't even invited to the wedding.'

'And what was his excuse for that?'

'There were no excuses. He'd see no need for them. We learned all about it from a small scruffy cardboard box and a piece of wedding-cake and a printed card three weeks after the ceremony.' Joan's voice trembled.

'We wrote to thank him and sent him a beautiful watercolour which he'd always admired. A Bonington. But we never heard whether it had arrived. Not even a post-card.'

'And nothing from his wife?'

'Not a word. She probably didn't know that he had parents still living.'

'When was all this?'

'Getting on for a year ago.'

'And you've not seen anything of them? Nor even wedding photographs?'

'That's not quite true,' Lockwood said mournfully. 'One afternoon just before Bonfire Night last year we heard a knock at the front door. That's not quite true either. We thought we heard somebody fiddling with a key at the front door. We were interested and not a little frightened. We'd no idea who it could be. We just couldn't think. I knew they'd get nowhere because I'd changed all the downstairs locks recently. I do this once every two or three years. Silly, I know, but there you are. I feel a bit safer and I get some satisfaction from still being able to do the job.' Lockwood coughed drily, as if he was gathering the energy to continue. 'But that's beside the point. There was suddenly a thunderous knock on the door as if someone was trying to break the thing down. I went out to see if I could make out who it was through the stained glass.'

'I told him to keep the chain on,' Joan said. 'You never know these days.'

'I could see it was Charles, and so I opened the door. There he stood, grinning like an ape. And his bride behind him. I invited them in. He said, "I thought you were out. So I tried my key, but it didn't fit." Then, bold as brass, "Annie, this is my mother and father. You can see they aren't pleased. But never mind." He went up to Joan and kissed her. His mother wasn't exactly charmed.'

'You might have given us some notice,' she said. 'You know our phone number.'

'"To give you the chance to dress up?" he said. "Why, you look a picture, doesn't she, Anne?"'

'What did his wife say?' Mirabel asked.

'Nothing. Not a word. And a look on her face as if there was a nasty smell about.'

'I don't know who she disapproved of, us or her husband.'

'So you weren't very impressed?' asked Mirabel.

'We couldn't make her out. She hardly said a dozen words the whole time she was here. She looked and sounded uncomfortable. And Charles was as bold as brass, smiling and making remarks about changes since he was last here. He even commented on his father's hair-cut. Unfavourably, of course.'

'I'd only had it done the day before, by the same barber I'd been to for years.'

'They only stayed for perhaps three-quarters of an hour. Gilbert was just explaining something to him, something about repaving the garden paths, when Charles pushes back his cuff and says it was time they were on their way since they had two more visits to make. He was up like a start and outside to the hall to get their coats, which they had on in no time. I noticed he just pushed Anne's into her arms. There was no attempt to be polite and help her on with it.'

'I asked him when they'd be likely to call again. He said he didn't know. His business had made this present opportunity. I told him to give us a ring so that we could prepare to entertain them properly. "Oh," he says, "we're not complaining about the hospitality."'

'And that was that. They were off like a shot from a gun.'

'And into a great Mercedes,' Lockwood added. 'It pretty well filled the whole street.'

'Don't exaggerate, Gilbert,' Joan chided. 'But we were left here in silence. Gob-smacked as they say nowadays. Do you know the last thing he said to me as he passed me on his way out? "You've not forgotten how to make a cake, Ma. I'll say that for you. You could give Annie here a tip or two in that field."'

'And did his wife say anything to that?' Mirabel asked.

'No. She tried to smile and tripped off down the path.'

'We always tried to bring him up politely,' Joan said.

'Time wasted.'

'If he comes again, I don't feel like opening the door to him. Son or no son.'

'Did they come to visit you when he was married to Mirabel?' George Taylor asked his first question. 'I think you said so.'

'They did. You insisted on it, didn't you, darling?' Joan said.

'Yes, we used to come when we lived in London. He didn't demur. He knew I got on well with his parents. Of course, he wasn't perhaps so immersed in his work.'

'He wasn't on the Board then?'

'It seemed to me,' Joan said, 'as if he was getting above himself. He wasn't ever bothered to enquire from his wife what they were about to do or when.'

'He was always that way inclined when he was younger. We thought you were getting him out of it,' said Lockwood to Mirabel.

'I always had my say about how we spent our spare time. I don't remember that he was too unreasonable. Then again, he may have chosen Anne so that he could always do as he liked.'

'You were good for him. We often said so,' Joan told her.

'Or too good.'

'He always liked his own way. Didn't you think so, Mirabel?'

'All husbands do. It's different, I guess, when there are children.'

'Did you argue with him about that?'

'We didn't exactly quarrel. But he made it clear that he put his work first, above everything else. He'd say to me, "Let's make sure we can bring children up properly, not scraping round in poverty."'

'You weren't short of money, were you?'

'By no means. But he encouraged me to go out to work. "It'll occupy you," he said. By that time we weren't, we found, exactly suited one to the other.'

'How did that come about?' Lockwood asked.

'Charles arranged things, pleasant enough in themselves, without mentioning them to me until the very last minute.'

'And you didn't mind?' Joan queried.

'No, not too much at first. I enjoyed these entertainments, even business occasions. Especially when I had time to prepare myself for them. Later, I couldn't quite make out what he was up to. I remember one evening he came home and announced that we were off to New York the next morning. "It's only for a week," he said. There were three major social events, dinners, we had to attend. It was then that I warned him.'

'Did he seem surprised?' Lockwood asked.

'You never knew with him. I said that it meant missing two quite important interviews at the office next day. He mocked me. "Quite important?" he said. "*Quite* important. This trip is *very* important. It means big money to the firm, if it comes off. And big money to the firm means big money to you and me, my girl."' Her voice took on his sarcastic overtones. '"How long have you known about this?" I asked him.

'"I only learned the final details today."

'"Somebody didn't see it as so very important, if they only told you about it today."

'"I didn't say that," was his answer.

'"If you want me looking at my best, you'll give me a week or two to buy myself suitable outfits, and clear my work-desk," I said.

'"You'll look beautiful in the clothes you've already got packed into your wardrobes, darling." And I told him, politely, that that was up to me to decide.'

'Do you think it was deliberate on his part?' Joan asked.

'I do. It happened again, too often to be mere forgetfulness.'

'Why would he act so?' Gilbert Lockwood asked.

'He thought I'd spend, or overspend, a lot of money on clothes for the occasion.'

'It wouldn't be his money, would it?'

'No. It would be mine. But he thought I might outshine him.'

'Had you done so? Before, I mean.'

'I wouldn't have said so. But it was his crooked thinking.

37

If we'd been out, and somebody made a fuss of me or paid me particular attention, he didn't like it. He must be the star of the evenings, the centre of attention.'

'The cynosure of all eyes.' George Taylor offered the phrase diffidently.

The parents and Mirabel recalled occasions in their son's married life when he'd shown jealousy and arrogance. The Lockwoods now seemed to enjoy slandering their boy. Twice Joan broke into the recital to say how glad she was that Mirabel had seen fit to visit them, and how the home seemed brighter for her presence. She seemed to George to exaggerate, and not inconsiderably, but the old woman continued to speak freely.

After an hour, when the coffee-pot was empty, Gilbert Lockwood said he hoped the visitors could stay for high tea. Mirabel seemed to hesitate, but when George said he had the time Mirabel immediately accepted the invitation.

'It's too dark for you to see anything of the garden,' Gilbert mumbled.

'Not that there's anything to be seen,' his wife added.

'I like the spring flowers even when there aren't many of them,' he said.

'Would you like sausages for tea?' Joan now approached George properly. 'I've just discovered some in Sainsbury's that are tasty, really delicious. It's the herbs they use.'

'What are they called?'

'I've forgotten. My head's like a colander. But I'll show you the packet when we put them in the oven.'

'She's like a dog with two tails,' Lockwood said to George when the women were out of the way. 'My word, I've something to be grateful for. Joan's not been well since Christmas, so down in the mouth. This visit will be a real pick-me-up.'

'Your wife seems really fond of Mirabel,' George said.

'She thought Mirabel was beginning to sort Charles out as we'd never been able to.'

'It's a pity the marriage came to nothing.'

'I hope that's not altogether so. I don't think that they'll get together again, but the time they had together wasn't quite wasted. I think Charles was made to see the other side of any matter.'

'Were they unhappy?'

'She was. I don't think he wanted to lose her. As long as he

38

could have priority for his views, she was otherwise a perfect wife.'

'He'd feel the loss of her when she moved out?'

'I'm never sure. Yes, I suppose he did. Mirabel was one of his possessions, the sort of wife any man would want; beautiful, intelligent, good company and one who kept the home in perfect order. Joan says he didn't know how lucky he was, and that's about right.'

George Taylor enjoyed the high tea which followed. The recommended sausages certainly were delicious and unusual. The old people reminisced a great deal, and Gilbert Lockwood produced photographs of his early married life. Charles appeared on these, a small, very smart boy, with brilliantined hair, looking superior to the other people and the surroundings.

'He was so clever,' his mother said. 'And so charming. He'd go out of his way to be attractive to those he talked to, be they young or old. I don't know where we went wrong.'

'I don't altogether blame you or myself,' said her husband.

'There must be some reason,' she said. 'Even if what we saw and admired expanded and altered for the worse because we did nothing to prevent it and he became what he is now.'

This led to argument, fairly light-hearted, about from which parent he inherited these characteristics. Mrs Lockwood became jolly, exuberant even, as she put her point of view, to such an extent that George began to wonder if she was as normal as he had at first thought. Mirabel intervened only rarely, as if she had neither right nor knowledge to pronounce on her ex-husband's conduct.

'You're too generous to him,' Gilbert Lockwood said when she very mildly suggested that it was perhaps Charles's work, his status in the office, had caused his fall from grace.

'You wouldn't have thought so if you had heard the way I used to tear into him. When I think about it now, I feel quite ashamed.'

'I expect he deserved it.'

'I'm sure he did, but I don't think he was as capable of shrugging off criticism as I was.'

At these times a kind of darkness, grief even, settled on the table. They ate grimly, not venturing further into such swamps of depressive talk. It was usually Gibert who attempted, not always successfully, to usher them back to euphoria.

'This is more like a funeral than a reunion,' his wife objected.

'I'm not much of an expert on funerary matters,' George said, 'but at the few wakes I've attended, I've always been amazed at the cheerfulness of the whole affair.'

'Does that apply to the surviving partner?' Mirabel asked.

'Not exactly, but they don't appear as grief-stricken as I expect I would be if I were left a widower. Perhaps it's the appearance of all sorts of people who have turned up. They'd come, at some cost to themselves, to pay tribute to their old friend, colleague, acquaintance. And this had so surprised the relict that it introduced a new note to their grief.'

The conversation became thinner, with longer pauses, as the meal drew to a close. When they had finished and the table was cleared, Gilbert and George went out to the kitchen to wash the dishes.

'This afternoon is just what Joan needed. It'll set her up for weeks. She's not been well now, what with one thing and another. It'll be the subject matter of talk, breakfast, lunch and dinner. Get Mirabel to come again soon, won't you?'

'I hardly know her. It's by a series of coincidences I've become the means of escorting her up here.'

'You surprise me. I thought you were together. Engaged or near it. You talk like a married couple.'

'I've hardly said a word since we came.'

'You've let Mirabel have her own way. They're her friends, let her enjoy them.'

'I never thought of it like that. I could see your wife was absolutely delighted, and I'm not one for spoiling something that's going so easily and well.'

'You were damn' near perfect.'

'Oh, thank you.'

The four parted at the front door with a flurry of invitations, promises and hugs which were repeated *con brio* at the street gate.

A yard or two along the avenue, Mirabel, stepping quickly out, said, 'That's wasted your evening for you.'

'Wasted? Not the word I'd choose. You made old Mrs Lockwood very happy.'

'You think so? She's very like her son Charles. She exaggerates everything.'

'I don't think I've ever seen anybody look so pleased. If she didn't mean it, then she's a marvellous actress.'

'She reminds me of a girl in my class in infants' school. If you gave her your one last broken bit of your Radiance toffee, you'd think you'd just presented her with a diamond ring.'

'Perhaps she never had any treats at home or pocket money for sweeties.'

'May be. But that's no reason to go over the top.'

'You think not? Look, that girl did something that you remember all these years later. How long ago is it? Thirty?'

'More. But I only remember her to mock her.'

'Where is she now?'

'I've no idea. My parents took me out of the State system at the end of the year when I was eight. After that it was private education.'

'And you never ran across the girl again?'

'No. Not that I looked very hard.'

'What was her name?'

'Spinks. I think that was it. I can't remember her first name. Edna? Was that it? Elsie? No.'

'And yet you remember her begging for your throw-away sweets. We all wish to be remembered.'

'Even for the silly or wicked things we've done? You don't think so? You've some curious ideas, Mr George Taylor.'

'But worth remembering.'

They both laughed, if rather nervously. After a few more steps in silence he invited her to walk back to his flat for a drink.

'No, thanks. I'd love to, but I've some work from the office that I'd like to get out of the way so that I can have Sunday free.'

'And how will you spend that?'

'That depends on several things. The first is to make sure that the work I have is clear and I've left nothing to worry about.'

'Do you like the law?' he asked.

'Not really. Not at my level. There's nothing that's very exacting. It's all run-of-the-mill stuff.'

'Like reading the envelope properly and then putting it through the right door?'

'Something like that. A bit more demanding perhaps. And besides, I have to do it in a stuffy room while you stride along in the fresh air.'

'The fresh air in my case is often icy rain, though I hope

that's done for this season. But while I'm walking these streets now, there's one thing that puzzles me.'

'What's that?'

'Why the thing that so impressed me about Mrs Lockwood, and which you call exaggeration, is the very behaviour that made her son impossible for you to live with.'

'The subject matter. Joan Lockwood impressed you because you thought it good that she could praise me, even if she went over the top with it.'

'She didn't.'

'Have it your own way.'

They reached the confluence of the Lockwoods' avenue and his road. Here they stopped as if they wished to continue the talk.

'Are you sure you won't come in for a drink?' George asked again.

'Certain. But thank you all the same.'

'Will you visit the old people again?' he asked.

'Yes. In a week or two. I quite enjoy their company.'

'Even when they're exaggerating?'

'Gilbert doesn't. He's a sweetie.'

'Not anything like his son.'

'His facial expressions remind me of him. The way he twists his mouth. Gilbert must have looked like Charles as a young man. They're not much alike in temperament.'

George put out his hand to be shaken.

'Goodbye,' he said. 'Shall I see you again?'

'That I don't know. I've reported our meeting to Andy, but he was in his usual hurry about his own affairs that he didn't listen. Just like Charles. That's two of them.'

'Your friends are full of faults,' he said.

'Goodbye, Mr Postman.'

She touched his still outstretched hand, swirled about and was gone, walking stately down the darkened street. George, put properly in his place, followed her progress and smiled. He did not mind such insults from that source.

IV

After that George heard nothing from Mirabel. He told himself that he was not disappointed, that her silence was what he expected. He was nevertheless not displeased to receive a card from Andrew Barron. It was sent as a post-card, not enclosed in an envelope as so many were these days. The hand-writing was large and dashing.

> Thank you for taking Mirabel to the Lockwoods'; she said you were the perfect escort. When I meet with her again we'll discuss our visit to you, and try for a date which will not disorganise any previous engagements. Good wishes and apologies. Andrew B.

George slipped it on to a wooden letter-rack which he had made at school. He'd disliked woodwork and both its teachers, and his models were almost immediately broken up and thrown into the waste-paper basket. This one passed muster at least: 'C –, very fair'. He was allowed to stain it, and varnish then polish it. He was not altogether pleased; he could see its many faults, but he presented it to his mother who kept it for the rest of her life. When he cleared her house he took it together with a dozen or so of the antique pieces she had collected. It had none of their virtues, but it now stood, slightly more battered than when it had left the school premises, on his desk, still capable of holding cards and letters. George looked sourly at it. He upturned it and could still read on the bottom 'N.G. Taylor, VA Classical.'

Now he stared at Andrew's card, in its place of honour. He needed to stir, to get out of his flat, he decided.

He washed his hands and face; flattened his hair, straightening his parting in the process; and took out, for the first time this year his best, heaviest overcoat. Making sure he had money in his wallet, he set out for the pub. As he walked George decided against the nearest, a pleasant rather sedate place, and stepped out away from town towards the Tom Bowling.

This stood half a mile along the busy main road, a tall, slightly lop-sided brick building, both uninviting and out of place against the neat rows of terraced houses on either side. He climbed three worn stairs, and found himself facing four doors. Never having been in here before, he was at a loss for the moment. He decided on the left hand, which would lead surely into a room at the front of the building.

He was fortunate; he had guessed right. This was the main centre of entertainment, with chairs and tables, more than half unoccupied. The room was not well lit but the bar, bright with a wall of massed bottles behind it, seemed welcoming. The barman, busy with a cloth and glasses, glanced at him, nodded him forward, as if he had noticed, even approved of the hesitant entrance he had made.

George arrived at the bar at the same time as a tallish old man who wore a dark blue raincoat with large buttons and belt and, altogether out of match, a newish trilby hat of a rich brown, looking as if it had been dyed freshly by some half-blind novice that evening. George signalled the other man forward. He declined.

'No, thanks, mate. You were here first.'

The telephone rang. The barman turned to answer it.

'If you'll excuse me, gentlemen,' he said. 'There's nothing on this phone that'll occupy me long.'

'That's a curious sentence,' Trilby said. 'This phone. Perhaps there is another that will give him good news, or bad, or at least interesting.'

'He's usually an accurate speaker?' George asked.

The barman replaced his phone.

'Bloody fool,' he said. 'Now, gentlemen. Who's first?'

Trilby gestured towards George who, having ordered his pint of bitter, nodded his thanks and made for an empty table where he sat and looked about him. The other drinkers had glanced up but now returned to their own concerns: conversation, thoughtful silence or dominoes. Trilby was still engaged at the counter; both his head and the barman's were lowered, though to what purpose George could not make out. He raised his drink; took a further glance round him before tipping the glass. The beer tasted good; he closed his eyes. By the time he had taken a second mouthful and carefully replaced the glass on the table, Trilby was making his way across the room to stand in front of him.

'Mind if I join you?' he asked.

'Sit down.'

'You're sure you're not waiting for anybody?'

The man sat, removed his hat and placed it to the right of his beer on the table. He then lifted his glass, took a swig, made a face expressing satisfaction.

'I've not seen you in here before,' he said.

'No. It's my first time.'

'Is your beer good?'

'Excellent.'

Down to the table went the man's hand and glass.

'That's the thing I like about this place. They know how to look after their ale. The actual room,' he waved a critical hand, 'is about as attractive as a wet washday.'

George did not answer, but tried his own beer again.

'There's nothing comfortable in this place. The pictures on the wall make that lime-green paper even more drab than they are. And the mirrors. They're too small to be useful, and are hung just where people can't get to them. And the lights. Dirty, undusted forty-watt bulbs.' He breathed deeply. 'It's as if they set out to put you off.'

'But there's no music.'

'Ah, yes. I take it you don't like music, then.'

'Not the sort they play in pubs. And it's either too loud or too soft.'

'What would you like?'

'Bach.'

'And loud?'

'I'd want to hear it.'

Trilby nodded, almost violently.

'I'll introduce myself,' he said. 'Francis Smith, known by my second name, Jim.'

'Thank you. George Taylor.'

'I've seen you somewhere. Do you live in these parts?'

'A quarter of an hour's walk away.'

'But you don't come in here. They look after you once they know you. You can get a superb lunch in the middle of the day. Goes on to three-thirty on Sunday.'

George looked hard at Trilby Smith and guessed him to be much older than he appeared.

'There are some streets not a million miles from here that are not fit to live in on account of the young hooligans and their thoughtless parents.' He had half-a-dozen anecdotes all ready for the telling, with which he must have regaled audiences before. He clearly enjoyed his rôle as raconteur.

'Is it worse now than it was when you were a boy?' George asked.

'Hard to say,' Smith answered, raising his pint. 'There's more money about now. And more guns and knives. And more immigrants.'

'Are they responsible for the trouble then?'

'Some of it, though I often wonder how I'd feel if I applied for a job and someone no better qualified than I got it because his skin was whiter than mine.'

'Is that often the case?'

'Often? Almost invariably.' He smacked his lips over the adverb.

'Did you start your working life here?' George asked.

'Yes, I did. In the Lace Market, though we produced high-class clothes. The firm's still there. Lockwood's. Have you heard of it? I had my first job in the offices. I was top of my class when I left, and my form-teacher promised me he'd write to Mr Lockwood, whom he said he knew, to recommend me for a job. He gave me some advice on how to stand and dress for the interview. We broke up on one Friday and I started work Monday morning as everybody's dogsbody.'

'Were they good employers?'

'Yes. They sent me to night-school, and I took several courses they recommended. Showed real interest in me, did Mr Lockwood.'

'That would be the father of the present Mr Lockwood?'

'Gilbert?'

'That's the man. I was talking to him the other day. They'd had a fire, a small affair in an unused bedroom. But they were coping pretty well.'

'Is his wife still alive?'

'Joan? Yes.'

'She was a very pretty girl. And if I had to deliver something from the factory to their home, she always rewarded me with a slice of delicious fruit cake, sometimes with icing on it. At home we only had that at Christmas, not even on birthdays.' Trilby sighed. 'Ah, times have changed. There weren't too many treats about at that time, or not for the likes of me. Strict economies, coupons and the like. Nowadays kids don't know they're born.'

He led off for the next five minutes about the use of knives and guns, George returning from the bar with their second drinks.

'I hear that some experts talk of rewarding repentant wrong-doers in schools,' Smith said. 'All carrot; no stick. Bloody ridiculous, if you ask me.'

'Spare the rod, and spoil the child?' George asked.

'Who said that?'

'The Bible. *Proverbs*. And Samuel Butler. I know because I had reason to look it up only a few days ago.'

'Wasn't he a local man?'

'No. That was another Samuel Butler. This one wrote a poem called "Hudibras". Your man lived in the Victorian period. Wrote *The Way of all Flesh*.'

Smith seemed to shrink at this correction.

'You don't mind my asking, but are you a teacher?'

'No, I used to be. I'm a postman now.'

That also put Smith on the back foot. He frowned, as if he was finding difficulty in assembling words for the next question or observation.

'Did you teach here?'

'No. Out at Mansfield. In the grammar school there.'

Smith made curious noises as an introduction to coherent speech.

'Isn't that . . . I don't know quite how to put this . . . I mean, it's no business of mine to be poking into your private life, but isn't it a bit of a come-down? You need a degree to teach at a grammar school, don't you? I've nothing against postmen. It's a responsible job in its way. Very much so. You don't mind my asking, do you? I've always worked on the assumption that if you want to find something out, the best way to do it is to ask plainly about it.' When George did not immediately reply, Smith shuffled his feet, and cleared his throat noisily. 'It's got me into trouble, I must confess, more than once.'

'I don't mind your asking. I didn't get sacked for interfering with boys or helping myself to the school funds.'

'Oh, no. I didn't have any such suspicions.'

'I think I would have done. No, I had trouble with my lungs and the doctor suggested that I'd do myself some good by working out in the open air. I'll tell you, my chest was giving me hell at the time, and I was only too glad to work on a round out in the country.'

'Did it do the trick?'

'It seems to have done so. Whether the improvement is permanent I can't say. Nor can the doctor. I was also lucky insofar as I wasn't short of money. I owned my own house in Mansfield, and bought a convenient flat in town here.'

'Don't you miss teaching?'

'I teach an adult class once a week in Mansfield.'

'What do you teach them?'

'Literature. Victorians this year. Mainly Shakespeare.'

'Is he, in your opinion, the greatest of our writers?'

'Yes, I think so.' George Taylor then stood, and leaning on the table, supported by his spread fingers, said, 'I must go now. I have to be up early, Shakespeare or not. That's one of the disadvantages of a postman's life.'

'But I'd like to buy you another pint.'

'No, thank you. Two is my limit, otherwise I'll be up all night.'

'Then I hope to meet you again before long and fulfil my obligations.'

George smiled at the phrase.

'Good night. I've enjoyed our conversation. And if I see Mr Lockwood I'll tell him I've talked to you.'

'That's Gilbert Lockwood?' Trilby asked.

'Yes. Will he remember you?'

'I'm certain he will. He didn't like me very much.'

'Was he one quick to take offence? That's not the way he struck me.' George re-seated himself.

'You must remember,' Smith said, 'that all this is getting on for fifty years ago. I was a sensitive youth of seventeen and may well have read things into the situation that weren't there. I've told you that old Mr Lockwood thought highly of me and said so – sent me on courses, explained things about running the firm that were, to say the least, unusual. He used to tell me that I was doing well, and that if I went on like that I'd be in

48

line for promotion and end up as a manager, at least, in my twenties. Then young Mr Gilbert arrived on the scene.

'He'd been to Oxford or Cambridge or somewhere of the sort and then taken a position in our biggest place, the Loughborough factory, and from the men in charge there he didn't get very good reports. He wouldn't be told by people he thought of as underlings. So his father had to take him back to our place. And old Mr Lockwood was always praising me . . . A clever boy who worked really hard and was quick to learn. Well, Mr Gilbert Junior didn't like it, and he treated me like dirt. If I explained our way of doing something, he'd find something amiss with it. Or that's how it seemed to me. Perhaps I was wrong. When I think about it now, Mr Gilbert treated all his underlings and employees in the same way.'

'Is that why you left the firm?'

'Yes. In time. I didn't think I'd get anywhere there with the young squire about, and it wouldn't have been too long before they'd have thrown me out.'

'You didn't get any promotion after the son arrived?'

'No. I was promoted by Mr Lockwood, Senior, but promotion in that sort of old-fashioned firm was slow. You never reached any sort of managerial position, even foreman; these only came to you when you'd reached middle-age.'

'My impression of Gilbert Lockwood is of a mild, unaggressive person.'

'I may have been wrong, over-sensitive about it all, but I left. And it turned out to be a good move.'

'And how did you end up?'

'In the property market. With Drew and Walmsley. In the end I became a partner there, and I still am, which I wouldn't ever have been in the case of Lockwood's.'

'And have you seen Gilbert Lockwood recently?'

'Not once in all that time. No, I did see him on one occasion in town, not so long back. He passed me by without so much as a flicker of an eyelid.'

'You were ready to speak to him?'

'Yes. We'd worked together for three or four years. It's quite possible he didn't recognise me, though.'

'Have you changed much?'

'I wouldn't have said so. His eyes may be failing, for all I know. If you do mention my name to him, now I come to think

49

about it, he may not have the slightest notion who it is you're talking about.'

'I'll try it, it all sounds so interesting.' George rose again.

'I don't mind. You please yourself. I hope we meet again. It's been a fascinating evening. You're the sort of man I can talk to. And that's not always the case.'

Smith stood up uncertainly and put out long, delicate fingers. The two men shook hands before George pushed brusquely out of the building.

In the street a chill wind blew into his face, and he hurried to reach home.

V

Some four days later George received a telephone call from Andrew Barron enquiring about a suitable date to call in.

'Will any day of the week suit you?' George asked.

'Well . . .' The voice hesitated.

'I'd like you and Mrs Lockwood to come for a meal in the evening. Any day except my Tuesday teaching night will do, so long as we don't stretch it out too late. We postmen have to be in early to see you get your first post in time for you to go to work on it.'

'You've not been so regular lately. Not that I'm complaining.'

'It would be a waste of breath complaining to me. I just do what I'm told.'

'I doubt that.'

They decided on the next Saturday at seven o'clock.

'Is there anything you don't eat?' George asked.

'Not really. Do you ever cook vegetarian meals?'

'Yes, but only rarely.'

'Is it a lot of trouble?'

'No. Less if anything. It'll be nothing out of the ordinary. Plain cook, that's me. Are you big eaters?'

'We'll do justice to it, I can assure you.'

Andrew Barron spoke cheerfully, and their arrival on Saturday was equally jovial. Andrew had dressed in a very decent dark grey suit with a white shirt and some sort of club tie, which George could not identify.

Laughter seemed to rebound from the walls as he took their coats and hung them away. Mirabel described the difficulty she had in getting Andrew to dress like a 'Christian and a gentleman' to pay this visit.

'She knows I'm neither,' Andrew said.

'That's why you need disguising.'

They sat in the large sitting-room and drank, their choice,

51

dry sherry. They talked about the weather which had changed from sunny, mild days at the beginning of the week to cold, windy, showery rain which rattled the windows.

Talk came easily. George explained why he thought *King Lear* Shakespeare's greatest play.

'Not *Hamlet*?' Mirabel asked.

'I'm not really competent to judge between such high master-pieces. But to my failing senses the tragedy of an old man and his hateful daughters, his madness, the misjudged Cordelia's death, affect me more than the young prince of Denmark, though I am greatly moved by both. I'm afraid that's not a strong argument, I know.'

'Did your pupils never try to rank plays by merit?'

'No. Their examiners want to find out how well they know the text. In my view that's quite sufficient. If they are then asked to choose between two plays, at least they have a sound knowledge of the words.'

'Do you think literary fashions change?' Andrew asked.

'I'm sure they do. The critics who followed Shakespeare in the next hundred or so years would have made it clear that they thought he was at his best writing comedies.'

'You don't think that, surely?' Mirabel asked.

'No, I don't. But I can easily imagine that if I had lived in the seventeenth or eighteenth century I should have had such a belief.'

Both visitors seemed much taken by this statement, and began to argue. In the middle of a quite hectic disagreement about Shakespeare's language, George stood quietly, excused himself under his breath, and went out to bring in the first course. When he returned he was carrying a huge tray with three bowls of soup and a plate of toasted croutons on it. They took their places eagerly enough, unwrapped their napkins, and began. He rested the tray against the unoccupied end of the table. The guests wasted no time.

'Delicious,' Andrew said, after suspiciously testing a spoonful of soup. 'What is it?'

'Home-grown cabbage,' the host said, enjoying his first mouthful.

'It isn't borscht, is it?'

'I've never had borscht, so I can't say.'

'Borscht has beetroot in it,' Mirabel told them.

'It's from an old recipe of my mother's.'

'Is it still in print?'

'This is from a note-book in her own handwriting. Heaven knows where she took it from.'

Andrew helped himself to a further delicate handful of croutons. He did not speak again until he had cleared his bowl.

'That's a winner,' he said, partially stifling a belch.

'Positively in the Shakespeare class,' Mirabel said. She was still engaged hard with the soup. 'Your own cabbages?'

As he collected the plates, George described, pedantically, the small stretch of garden where he cultivated his vegetables.

'A man of parts,' Andrew said.

'The next course, I'm afraid, you'll find rather bland,' George said, as he made for the door.

'It's not from your mother's note-book, then?' Mirabel asked.

'No. It's from a little paperback pamphlet called *The New Housewife's Cookery Book*. I found it in her cupboard. Presumably she approved of it or she would have thrown it away.'

The guests were talking quietly when he returned with three plates of vegetables, theirs filled high, all topped with Cheddar cheese, richly melted. A jug of chopped tomato he placed between them on the table.

They ate heartily. He felt pretty certain that they would have preferred something spicier, more tongue-tingling, but they cleared their plates and seemed sincere in their praise.

'I cooked you that not only because it's easy, but because I was sure you were people who insist on five vegetables or fruits a day, and with this you could exceed the limit.'

'Excellent,' Andrew said. 'I feel full already.'

'Yes, I could have chosen something more filling. But I wanted to leave space for the pudding.'

'What is it?' Mirabel asked.

'Guess.'

'Fruit salad.' George shook his head.

'Meringues, peaches and cream,' Andrew called out.

'You are both wrong. It's Christmas pudding, custard and cream. I did my neighbour up above a good turn and she presented me with two puddings. "If you don't want them now, they'll keep," she said. I ate one slowly over the Christmas week, seven whole days. And now, on the brink of spring, we'll test the other tonight.'

'Test?' Mirabel said. 'Is it likely to have gone off?'

'Not the way I've nurtured it.'

'Nurtured?' asked Andrew.

'That's not the right word perhaps. It's been in the freezer and I've looked at it from time to time. I wanted it ready for your visit, because it would remind me, if not you, of our first meeting on Christmas Day. But then I began to despair of you; I thought you'd never come.'

'I told you he'd rub it in,' said Andrew.

'And quite right, too,' Mirabel answered.

'We'll make it up over the pudding,' George called back as he left for the kitchen.

He served the pudding and encouraged them to have both custard and cream.

'That surprises me,' Mirabel said. 'I had guessed you'd be the sort of person who thought one can spoil something very good by overdoing it.'

Both she and Andrew confined themselves to custard. George, partaking of both, felt he'd be judged as a sybarite.

'I don't get the hang of you two,' he said.

'That's how we like it. To be persons of mystery, not to be immediately figured out.'

Mirabel helped him carry in the coffee to where they found Andrew Barron almost asleep in front of the fire.

'I don't know what's wrong with him,' she said. 'He's been idle all day.'

She hovered, like an examiner, round the table, where George poured out the coffee. Mirabel carried a cup over to Andrew and shook him, none too gently, then placed it on the table by his chair.

'Thanks,' he said. The other two seated themselves.

They sat for a minute or two in a warm silence, studying the fire. They felt at ease. George was sure he had satisfied his guests, that they'd be sorry to leave.

Andrew sat up straighter in his chair. Now there was nothing lethargic about him. His fists were clenched, and he looked ready to leap to his feet. Still in this position, actively sitting, he spoke to George. His voice had an almost threatening ring.

'Now, young man, we have a little matter to discuss with you.'

George made no attempt to answer.

'Mirabel and I have talked this over together, and for once

54

we agreed. After our meeting on Christmas Day we decided that we liked you. You impressed us. This is not a common occurrence in our variable lives, but we'll not tell you why at any length. We both said we'd like to meet you again. Now at that time we were particularly busy, one way or the other, and so, feebly, we never came round to arranging contact again. You weren't forgotten, I can assure you of that. We mentioned you time after time, but never got down to discussing the day and nature of a meeting.

'Weeks seem to slip past us at that time of year, winter beginning to become spring. You may think, I know I would, that the meeting with you could not have been of much importance to us or we'd have done something about it. But we were both very busy, and Mirry had a bad attack of 'flu.'

Here Andrew took in a great breath as if to signal that the end was in sight. 'Then Mirry met you and told me about it, and we both felt desperately guilty. We'd treated you shabbily. We had promised to get in touch, and had left it dragging on for four months. It was bad manners, grossly impolite. Then you invite us here. I won't say I felt too ashamed to come, for I knew I'd be interested to meet you again. We discussed it. We came. You do us well, not showing rancour, but heaping coals of fire on our already troubled heads. And we decided on something, and our decision seems confirmed by our reception here tonight.

'Now, here's what we decided, what we suggest. You needn't give us an answer immediately. We've no idea of your circumstances, your arrangements. What I'd like to suggest humbly, with no pressure on you to agree, is that the three of us, Mirabel, you and I, should spend a holiday of three or four days together, really to get to know each other. How does that seem to you?'

George said nothing.

'I know we've treated you badly.'

'No, you have not.'

Andrew frowned as if annoyed at George's answer.

'Let Mirabel plead our cause then,' he said, rather stiffly.

'We would really like to spend a day or two in your company. I realise that our invitation must seem odd to you. But we mean it. Could we arrange something?'

'That's kind of you.' His answer sounded ironic.

'Do you agree? You accept the idea in principle?' She leaned forward towards him.

'Yes.'

'Then we can work out the detail. Unless you have an idea you'd like us to try.'

He shrugged. Disappointment showed in her face at this apparent lack of enthusiasm.

'We have two suggestions. Turn them down if you wish, and we'll try again. Andy has a biggish caravan and we can take it anywhere. I have a cottage in Derbyshire, miles from civilisation. Do they sound anywhere near your choice? Or do you prefer the seaside?'

'Your caravan could go to the coast, couldn't it?'

'If you so wished.'

'I see you are intent on pleasing me, and I'm grateful. But there's no need to go out of your way. You owe me nothing. I would like to spend a few days with you, but for the sake of your company not for the venue.'

'Does either of our suggestions appeal?'

'Is there room in the cottage?' he asked.

'We shan't be sleeping three to a bed,' Andrew said, laughing. 'Could you get yourself three days off, let's say at the end of the month, and we'll fix it? That'll give me or Mirry time to go over to the cottage and warm it up. It's hardly been used this winter.'

The rest of the evening was spent in talk on subjects randomly chosen. Whatever they chose to chat about seemed to come easily to all three. Andrew and Mirabel were not averse to crossing verbal swords, but strongly as they argued, or criticised their opponent, it neither dispersed nor lessened their appreciation of the other. Mirabel talked to George about Bach, and he in return answered her with a performance on his piano of a fugue from the 48 in *The Well-Tempered Clavier* no xi, in F. He was making an obvious point that Bach's subjects were interesting, memorable in themselves, never mind what the Master made of them. Mirabel did not seem convinced. His guests were moved by the demonstration, however; they had not expected it, but it strengthened their already strong opinion that George Taylor was an acquaintance worth cultivating.

George had set the time for breaking up at ten o'clock, but such was the general enjoyment that they did not leave until well past eleven. Andrew rolled out the old cliché about their evening: 'the feast of reason and the flow of soul', and sober as they were the others did not laugh at him.

'Who wrote that, Andy?' Mirabel asked.

'Hanged if I know. Pope, probably.'

'What about it, George? Who was responsible?'

'Pope.'

'Where, pray?'

'*Imitations of Horace.*'

'How in hell did you know that?' Andy was struggling into his topcoat.

'By chance. I looked it up for a friend only last week.'

Mirabel clapped her gloved hands.

'That's our sort of man,' she said. 'He looks up the answers to our questions a week before we ask them.'

George stood bemused behind the closed door, listening for his guests outside. He heard Andrew Barron's four-wheel drive start up and the sound of tyres on gravel. He felt lonely; he begrudged his friends' absence, as if he and his house had been robbed of something precious and long-standing. With no attempt to clear away he made straight for bed.

By the end of the month the arrangements had been made by telephone for George's stay at Mirabel's cottage.

On the selected day, Wednesday, Andrew called for George, who climbed into the 4 x 4 with something like excitement. He had done a round that morning, and had gone straight to bed after lunch, and was now speeding in comfort towards Derbyshire. They talked as they travelled, while George admired his host's fast but skilful driving.

'Will Mirabel be ready for us?' George asked.

'I hope so. She's been there since Monday night. The place needs some looking after. I don't know the exact ins-and-outs of it, but it was her grandfather or great-uncle who'd left it to her. He'd spent a lot of money on it. When they took electricity to the cottages he had them extend the cables over. He had the place put in order, decorated and so forth.'

'What was the idea?'

'As far as I can gather, the old man had the thought of spending time there himself. He had holidayed out there as a boy, and now he was old looked back sentimentally to that time. It didn't altogether work, because the place was too out of the way. He had a big car, a Bentley, so it was easy enough to drive over to the shops, or so I'd have thought.'

'But it didn't suit?'

'He managed one winter. But as soon as spring appeared, and the bad weather was over, the old man took ill. He was rushed back home to hospital, and died in the late-summer. Sometime at the period of his illness he changed his will and made the place over to Mirry.'

'Was she a favourite of his?'

'Not particularly, as far as I can make out. But if Mirry sees anybody in need of a helping hand she'll move in sharp to give it, and I guess she did in this case. Or it may be that back in history, her family had done him a good turn. I don't know. Whatever the reason, he left her the cottage and quite a sum towards its upkeep.'

'Was she pleased?'

'Surprised. Didn't expect anything except a keepsake or two or a few hundred pounds to dress herself suitably for his funeral. She'd never seen the place, never visited him there.'

'Taken aback, was she? It doesn't do to help too many lame dogs.'

'There was also a long codicil in his will saying what she could or could not do with the place if she decided to accept the inheritance. The most important of these clauses was the one which said she could not sell it. She could do what she liked with it as long as it remained hers. If she decided she didn't want it, it went to some charity, the National Trust perhaps, I don't know.'

'Why did he demand this?'

'He wanted the house looked after, and thought she was the person to do it. I'm a bit vague about it all because I saw little of Mirry at the time. It was during her divorce.'

'And did she take the bequest seriously? Once the house was hers?'

'I believe so. She drives out to the place every free weekend. And occasionally in mid-week. Of course, electricity and a modern, efficient central heating system made it easier to keep the damp and wildlife at bay. She even planted a bit of a garden: shrubs and a fruit tree or two. It must have been a burden. I would have hated it, but in the blank period after her divorce it gave her something to do.'

'I'd have thought, on my short acquaintance, she wouldn't have been short of friends or cultural activities, theatre, music, books.'

'You may be right. But I think the split with her husband hit her hard, and she wanted diversions of a different sort from her usual ones. It depends. Divorce, which is so common these days that one almost expects it amongst one's friends, affects a few people very strangely. And she's an unusual woman.'

'She hasn't met anyone else she wants to marry, then?'

'Not to my knowledge. I tell you, I wouldn't have minded marrying her when I had the chance.' Andrew slapped the steering wheel. 'I made a move or two in that direction, but after a good beginning on my part, she soon made it clear I wasn't in the running.' He paused from confession to overtake a mini-bus on the narrow road. 'Bloody fool,' he hissed at an eccentric move by the driver as he squeezed past. 'Once she saw I'd accepted this it all became easier. We saw each other more often. She insisted on paying her way if we went anywhere special.'

'And you weren't disappointed?'

Andrew took his eyes from the road.

'Not so much as I expected. Perhaps I'm not the marrying sort.'

'What sort of husband would you say she wants?'

'I don't know. She's clever, did very well at her law exams when we were at college, and deep. Thinks about things. What are we doing here on earth? What's the purpose of our existence? Or isn't there one? She can also be very good company, funny, hilarious sometimes, but sometimes I suspect that behind it all is a woman who is really concerned with what she's doing here, in a way that I never am.'

'And Charles Lockwood fitted the bill for her?'

'I've thought about that. He was our tutor at university, though not at the same time, and seemed so clever, sophisticated, immersed to his advantage in the ways of the world. And good-looking too. Never at a loss.'

'She wasn't smart enough to realise he'd have drawbacks as a husband.'

'She hadn't the experience at the time. How could she know? And another thing I've noticed. Some people who are highly intelligent and very gifted in some ways are stupid when it comes to the straightforward snags of ordinary, day-to-day living.'

'Did you like Lockwood?'

'I was impressed by the man. He thought highly of himself. Now I know he treated Mirry so badly, my opinion of him has been radically changed.'

They drove quickly along the narrowed roads, always safely. It was Andrew who opened the conversation again.

'I wondered,' he said, 'if she wasn't struck on you. She got on to me time and time again about meeting you as we had promised.'

'That was perhaps politeness.'

'Maybe. It seemed more than that. Or perhaps I'm no sort of judge. Or jealous even.' He stopped for thought between each sentence.

'Surely you'd think she'd choose someone with more about him than I have.'

'Don't you run yourself down. I'm just saying I wondered, not that it was so.'

'If she's as gifted as you say she is, she'd be aiming a bit higher than love for a postman.'

'You're an unusual postman. A graduate. A man with a knowledge of literature. You're on the postal rounds not because you're lacking in talent, but because your lungs are not working too well. I shall be watching the pair of you with some interest.'

'I'm flattered.'

From that moment to the end of their journey they talked of other matters: food, local news, house prices, some legal intricacies.

'Here we are then,' Andrew announced.

They had stopped before high iron double gates set in a brick wall. They stood open on to a drive which led to their destination. Once inside the gates Barron stopped to invite George to scrutinise the outside of the 'cottage'.

'It's pretty big,' George said. 'I'd expected something rather more modest.'

'It was originally two, if not three, shepherds' houses.'

'When would that have been?'

'Eighteenth century, perhaps even earlier. It's been altered several times, not least by Mirry's relative. There are five bedrooms now, a kitchen fit for a palace, and two big reception rooms. You'll find it all very comfortable. I've not brought you out here to rough it.

'I'll not put the car away into the garage because if I do Mirry will tell me she's short of butter or gravy-salt and send me belting away to buy some.'

'Will the shops be open?'

'There are no shops here. I shall be sent off to the nearest town where the Co-op or Asda will be open as late as they are in Beechnall.'

They lifted down their luggage and made for the front door with its elaborate porch, which George praised for its originality of design.

'That's where you remove your boots and scrape the mud off after you've been out for a walk. There's even a seat installed for this purpose.'

Lights came on in the porch and the hall behind.

'We've been spotted.'

Mirabel opened the door of the porch and stepped out into the cool of the spring evening.

'Welcome. I thought you'd got lost. Dinner's been ready for some little time.'

'That would be my fault,' George said, not knowing why.

'And I drove very steadily,' Andy said. 'I wanted to deliver our guest safely.'

'I don't believe it,' she said, kissing them both lightly on the cheek and ushering them into the hall. The warmth of the house lapped them in comfort.

'Would you like a wash and then we'll eat?'

'Yes, I could go a pee,' Andrew said.

'I'll serve the soup, so don't be too long.' She disappeared.

Five minutes later Andy led the guest of honour into a large dining-room. He pointed out a chair to George.

'She'll be here any second,' Andy prophesied. 'As soon as she heard us shuffling about here she'd pour the soup. Piping hot is her motto.'

George, once seated, looked about him.

Mirabel brought in the tray of soup, and as she handed out the plates instructed Andrew to light the candles. He did this at once, obviously not for the first time.

'I see we've brought the family silver with us. My word, you're honoured, George.'

He took notice of the magnificent damask tablecloth, the superior knives, forks and spoons, the silver serviette-holders decorated with what seemed like ancient Greeks, indulging nakedly in athletic rivalry. He wondered if these were part of Mirabel's inheritance. She and Andrew kept conversation alive, if with pauses as they enjoyed their tomato soup.

They cleared the soup dishes and noisily prepared the next course for the table. While they were thus occupied in the kitchen, George examined the room. Portraits in oil occupied the long wall. From their clothes he guessed, a little uncertainly, that the sitters had flourished in the late-eighteenth century. The pictures were rather dark, for Mirabel had switched off the electric lights once Andy had lit the candles. George thought hard about his hostess. She had impressed him with the rich colour, a kind of imperial purple, of her beautifully cut dress; its deeply plunging neckline somehow complemented her hair, piled thickly on top of her head. Two long ear-rings sparkled in the semi-darkness and seemed to reflect the jewelled light from the broad bracelet on her left wrist.

Thinking of what Andrew had hinted, he sought in her face or in the tone of her voice some sign of a love for him. He was disappointed. There was nothing.

What did he expect? What could he expect? He did not know. She was a beautiful woman with no more than a marginal interest in him. She let Andy in, he with three steaks on warmed dinner plates, she with a tray of tureens of gravy, vegetables and sauces. Whatever else she was, she was a marvellous cook. George, who thought he detested all culinary extras, saying that if something was worth eating it needed no extra flavouring, found himself ladling sauce on to his meat, and enjoying every delicious mouthful. The first ten minutes of their attack on this main course silenced them. George felt himself capable of some kind of pianissimo, an animal humming to demonstrate his satisfaction once he realised how hungry he was. He tried to slow down, but found this task beyond him.

'Do you like this?' Andy asked, pausing from his equally gargantuan swallowings. 'Suits your taste?'

'Wonderful,' George said, laying his knife and fork on his plate. 'There's wine in the sauce. I hardly touch alcohol. But this is delicious.'

'Good boy,' she purred as to a small child or animal.

The men allowed Mirabel to finish her course. She chewed delicately, looking almost regal as she ate. Bolt upright at her end of the table, she carried each tiny forkful towards her mouth, paused and smiled at her men as she made them wait. George refused a re-filling of his wine glass. Mirabel waved away the proferred bottle with a small, grateful gesture of her left hand.

Andrew filled his glass to the brim, but spilled not one drop as he took his first huge sip. He lifted his glass and held it near a candle.

'Ah,' he said. 'That's something like it.' And to George, 'You don't know what you're missing.'

'I'm afraid I don't.'

'Don't you drink at all?' Mirabel required.

'Not much. I haven't the time, really. And drinking's a social activity. If I go in the pub, a pint and a half suits me. I'll stretch it to two if I find somebody who'll talk to me.'

'Which pub do you favour?'

'None particularly. The last one I patronised was the Tom Bowling on the Boulevard.'

'The beer there's reputed to be very good,' Andy told them.

'Did you have decent company?' Mirabel asked. 'To tempt you towards that second pint?'

'Yes, I did. A funny old chap. He worked for a time with your ex-father-in-law. Called him Mr Gilbert. They didn't get on very well.'

'And why was that?'

'Mr Gilbert had just come down from university, and went first to join the family branch at Loughborough. Apparently he threw his weight about there and upset the management. So his father had to bring him over to the Lace Market factory, to keep an eye on him.'

'And?'

'My man got on very well with old Mr Lockwood, was a bit of a favourite, and he perhaps compared the son's efforts to learn the business unfavourably with his own. Gilbert was a bit touchy and didn't like this. Treated him like dirt, criticised his every move.'

'What was your man's name?' Andy asked.

'Francis Smith, called Jim, he says.'

'This was all long before my time.'

'He spoke as if Gilbert was a bit of a tartar,' George said. 'Now, on my short acquaintance he seemed a quiet, polite, unassertive sort of man. So either Smith's story's all wrong or Gilbert has changed his character.'

'He's a lovely man. I'm very fond of him. And his wife. That's why I'm so grateful to you for letting me know that they'd welcome me back. Your pub acquaintance's story doesn't convince me.'

'Did your father-in-law take over the management of Lockwood's?'

'Yes. He was the head of the firm. I don't think he was over pleased when he retired.'

'Did he have to?'

'Retire? Not on account of illness, no. I think, and this is only my impression, that it was his wife who forced it on him. She used to tell it to him straight, "You've had your day. You're sixty-five now and you've done enough for Lockwood and Son. It's time you eased up on work and enjoyed yourself."'

'Perhaps that was his style of enjoyment?'

'Yes. They say he was very good at it. Profits soared when he took over. He's still got a substantial financial stake in the place. His wife used to tell me that he didn't know how to spend his money. He had plenty, and so had she, and Charles, my ex, had a more than comfortable income. He was into property amongst other things. Charles had an eye for profit.'

'Interesting,' Andrew commented. 'Here's this kindly old gent we know, and we find out he was once a rip-roaring young terror.'

At this the topic was dropped. Instead they questioned George about his jobs. Was pushing correspondence through letter-boxes less interesting than teaching thick-heads for GCSE or A-level? He explained, not for the first time, that when he walked the streets he could breathe; in the classrooms his chest was clogged and breathless.

'I've no regrets about losing status,' he said. 'If that's what's worrying you.'

'You won't go back even if your chest clears?'

'I don't imagine so, or not as I think now. I do my bit of evening teaching once a week, and that keeps my hand in. Of course, when I'm getting on towards sixty and retirement, walking the streets may not seem quite so attractive.'

'What about pensions?'

'I think I shall be covered. My father was a very careful man and put his and my mother's savings in houses. That proved a very good investment.'

'But suppose you marry,' Mirabel asked, 'and have a family to care for?'

'I'll have to work longer. Unless I marry some well-to-do lady.'

'Have you one or two in mind?' Andy asked.

'No. My path doesn't seem to cross that of the well-heeled.'

'Would you like to be married? Mirabel asked. Her face demonstrated no more than mild interest.

'Yes rather than no. Though it doesn't seem a very urgent decision.'

'Have you been serious about a wife or woman before?' Andy asked, brazenly, George thought.

'Yes.' He was not pleased with the direction of these enquiries. He tried not to show it.

'Have you lived with a woman?'

'Yes, but it did not last, I told you.'

George looked over at Mirabel. Her face showed no more interest than if he was being questioned about his taste in puddings or neck ties. Andrew was now nodding as if carefully considering George's answer. He might well be a judge demonstrating to his court that he wasn't prepared to let one word escape his minute attention. Then he suddenly seemed to liven himself and ask George which of the local soccer teams he supported. This bore no relationship to what they had just discussed. Relieved, he said he was not interested in either.

Mirabel brought the topic neatly round to poets and poetry.

'Who's your favourite twentieth-century poet?' asked Andrew.

'Guess,' George said, beginning to tire of his direct method.

'I'd say T. S. Eliot.' The answer was immediate, confident.

'That would be my guess too, I think,' said Mirabel.

George waited, made them wait.

'You're both wrong,' he said pacifically. 'Because I'm not sure myself. My mind tells me it ought to be Thomas Hardy, but the man who affects me most of all is Yeats. He's histrionic, a bit of a strutter on the stage.'

'Give us an example.'

'Well, take the first few lines of "The Wild Swans at Coole".

'Quote us a bit,' Andrew ordered.

> '"The trees are in their autumn beauty,
> The woodland paths are dry.
> Under the October twilight the water
> Mirrors a still sky.
> Upon the brimming water among the stones
> Are nine-and-fifty swans."'

'Very good,' Andrew said.

'I don't know why I chose that,' George said. 'I'm roused by it, but the language is hardly extraordinary. It's even got an old poetic word "upon". "Brimming" is good. It's perhaps the rest of the poem.

> "Unwearied still, lover by lover,
> They paddle in the cold
> Companionable streams or climb the air;
> Their hearts have not grown old."

'Yes,' said Andrew, dully, distantly.

'I've been there in Coole Park and stood there by the lake as Yeats did. I've even seen the wild swans. It's not astonishingly beautiful. A bit less civilised than in public parks, but Yeats has made the place unforgettable for me.'

'And that's his strength.'

'Yes. He can make the people he knew into great figures of myth: Cuchulainn, Oisin, and the old Irish heroes.'

'But were they the equivalent?'

'In some ways. If we had known them and admired them they would still have been men, not the heroic figures of great poetry. And clearly that's what I choose as my poetry. Hardy had perhaps more to say about the human race than Yeats, was nearer our life, our victories or tragedies.'

'And this heroic verse is what you admire?' Mirabel asked. 'Are you, or do you consider yourself, one of them?'

'No. But poetry should not be prosaic, everyday, humdrum, however accurate. The language should lift it. Of course, there are some critics I've read who mock Yeats and his expressions. When he refers to Synge, whom he admired and put in the right way of subject matter for his greatest work, he always calls him "that 'something' man" and the chosen adjective, whatever it is, annoys some critics.'

'But not you?'

'No, it opens my eyes. When Yeats is walking round the Municipal Gallery looking at the portraits of his friends it seems well-nigh perfect.

> "And here's John Synge himself, that rooted man.
> Forgetting human words, a grave, deep face."

66

'Or again, from his poem "In Memory of Major Robert Gregory", he's talking about his friends, his dead friends, whom he'd like to invite to his house. And Synge is one of them.

"And that enquiring man, John Synge comes next
That dying chose the living world for text."

Andrew and Mirabel looked at him with some surprise. George had no idea whether they agreed with him or thought him an exaggerator, showing off.

'Do you lecture on Yeats for the WEA?' Mirabel asked. 'I'd like to come and hear you.'

'It's out at Mansfield,' George discouraged her.

'That's no drawback.'

'These days at the WEA they expect you to do written work and score points, which in the end are totted up. After some years, if you've done well enough, the university will give you a degree.'

'And are most of your students keen on this?'

'I don't think so. They are on the whole aged and retired people who want to be introduced to some branch of culture. It's good that some of the younger people can and deserve to win a degree, to better themselves career-wise.' He looked hard at his interlocutors. 'I preferred it when they were there to improve their minds though, think about some new aspect of human life. Besides, quite a few of my class are already graduates.'

'Not in English Literature?'

'Not as far as I know.'

'I'll be on the look-out for your next series,' said Mirabel. 'I ought to struggle out of the grip of the law at least some of the time.'

They questioned him and he enjoyed being quizzed by intelligent people who know a little about the subject. Returning from a visit to the lavatory, he paused outside the half-open door of the room where Andrew and Mirabel were sitting. From the corridor he could clearly hear what they were saying; he stopped to listen. They had not heard his approach and were talking about him.

'He's a bit of a mystery to me,' Andy said.

'Why's that?'

'He clearly holds some of his views strongly, but doesn't seem to know exactly why. Take, for instance, that poem about the wild swans. To him it is a powerful piece of writing. He's moved by it. You could see that. His eyes filled with tears. Now if I were as shaken as he is by that work, I'd want to know why.'

'Perhaps poetry is like music to him. One is gripped but one doesn't know why.'

'Poetry's not like music. It has words which mean something. Music, apart from a title or a setting of verse, doesn't.'

'Why are you moved by music?'

'I don't know that I am. A catchy tune might stay with me for a few minutes. Or a piece in a certain context, a funeral or a powerful film or play. Otherwise I'm not much influenced by music. I'm neither stone-deaf nor tone-deaf. It's just that I've not listened enough, am ignorant how to listen, but . . .'

'But, what?' She gave a trill of laughter.

'He has words. He's studied literature for years. He ought to be able to say what it is that moves him.'

'For him the words as subject matter are not the be-all and end-all of the matter. The music, the sound and rhythm of the treated words, are important to him.'

'Why?'

'They somehow chime or echo with his experience of life, so that they are important enough . . . Shhh.'

'He's coming back.' George had neither moved nor made a sound. He waited a few seconds as the two of them sat in silence then moved towards the door, dragging his feet to warn them of his arrival.

'We were just talking about you,' Andrew breezily announced.

'I hope it was complimentary.'

'Andrew,' Mirabel said, 'could not understand why those lines about the wild swans meant so much to you and so little to him.'

George scratched his chin.

'I don't know him, his character and background, well enough to lay down the law about that. Some people like strawberries rather than raspberries, and don't know why, don't even think about it. There must be a reason. There's a reason for everything. But it seems of no importance why you prefer one to the other, and so you don't give it a second thought.'

68

'But it's your subject,' Mirabel said. 'You should give it more than a second thought.'

'I know I'm a poor critic. Or at least I appear so to myself. But decisions about poetry are not like decisions about addition or multiplication. There's a right answer or a wrong with arithmetic. But with poetry you'll find that critics will scorn the opinions of those of a former generation. I don't for a minute conclude that the new judges are so much more clever or learned than the old. Life has taught them to view matters differently, to value today things that were not thought highly of only a few years before.'

'Doesn't that make these aesthetic judgements of less value than, let's say, arithmetical ones?'

'No. It makes life more interesting.'

They argued like this for some time. George was convinced that Andy had drunk too much of the wine. Mirabel once tried to make them change tack by asking if it wasn't true that there was something magical about great literary master-pieces. Andy then asked her to define magic. She tried, but he, like a schoolmaster with a stupid pupil, loftily dismissed her. 'All you're saying,' he pronounced, 'is that you think Shakespeare has done the job much more competently than you could.'

'I certainly believe that, but is that the answer you want?' she asked.

George enjoyed this talk, which had about it the form of an oral examination. Andrew made his questions as awkward as possible so that the candidate could show the breadth of his knowledge and the uses to which it could be put. What George could not decide was whether Andrew questioned him in order to display his own superior grasp of the topic or to give George the chance to display his intelligence and thus to impress Mirabel. She put her few questions, he thought, with the intention of helping the listener out of awkward situations. Her voice was low and friendly, and her expression smilingly keen, as if she wished to learn and profit from his answers. Whether this meant that she was attracted to him as Andy had suggested, or was from her usual politeness, he did not know; could not, try as he might, decide.

They talked in this way for an hour before Mirabel announced it was time for bed. She offered the men a bath, but both refused.

Andrew showed George to his room and ensuite bathroom and lavatory.

He wished him good-night when he had made doubly sure that all the guest's needs were catered for.

'What time do we get up in the morning?'

'None of your crack of dawn postman stuff. Breakfast will be at nine. If you're awake and want no more sleep, let yourself out by the back door and have a tramp round outside. As long as you're back for nine, you'll be in no trouble. Anything more? Sleep well, then.'

George noted that Andrew seemed quite sober now, stood solidly on the floor. He seemed rather patronising in the way he offered hospitality on Mirabel's behalf. I know this place and her ways, he seemed to say. I've been here often enough before.

George's bedroom was pleasantly warm, as was his bed, but he could not sleep. He could not make out what Mirabel and Andy intended by their hospitality to him. It was midnight before he went to sleep, and then his rest seemed broken. He looked about the room but there was no reading matter to be seen, nor was there a television or radio. He lay quite still, but there were no sounds from other parts of the house. Ten minutes on his back, eyes closed, made it clear that he would sleep no longer, so he reluctantly thrust his feet to the floor.

Half an hour later he had washed and shaved, dressed and made his bed. He glanced at his watch. Twenty to nine. Someone tapped lightly on the door. He invited them in. Mirabel entered, a cup of tea in her hand.

'Good morning,' she said. 'I thought you'd like this. Did you sleep well?'

'Not at all badly.'

'Good. I find it hard work to get a full night's sleep in a strange bed.' She smiled largely as if this were some kind of joke. 'We're going out to lunch today. To a neighbour. Ten minutes' drive away. He's an interesting man. He teaches at Derby Art College, and is making quite a name for himself as a sculptor and painter.'

'Was he featured in the *Sunday Times* magazine a month or two ago?'

'That's right. You've a good memory. Howard Clark. I told him about you, and he said he'd like to meet you. He fancies

70

himself as a cook, so you won't starve. He and Andy usually are at loggerheads about something, so you'll be kept amused.'

Breakfast was dull. Andrew ate hardly anything and spoke even more sparingly. Mirabel coaxed George to join her with a freshly boiled egg.

'I haven't had such a thing since I was a boy,' he said.

She told him the name of the farm they came from. Andrew breathed heavily. Immediately afterwards he pushed his plate away and with a muttered excuse, left the room.

'Is he not well?' George asked.

'He's always like that first thing in the morning. It's the wine, in my view. By the time we reach Howard's soon after twelve he'll be himself again, laying the law down and questioning us all quite mercilessly.'

George helped her clear the table and wash the dishes.

'That was all very dull,' she said.

'No. You've introduced me again to the joys of a boiled egg.'

'You don't take much pleasing,' she said.

He could not decide whether this was praise or blame.

VI

George offered to help Mirabel about the house.

'No, thanks. There's little enough to do. There are books about the place if you'd like to sit and read. Or you could walk round outside. The day's not promising, it's rather cold.

'Where's Andrew gone?'

'He'll be down at any minute.' Mirabel held up a finger for silence and he heard footsteps descending the stairs. The door to the dining-room where they stood was stealthily opened and Andrew, dressed for outdoors, hat on head, appeared.

'See you just before noon,' he said. His voice was hesitant, catarrhal.

'He's off to see a client,' Mirabel explained once the door was shut. 'He'll never close his eyes to the opportunity to make money. Once he knew we were coming here, he phoned the man. I don't know what about.'

'Surely the man could have found a solicitor nearer home.'

'You'd be surprised. People often think it's wise to stay with someone they know, even if it makes difficulties. And recently solicitors have been reported in the newspapers as playing fast and loose with clients' money.'

'I thought that solicitors were like parsons, all honest.'

'So they are. But our society is askew in many ways, especially where money is concerned. And a few have been tempted and fallen.'

'But not our Andrew?'

'No. He's in his family firm, as old and strait-laced as you like, and they make enough not to have to bother with fancy work if you know what I mean.'

'And your brigade?'

'Never. Younger men. We're doing well financially and getting a good reputation. The two principals are both in their fifties, and are keen to give value for money. We've had a lot of new business since I joined them.'

'On your account?'

'No. I didn't mean that at all. But what it means, now I'm there, is that I do the less well-paid jobs that all solicitors get. I don't mind. There is plenty of interest in the work I do, and I can clear it up. They, the partners, thought they would employ some young, not very ambitious person or some old, stay-at-home, experienced provincial man near his retirement. They chose me – youngish, but fairly experienced. Former wife of a very ambitious lawyer. And I'd worked in London, would know a guinea from a brass farthing.'

'Did they tell you all this when you applied?'

'Not they. They're not stupid. But they'd know what I thought. They made sure I'd do the humdrum work thoroughly, and after a time, when they saw how I was shaping, they upped my pay and would even drop an interesting bit of their work in my direction.'

'You don't like them much?'

'I can't say that I do. They are both tremendously hard workers and have had one or two spectacular successes. They both have ambitious wives, too, who don't begrudge them the time they put in at their desks.'

'Were they lawyers?'

'No, I don't think so. Both good-lookers; both know money doesn't grow on trees. They like to hear the till ringing. They live in very superior houses now and will soon be pressing for something more, let's say, aristocratic.' Mirabel laughed. 'I'm making more than half of this up, but just you watch them when you get the chance.'

George was much taken with this and again volunteered his services at housework. They stripped the beds, worked over carpets with the vacuum cleaner, polished the silver.

'One can get a great deal done when there are not meals to be prepared and cooked,' she commented as they hung out bed clothes. 'I can see you are well versed in this sort of domestic work.'

'Isn't Andrew?'

'No.' She pulled a sour face. 'He has a woman in for an hour every weekday morning. And he gets his pound of flesh out of her. Now Howard Clark, the man we're going to see this morning, does his own housework. He has a woman in for three hours on Friday morning to see that his house is spick and span for the weekend, and I guess that she won't be overworked.'

'He's an artist, isn't he?'

'Yes, and a very neat and trim one. Until a year or two ago he mainly did sculpture. Then he was ill, really ill, and since that time he's concentrated on watercolours. He's very good.'

'And he lives on his own?'

'Yes. He was married, but they didn't hit it off. And she went off with another man.'

'An artist?'

'No. A banker, a widower. He's rolling in money. He bought statues from Howard, and a bust of his wife, that was before the marriage broke up, and a good number of his sketches. Now, or so people say, his wife, Janice, won't let him buy anything from Howard.'

'Would he want to?'

'I guess so. Everybody says how talented Howard is.'

'With watercolours.'

'Yes. He still has plenty of work. You might have seen some in the newspaper. He's one of those individuals who seems to be driven. He must fill every one of his waking hours. It annoys Andy. Not that Howard will mind that. I think the dislike's mutual, reciprocal, whatever the word is.

'Howard invited me to lunch today and I told him I couldn't come because I had you and Andy staying with me. He asked what manner of man you were, then he said you'd do, you sounded interesting. And, in any case, you'd act as a foil or a brake on Andy. "That school-yard bully you cart about with you." That's how Howard described him.'

'Does Andy make a lot of enemies? What's his trouble?'

'He's like most clever people – curious. He asks questions. But he hasn't yet acquired the art of doing it tactfully, or even politely. Perhaps he doesn't want to. He likes to stir things, likes to see people embarrassed or angry. I'm not sure.'

'But it's you, not Andy, that Howard Clark's interested in.'

'I think he likes female company, and I seem harmless to him.'

'Harmless? That's hardly a compliment.'

'He's never declared just how he stands with me. I'd guess he thinks that Andy and I are an item, but that we shall part before too long.'

'And, if I may risk an Andrew-like question, how do you find Howard?'

'No. Not my type. No sexual attraction. And as with all people who are good at their job, and in his case I should have said "outstanding", he puts that first. I don't think I'd like that.'

They took a cup of coffee, and after that she went upstairs to dress herself for lunch.

'He likes that, does he? Should I put my glad rags on?'

'I don't suppose he'd notice,' she said.

George put on a clean shirt, and a chaste tie round his neck. He polished his shoes and noticed how sharp a crease ran down his trousers. Soon after twelve Andy arrived and said he was ready to go out.

'You're late,' said Mirabel.

'He won't notice a minute or two.'

'No, but I do. You said you'd be here before twelve.'

They put George in the back seat of the car, and took the hilly roads. Andrew drove with his usual skill as he outlined to Mirabel the business which had occupied his morning, the possibility of selling two cottages. Any trace of ill feeling disappeared as he outlined the advice he had given his client.

'He doesn't know whether he wants to sell them or not. The tenants he has in are ideal. They look after the place, pay regular rent, and only rarely do they call on him to do repairs which will cost much.'

'And what did he decide?'

'He didn't. I told him to hang on for the time being. In my view the cottages will rise steadily in value in the next year or so.'

'And will he do so?'

'You never know. He's not got an ounce of the gambler in him. He wanted me to spend the whole afternoon advising him. I told him I was out to lunch with Howard Clark, but he behaved as if he'd never heard of him. If he believed his own suspicious mind, I'd just be making the lunch engagement up. It's pitiful to see him, on the horns of a dilemma of his own making. I tell him there's no certain answer to his question, but I don't think he believed me.'

They stood together on the drive, straightening their coats. It took Howard Clark some time to answer the doorbell.

'Hello, hello,' he greeted them at last. Andrew made the introduction of George. George and Howard shook hands heartily. 'Delighted to meet you.'

Clark was tall, strongly built. George had been told that the man was nearly seventy, though he did not look it. His thin face was tanned as if he'd just returned from a holiday in the Greek Islands. He ushered his guests inside, and once there Andy began to move from picture to picture hanging on the walls of the corridor. He tapped the glass of one.

'A beauty,' he said. 'Where is it?'

'Rhodes,' Clark said. 'I was over there for Christmas. I've only just got these two back from the framer's.'

'Aren't you going to have prints made?'

'I expect their representative will be round before too long, to see what I have to sell.'

'You don't chase them?'

'I have an agent.'

He led them into a sitting-room, and poured out sherry for all. George watched him as he prowled about the room, bottle in hand. He offered no choice. Clark moved from guest to guest with hardly a sound. He seemed to stoop, almost deliberately, as if to diminish his height.

'Have you been painting this morning?' Mirabel asked.

'Yes. I got up early and prepared the lunch straight after breakfast. By that time it's light enough to paint.'

'I'm sorry,' Andy said, staring at his glass of sherry which he held up towards the window, 'that we are putting you off your morning's work.'

'You're doing no such thing. It does me good to break from my routine. It gives me ideas, makes me look harder at what I'm doing.'

'Do you paint all day? I mean, usually?' Mirabel again.

'Yes. And I eat my main meal in the evening.'

'Does Mrs Burney not come in to clean?'

'Yes, twice a week now. Monday and Friday. I'm a man of habit.'

'Does she clean your studio?' Andy asked.

'No.' The answer was snapped out as if the man was angry.

Andrew pulled a sour face.

'I'll take you round my studio after lunch. It doesn't need much cleaning. After what it was like when I was sculpting or even oil-painting, it looks really tidy. She's let in when I am doing my shopping.'

'Does she show any interest in art?'

'Yes. In an amateurish way. She'll ask me questions from time to time. And I've used her as a model. Luckily she's good at that. Knows when and how to stay still.'

He pointed at a statue which was half hidden behind their chairs. It was of a naked young woman, standing angrily pointing downwards.

'She stood like that one day when I had accidentally and clumsily kicked over the bowl of water and vinegar she was using to clean the windows. I was very taken, and made a quick sketch or two in my rough-book.'

'That made her even more angry?' Andrew asked.

'No. Why should it? I asked her if she'd stay the afternoon while I did more sketches.'

'Does her husband know she poses for you?'

'Yes.'

'In the nude, I meant.'

'I said yes, I meant yes.'

There was a minute or two of awkward silence before their host led them out to the lunch table. He served a summery meal: roast beef, boiled ham and salad, new potatoes.

'I haven't had the time to prepare anything complicated,' he apologised. He need not have said this for the food was delicious.

After lunch they retired to the sitting-room for coffee. Now was the time, it appeared, for talking.

'People we know in this small world . . .' Clark left them waiting while he considered his conclusion. He turned, fully to face Mirabel. 'The local manufacturing firm, Lockwood & Son. Any relation to your ex-husband?'

'Charles is the son of Gilbert Lockwood who was head of all the factories. He is semi-retired now, of course. Why?'

'They want some artwork of mine. Though I was born in Beechnall I've lived most of my life away, London, Cornwall. But Derbyshire suits me now. Anyhow, I came across Gilbert when we were both young men. He was a few years older than I.' Howard bit reflectively on his lower lip. 'When I knew Gilbert Lockwood he was renowned for his shortness of temper. Get across him on the most trivial pretext, and he'd blow his top like a lunatic. And it didn't matter where he was, indoors or out in the street.

'I remember once I annoyed him. It wasn't about anything important. I'd replied to a letter from him asking about a statue he'd seen in the local museum, which had caught his interest. He never replied. I'd taken some care about my answer, I'd had to look things up. I spent a whole day in the library reading-room chasing up one topic. But that was like me as a young man. I hardly knew Gilbert at the time, but the questions he asked were really relevant and I took trouble with the answer. He didn't reply.

'I mentioned this months afterwards to a man who knew him well and asked if this was typical. He'd never written to Gilbert, he said, so he didn't know. Not more than a week later I came across Lockwood at a party, and he suddenly turned on me and said I had no business to criticise him publicly because he hadn't bothered to reply to me. I did not, he excused himself, know his circumstances or why he hadn't written.

'I said it would only have taken five minutes to thank me by letter politely, or by phone. I told him that I had taken time and trouble to answer his queries. He had written to me out of the blue, and I'd done my best for him. This, which I delivered very quietly, seemed suddenly to anger him. I had no right to tell all and sundry that he had not replied to my letter, he insisted. I told him that, far from publicising his lack of courtesy, I had mentioned it to one person only, a man he knew pretty well, who might know if I had been helpful to him or not.

'At this his face turned red, and he said he was very busy, at the time, but in any case that was not his complaint. It was my spreading the story about. I asked him if what I'd said was the truth, and he suddenly lost all sense and reason. He swore at me, and remember this was in mixed company, but it made no difference to him. I was on the watch all the time. I thought he sounded so far from sanity that he'd aim a punch at me, though I was bigger and heavier than he was.'

'How did it end?' Andy asked.

'Two of his friends who heard it all dragged him away. I just stood my ground. They got him out of the room. "That's just him," the host told me. "He looks and sounds so quiet and sensible," I said. "He's mad." They kept us apart for the rest of the evening.'

'Did you meet him afterwards?' Andy asked.

'Not often. He'd nod and acknowledge me, but that was about all. I left the district, and forgot all about his behaviour; when I came back hereabouts ten years ago we never met, even casually. People spoke highly of him, said what a decent old chap he was. I wondered about this, and why he had changed.'

Again they snuggled into the comfort of their armchairs. Clark seemed engrossed in his thoughts.

'Is it possible that a man can change so radically?' he asked, shaking his head. 'From touchy, wild youth to saintly old age.'

'It does account,' Mirabel said, 'for Charles. He was a real devil, or could be if he wished. That never seemed to tally with such quiet parents.'

'Yet when we visited them,' said George, 'they weren't afraid to offer a poor opinion of their son, in front of me, a stranger. Perhaps they thought they were just talking to you, needily. But it was oddly awkward. Will you really want to keep in touch with them?'

Mirabel ignored the question.

'Tell you what,' Andrew said to Clark, 'Mirabel or George could invite you over and include Gilbert and Joan. See if it was Gilbert who wants your work now.'

'And you could put him through one of your cross-questioning bouts. You're fond enough of that sort of thing.'

George wondered whether Clark was trying to annoy his guest.

Andy took it no further, and this time Mirabel came to his rescue.

'You said you'd take us round your studio,' she said to Howard.

'So I will, but I warn you it will be a lot colder than it is in here.'

'Anything for the sake of art,' Andrew said, sarcastically.

They put on their outdoor clothes, crossed the grey-flagged back-yard, now flooded with electric light, and moved towards a large stone building which stretched out at an awkward angle to the back of the house.

'Which is older?' Andrew demanded. 'This,' he waved his forefinger stiffly along the outline of the studio, 'or your house?'

'The house, by a hundred years. This,' Clark mocked Andrew's pointing finger with a similar awkward movement of his own, 'outbuilding would have been a store-house of some kind.'

'Why so near the house?'

'Convenience, I expect. They wouldn't be interested in pretty gardens of flowers in those days. What they originally kept in it I don't know, but it was something that they needed quickly in the house. Don't ask me what. Fruit, perhaps, or fuel.'

'It's a big place for that bit of Christmas cheer,' Andy said.

'You can't make it out in this light but it was built in two parts – this and then a further extension, three times the length.'

'Who was responsible?' Andy queried.

'I don't know. The place changed hands several times during the nineteenth century. But who stuck the tail on the dog, I'm not sure.'

'He'd no sort of eye,' Andy said. 'It's not even straight.'

'It's not ugly by daylight, and it presumably served its purpose.' Clark took in a noisy lungful of breath in the oddly lit dark. 'I must say, I like it.'

'The look of it?' Andy sounded affronted.

'Yes, the look of it. I am not overfond of these modern, symmetrical pieces of geometry. If they're big enough they're impressive, but for a bit of domestic building one needs something else, and that's where the artist's eye comes in. And whoever was responsible for the second stage of the building here had the gift.'

'Would he have been an architect, do you think?' Andrew asked.

'I doubt it. Not that I've anything against architects. They know their business. But whoever put this up knew the ground here, and the hills round about, and took these into account when he knew what the owner wanted. He used local stone to effect. You wait until you see it by daylight, without the aid and the shadows of artificial lighting, and you'll understand what I mean.'

Clark now fiddled with the padlocks and locks of the building. He pushed inside and flooded the place with light.

'In you come.' They obeyed. The inside, without any partitions, seemed spacious as a church. The visitors stared round, wondering at the size.

'Here's where I'm working just now,' Clark said, pointing to a large, flat-topped desk. 'I'm dealing with water colours. I could easily do them in one of the sitting-rooms in the house.'

'Why don't you, then?'

'When I first came back to this part of the world, water colours were a poor third on my list of priorities. First was

80

sculpture, then oils. I like a biggish place when I'm carving, so I can do it in the fresh air, so to speak, not choke myself. This seemed ideal. I had plenty of room, whatever I chose to do, and beyond that space enough to build a railway engine.

'A year or two ago an agent approached me to do quite a large advertising job, watercolours, for a holiday firm. I must have suited them because I'd no sooner finished than there they were with an equally large offer. I took it immediately because they paid well, and because when I came here I was not selling a great deal.

'I suppose that's always the trouble if you're working for yourself. I'd made my name as a sculptor, but art's like everything else in this world. Fashion makes the demand. I ought to spend more time on my other two areas of expertise, but I need to live.'

'You don't think watercolour painting is what you're most gifted at?' Andrew asked.

'No. I'd say I'm a sculptor primarily. Presumably you think I should starve in my attic, working on masterpieces even if nobody will buy them? But I don't feel I'm demeaning myself by working on commercial advertising material. I've learned a great deal from watercolour painting. And they're in favour just now. Don't ask me why, or whether it's right or fair or just or the will of God, that it is so. They're cheaper than statuary or oils. Twenty pictures sold for a thousand pounds each are just as good to me as twenty thousand for an oil painting or a bust, even if I could get that, which I very much doubt. And they offer me artistic opportunities which I didn't think were there. I'm satisfying myself as a creator of works of art. Now I'm also in favour with my bank manager. I can afford to sculpt or paint in oils when I want to, even if I lose money by so doing.'

'Without feeling that you are letting yourself down?' Andy enquired.

'That's what I said.'

'You're the last person I'd expect to be so commercially minded.'

'What makes you say that?'

'What people have said about you. Admirers of yours. They gave me the impression you'd sooner starve in your attic than throw over what you're good at and do jobs which just bring in the money. And, anyhow, you seemed to be making a fair living at sculpture. It just goes to show.'

'But it's not so?' Mirabel intervened.

'Fortune's a fickle jade. The sort of work, both in stone and oils, that I did for thirty years won me both money and praise, and I thought, in my innocence, that this would always be so. I've been lucky so I'm not complaining, but by the time I sold my house in Cornwall and bought this one up here, I knew I should have to live carefully. This doesn't suit my character. I think I deserve something from this rough old world.'

'Why?' Andy.

'To make up for my childhood. My father abused me. Physically and mentally, not sexually. He thought everyone and everything had it in for him and he took it out on my mother and me.'

'You were the only child?'

'Yes. My father wasn't fit either to be married or to have children.'

'He had a job?'

'Yes. He was wages clerk to a building firm owned by two brothers. It was quite a large concern, but so far as I can ascertain he was on top of his work. The two brothers he despised as illiterates. They were hard workers and talented and took on some large concerns. But my father was a grammar-school boy. He wasn't qualified as an accountant, but that was because nobody had encouraged him to study for the exams. He had a good School Certificate, but didn't stay on into the sixth form. He held this against the world. In his office there were two or three women. He did not think highly of them.'

'Was he badly paid?'

'I don't think so. He was buying his own house. A new semi-detached in a decent district. That would have satisfied most people of his standing in the world. But not him. He kept my mother short of money and beat her if she crossed him or served a meal he considered not up to standard. If I did anything wrong then he'd set about me. He'd do so for the merest misdemeanour. Or he'd tick me off for some slight fault and, before a minute or two was out, he'd be shouting at the top of his voice and hitting and kicking me. My body was covered with bruises. He'd never hit me on the face where the marks could be seen.

You talk about a sadist. And yet when my mother died, there he was at the funeral, sobbing and moaning.'

'How old were you when she died?'

'Sixteen. I'd just left school. I had a job in a bank. But I kept up with my art. The school art master ran a class at night and he encouraged me to apply for a bursary at the art college. I did so, and when I told my father he was furious. Here was he, paying out money he could ill afford to give me a decent start in life, and here was I, with my usual witlessness, proposing to embark on a course with nothing at the end of it, no chance of employment. What did I think he was? A millionaire? His shouting got louder and louder, his face redder by the minute.

'I was slightly surprised because he'd been quieter, more like a human being, since my mother had died. I'd thought that her absence, especially after all that publicly expressed grief, had taught him a lesson, but I saw I was wrong. He had the same unbridled anger he'd always had. One thing I did notice, though; he flung his fists about in the air, but he never attempted to lay one on me. Just at this time I'd had another spurt in my growth and I was bigger now, broader, than he was, and I presume that his temper allowed him to act circumspectly in case I hit him back.'

'And that never happened?'

'Yes, it did. In the first Christmas holidays from college. I wrote regularly to him in the first term, telling him what we were doing. I never had a word back from him. I was costing him nothing. I'd won scholarships to keep me, just about, and the college authorities were sufficiently impressed by my first term's work to grant me another, for which I was grateful.'

'Were you the best of your year?' Andy asked.

'Presumably my teachers thought so. I didn't. There were two other boys just as good as I was, but there. The college perhaps knew of my circumstances, and handed me the extra money. I was very grateful, I can tell you.' Clark dabbed at the sweat on his forehead.

'And that Christmas, what happened then?'

'Things seemed to be going as well as I could expect. He didn't charge me anything for bed and board. He did little to welcome me. I seemed to be expected to clean the house, and to prepare the meals and serve him. There was never a word of thanks, but at least I learned what comestibles were about in the larder, and I did my best with them.'

83

'Was your mother a good cook?' Mirabel asked.

'In a plain sort of way. He never gave her enough money for anything fancy. But she always served up something worth eating.'

'And you followed in her footsteps?'

'I make no great claims for myself. The old man complained from time to time, but he'd the sense to see that it was to his advantage to have a hot meal on the table five minutes after he came in from work. He was probably pleased, after his fashion, though he didn't tell me, when I came home on holiday.'

'He never thanked you if you'd made a good meal, then?'

'Never. He'd push his plate away, leave me to clear the table and wash up while he went off to his newspaper.'

'Was he like that with the underlings he worked with?'

'I guess so. I never questioned any of them, but I heard at second hand that he could never be satisfied.'

'He never went round punching sense into them?'

'Not that I heard. They were mostly women, anyway.'

'Did he take advantage of his superior position? Sexually, I mean.'

'No. He would have been against that. In principle. It's odd, but I can't imagine his having sex, even with my mother.'

'And this Christmas when you hit him?'

'He'd been back to work after the holidays, and I guess the employees, his underlings, had been awkward, or if not them the bosses. And he came home in something of a temper. Not that that was anything out of the ordinary. I put his dinner in front of him, and went out to the kitchen to fetch mine. I always dished it up in the kitchen. When I came back he was staring at his plate as if it were poison. I sat down, and he said one word.

'"Sauce."

'"I beg your pardon?"

'"Sauce. H.P. Sauce."

'"Where is it?" I asked.

'"In the pantry. Where do you think?"

'I got up and went out to look. I couldn't find it. I came back and told him so. He had not started to eat, still sat as before staring down at his plate.

'"You're just like your bloody mother," he said. "If something had been moved half an inch from its usual place she could never see it, even if it was just in front of her nose."

'"*You* go and find it then."

'"What did you say?"

'"You go and find it then."

'I thought he'd hit me, but he got up and went out. I started on my dinner. I could hear him moving things about. And once he knocked something over, a glass jar, or dropped it. He came back with a face like thunder, but carrying nothing.

'"There isn't any," he said.

'"No. I couldn't find anything."

'"You could have brought some in when you went out to the butcher's."

'"I didn't know you wanted it," I said.

'"You've been living in this house eighteen years, sitting at the same table, and you don't know what I like yet? Typical."

'"You should tell me what you want. If I went out choosing things myself, you'd soon be accusing me of wasting your money."

His father was now glumly and sullenly eating his meal, in small forkfuls, as if he loathed the taste. He sighed often and breathed heavily, and when he finally clapped his knife and fork on to his plate, to indicate he'd finished the course, he'd left a quarter of his food uneaten.

'Have you finished?'

'Eh?'

'A saucy plate,' the boy said, pleased with his wit. 'You'll have to be satisfied with that.'

His father's face creased into anger as he stumbled up towards his seated son. His right arm was drawn back to deliver punishment. Slickly Howard slipped from his seat so that he was on his feet and side-stepping when the blow whirled. The punch was large; his father pulled his arm back and sprung in a huge half circle so that the clenched fist landed not as he had wished, not on his son's face or ear but on his shoulder. The son felt its weight and his anger leap like flame. He led with his left and his father sluggishly swayed away from it, making himself and his face a target for the swift, well-delivered right which followed like lightning, the knuckles biting into the older man's cheekbone. A gasp escaped the open mouth as his body toppled backwards and collapsed bonelessly to the floor, where he lay, limbs awry.

Howard looked at the old man, shocked at what he had done. He knew he was fit, could hit hard. At college he had played

85

rugby and fought his way to the finals of the heavyweight boxing competition. At the local fair he had lasted the three demanded rounds against a professional thug in one of the booths. He'd done it by strength, and speed, and was still on his feet at the end of the contest. One eye was closed, and he was, he later discovered, a mass of bruises. He took the money, a begrudged twenty-five pounds, cheered to the echo by the locals, but his evening was spoilt. The pro knew how to punch his weight, and only a heavy blow from Howard toward his opponent's neck at the beginning of the third round and the speed of his feet kept the boy in the contest. His body, he remembered, pained him for over a week. He wondered if he had broken any bones, but did not dare consult the college doctor.

Now his lips trembled as he stared down at his father, whose grey, rather long hair hung over his face. He knelt down beside the body and, speedily awkwardly, turned it face upwards.

'C'mon, Dad. Get up.'

No movement from the lying figure, whose face seemed drained of blood.

Uncouthly, he felt under his father's pullover. The heart was still beating. Howard pulled the old man's body into a sitting position, where he propped it against a heavy chair. His father made no motion.

'Let's have you up in the chair where I can see you.' This he managed in one lift. His father was not nearly as heavy as he'd expected. He lay there at an uncouth angle, but breathing now audibly. His clothes were creased, seemed to have lost all credible shape.

Howard watched again, then shook him. 'C'mon, Dad.' After a minute or two of such treatment, the old man opened, closed, then opened his eyes; the lids moved sluggishly as if driven by rusty machinery. A groan bumbled from his lips. The boy put his hands under the armpits, and heaved upwards, shifting the body gracelessly so that both soon collapsed back into the chair, one on top of the other.

'Can't you stand?' Howard asked, having scrambled upright.

The eyes clumsily opened again. A huge tear-drop ran from one and down the cheek, followed by a second. Howard stood back, shocked. The old man had his vein-thick hands on the arms of the chair.

'Are you all right?' the son asked.

He received no answer but a tightening of the fingers. 'Would you like to go through to your room?' Again no answer. 'I'll give you a hand.'

The father's eyes were closed, but not comfortably.

'Let's go through to your study. I'll bring your pudding in there.' Silence again. 'It's Christmas pudding today, your favourite.' Again the boy straightened himself and pushed out to the kitchen where he cut a decent slice from the pudding, warming it in a saucepan on the stove. He flooded it with a helping of thick, yellow custard. It looked rich, enticing. He picked the plate up and slowly made his way out to where his father huddled in the arm-chair.

'Hello, dad. Your pudding. Your favourite.'

This time the old man opened his eyes as if he understood what the boy was saying.

'Where do you want it? In here or in the study?'

The father made a kind of nod in the direction of the study door. Howard placed the plate in safety on the table; took the old man's arm.

'Sit up.' He heaved the helpless body, or so it seemed, a foot or two higher. For a few seconds the father held the upright position, then suddenly, almost convulsively, rose to his feet, stood, then made for the study. He moved quickly, but unevenly, staggering from side to side so violently that the boy expected him to fall, but he reached a chair by the table and collapsed gracelessly into it. Arms on the table he stared forward. Howard silently placed the pudding, spoon alongside, on the table. The father dragged one arm back, picked up the spoon which, once it was clear of the table-top fell from the nerveless fingers. Howard darted round, examined it.

'I'll get you a clean one,' he said. 'Just hold on.'

He returned, placed the spoon on the table. 'There you are. Will you be all right then?'

This time the old man seemed to understand, and nodded his head.

'I'll come back in when you've finished that to see if you want any more.'

When he returned, ten minutes later, he found his father had eaten a spoonful or two of his pudding and then pushed the dish aside and laid his forearms on the desk before placing his head on the outstretched limbs. Now he seemed fast asleep.

'Do you want anything else?' Howard whispered. 'A drink?' No response, beyond a shuffle, and he left the room and went to the kitchen where he set about washing the dishes.

George admired the way Howard Clark told them this. He recalled the detail of each incident so closely that one could easily imagine it. Andrew sat frozen-faced at the table, while Mirabel once dabbed at her eyes with a tiny, lace-edged handkerchief. Once he'd finished, the four sat silent, silenced. It was Andrew who spoke first.

'And what was the result of all this?' he asked. 'Did he kick you out?'

'No. He was very quiet at tea-time. But he made some slight attempt to help. Not that he was very used to it.' Howard Clark shook his head. 'I've often thought about it. In a way I felt ashamed that I'd hit him. He'd a little cut on his cheek, and a real shiner. His eye was blackened, closed, and the flesh round it terribly discoloured. He didn't complain. That surprised me, but I concluded that he'd decided I was too big to be physically punished.'

'Would he be thinking of some other way of getting back at you?' Andrew asked.

'I'm sure he was. But he was a crafty devil. And I think he must have decided that I was more use to him there, at home, than making my own way paying rent.'

'Was it never mentioned?' Andy again.

'Never. He'd felt at a disadvantage, and was embarrassed by it.'

'He never tried to put you to embarrassment?'

'No. And later he left all his money to me, which with the sale of five houses he'd bought totted up to a quite impressive total. He was careful with his money. Never indulged himself. Lived with exemplary thrift. That was his phrase. I never thought any of it would come my way. But he was suspicious of charities. Felt that the directors probably pocketed the money. Or that the causes were themselves not worth supporting.'

'Was he miserable?' Mirabel said.

'He was no ray of sunshine, but he kept well and fit physically, until the day he died. I guess he looked at his bank accounts and rent-books, and was pleased with himself. I don't think he ever considered how he'd spend it, in any way.'

'You met frequently?'

'Not infrequently, let's say.'

'And you got on well, or reasonably?'

'"Got on" is not the expression I'd choose. We never had an interesting conversation that I can remember. We spoke to each other like people sending messages.'

'What did you say?'

'How we were, medically speaking, and about our jobs.'

Howard Clark pulled an awkward face. 'There is one thing I should mention, though I never noticed it myself. By the time he came to make his last will, I had started to make something of a name for myself. In a modest way. After his death, several of his friends, acquaintances might be a better word in his case, told me that he was proud of me. I didn't know whether to believe them or not. People, I find, tell me what they think I want to hear.

'But when I came to clear his house I found two or three post-cards of my early carvings, and quite an elaborate note-book, big, nine inches by ten, in which he'd pasted cuttings from newspapers which made any mention of me, however small. And as they were from various newspapers, *The Times*, *Guardian*, *Daily Telegraph* and *Independent*, which I knew he didn't take, he must have asked people to cut them out and save them for him. I never thought he'd bother with a cuttings album about me. He never went so far as to buy a carving of mine. He'd think that a real waste of money.'

'That's good, though,' Mirabel said quietly.

Clark spread his arms, showed the palms of his hands, expressing doubt. But a crooked smile played on his face.

As Andrew drove them back in the early evening, they discussed this revelation. Andrew expressed the opinion that the two men must have been rather alike in temperament, parent and son.

'A complex of puritans, if you ask me, with not enough reading behind them to direct a series of excuses from characters in novels.' He looked shame-faced as he said this. George kept quiet. Mirabel questioned neither man.

The rest of the stay passed peaceably, without incident.

89

VII

A week or so later George received a post-card, sealed away in an envelope, from Mirabel.

> You'll be sorry to hear that Andy has been involved in quite a serious road accident. He is in hospital, and is said to be recovering, if slowly, from his wounds. Yours, M. L.

"Wounds" not "injuries" frightened him.

He rang her and offered to visit the hospital if that seemed appropriate. She immediately invited him to accompany her that evening when she intended to call in shortly to the ward. She hadn't yet seen Andy.

'I hate hospital visits,' she confided. 'I don't know what to add once I've said I hope the patient will soon feel better.'

She did not prolong the conversation. George said he'd drive them there, and arranged a time to pick her up.

'It's out of your way,' she said.

'I put myself out, now and then,' he answered, 'and feel the better for it.'

He was surprised at the size of Mirabel's house, an imposing Victorian villa. When he said that it seemed large for one person, she laughed.

'I can get plenty of exercise,' she said, 'without going out. This is the house where I was brought up.'

'It's a fine family house,' he admitted.

'I was the only child. And when I came back from London my father had died and so there were only two of us. When I was a child we had a live-in servant. She was called Milly and worshipped my father. When he died she left, apparently.'

'And your mother?'

'She died just over a year ago. I had some time with her and I was grateful for that. We both felt we could look after each other.

90

As we did. She was fairly fit. Heart trouble that didn't seem too serious, to her, or anybody else, but it finally killed her.'

'Was she overweight?'

Mirabel laughed at his question.

'No. She was slim and lively. I wasn't sure where I could get a job after I left Charles, but my mother knew people and talked me up to her own solicitors, who took me on. Right, I'm ready now.'

This conversation had taken place spasmodically as she rushed about the house. When she was near enough to the room where he was waiting she took up their talk where they had left off, and so naturally, easily, that George was amazed. He wondered what last-minute chores demanded such rushing about the place, and noticed again how suitably yet simply she was dressed.

As they left through the front door she said, 'I haven't got anything to take Andy, grapes or . . .'

'You don't know whether he's capable of eating anything, do you?'

'No. All I heard was that he'd been involved in a car accident and that he was fairly seriously injured.'

They were lucky at the hospital and found a parking space.

'I'll pay,' Mirabel said.

'No. Be my guest.'

She stood, beautiful in the dim lights of the car-park. The ward they wanted was only five minutes' walk away. Once inside the building she said again that she hated hospital visits.

'Have you done many?'

'I came every day for a fortnight before my mother died.'

'Wasn't it expected? Her death, I mean.'

'I suppose it was, but they didn't stress it. Not to me.'

George was carrying a bunch of flowers, chrysanthemums, which he had laid on the back seat.

'I don't know whether one should bring flowers for men,' he said.

'He'll like them. Not that he'll say so.'

Andrew lay in a small room off the ward. A nurse from whom Mirabel asked the way led them forward to it.

'Don't disturb him. He's possibly asleep.'

She entered the room first and straightened any slight irregu-larities of the bedclothes, then looked the patient over as if she were about to demonstrate some medical point to them, but all she did was to issue further warnings.

'Don't touch him,' she said, 'and if you talk to him, do it quietly. If he's awake he'll hear you, even with his eyes shut.'

She left them almost militarily; George, casting an eye about the place, seized the single chair. Carrying it across the room, he placed it near the head of the bed and invited Mirabel to sit. She did so and asked in a whisper, 'How are you, Andy?' to which he gave no answer, though he slightly shifted the position of his head as if he'd heard the question.

'How are you, Andy?'

Andrew lay still, his face pale and on one side slightly scratched, presumably from the accident. A bag of blood hung on a stand by the bed and was connected via a tube to his left wrist. On the other side a second tube led to a breathing mask over his mouth.

'Oxygen,' George gussed, uncertainly. He must try to be calm and collected, for Mirabel's sake.

She sat at the side of the bed, staring at the patient, who did not move until she sighed deeply and asked again if there was anything they could do for him. Andrew, pale as death, lay in silence. They could not make out any sign of life except for a slight movement George noticed, a momentary shudder, very slight, in the body which emphasised the stillness that followed.

George looked round and said, 'I'll go and ask the nurses if we can have a vase for these chrysanths.'

'Shall I go?'

'No, you stay here and see if you can get any response out of this fellow.'

She looked up pitifully at him.

When he returned, with a large, ugly receptacle, neither Andrew nor Mirabel had, or so it seemed to him, moved. She sat bent forward, her face almost touching the bedclothes in an awkward distortion which the elegance of her clothes did nothing to deny.

'Would you like to arrange these flowers?' he asked, sorry for her, giving her a small task she could manage and be grateful for. 'I'm no good at it.'

She made no attempt to sit upright, but turned her head in his direction as if she had heard his voice but failed to understand his request. Finally she took the jug from him and filled it at the sink in the ward. Then with swift, deft movements she tore off the florist's wrapping and, one by one, placed the flowers into the water. She stood for a short time, the flowers upright before her. There seemed no order or arrangement to them; flowers thrust haphazardly into an ugly pot. She had done no better than he, thought George.

Mirabel carried the bouquet across the room and placed it, almost with triumph, on the cupboard by Andy's bedside. As she walked she regained something of her poise and beauty, but lost these as she flopped back on to her chair.

'Good,' said George. 'He'll be able to see them there.'

'Yes.'

She bent towards Andy, asking again how he felt, if he was any better. This went unanswered. The visitors kept their positions for a few silent minutes until George shuffled over to the window.

From the third storey of a building on a hill he could make out a large sector of the north side of the city. Hundreds of street lights stood out boldly but did little to dispel the impression of blackness, like dark velvet, the buildings made. The headlights of buses and cars drew the temporary maps of their journeys, sketching dim sheets of light on occasional, well-placed walls. From the overhead cables of the tramcars bursts of electrical energy exploded briefly and silently. He tried to make out the shapes of buildings he knew, not always successfully, but he watched, satisfying himself with the electrical evidence of a living city.

In the end he turned away, walked back to Andrew's bed, and stood by Mirabel's chair in silence.

'Any signs?' he asked.

The question seemed to galvanise Mirabel, who sprang from her chair.

'No. Just you take my place here and speak to him. He might recognise a male voice.'

He did as he was bid, lowering his head as she had done. 'Hello, Andy,' he said. 'This is George. George Taylor. Can you hear me?' He waited in vain. He could just make out that Andrew was still breathing. 'Can you hear me? We came to see how you were shaping, Mirabel and I. We thought you might in some way know the sound of our voices. If you can, would you give us a sign if this is so? You might open your eyes. Or raise a finger. Or give a groan. So that we know that you can hear and understand what is going on.'

Both visitors stared at their friend. He shuddered. They looked at each other, wondering if this troubled trembling of the body was the only attempt at communication the usually loquacious Andrew could now manage. 'Can you hear?' Nothing in answer to their question. George shook his head towards Mirabel.

She raised a woe-begone face. 'Try him once more, please,' she said plaintively. She laid one hand on his shoulder as he bent over the bed.

'This is George here,' he began, 'with Mirabel. We've come to see how you are.' Though he did not raise his voice, he had tried to infuse it with power. The effort was wasted. He felt like an infant-school teacher, trying in vain to explain some moral point to a stupid, intractable pupil who understood neither his intention nor his words.

He shook his head.

'No chance,' he said.

'What shall we do?' she asked.

'We'd better go home.'

'Would you just try once more?'

Again he asked Andrew how he was shaping, then announced their names. He instructed the patient once again how to indicate that he had been heard and understood. As he expected nothing was given in return. George stood slowly up and edged alongside Mirabel, who slipped a hand into the crook of his elbow.

''Bye, then, Andy,'' he said, quite loudly. She repeated his words. They waited a minute, it seemed longer, for his answer, then made for the door.

Outside she clung on to George's arm as they enquired at the nurses' station about Andrew's medical condition. 'He's been badly knocked about,' one of the younger nurses answered, 'but his present condition's stable. He's fairly young and healthy. We think he has a good chance of recovery.'

'Will he be back to normality?'

'It's too early to answer that, but we're hopeful.' George thanked them. 'Visit him tomorrow. You'll see a difference.'

They walked solemnly out to his car. He suspected that Mirabel was quietly crying.

'Would you like to come round to my flat for a bit?' he asked.

94

'Would you try my house? I won't keep you up too late. I know you'll have to be out at the crack of dawn tomorrow morning.'

'If it's no trouble.'

Her house felt warm. She led him into a wide sitting-room, furnished with polished items. The impression of wealth was unmistakable. The chair she chose for him was large and thoroughly comfortable. Six men could sleep in this, he thought to himself. Mirabel went out to prepare coffee. He sat looking at two large prints of local scenes: a winding road through a wood and a village inn with a hunt meeting before the front door. He pushed himself out of his chair to read the names of the artist. Both were marked by a similar signature in the lower right-hand corner: J. Wentworth Dacres, 2005. The painting, in water colour, was strong, almost leaping off the paper. George had no idea who Dacres was; a local notable, he guessed, he'd never heard the name. He must ask Mirabel. They were very good, from margin to margin. Amateur painters soon let themselves down; would paint like angels at high points – a near tree, the master's house, a threatening cloud – but leave parts of the painting uninteresting. Painted, yes, but below standard. He went back to his chair. He wouldn't mind owning these pictures. They'd be worth something now, and much more later on. Good investments but, best of all, works of art, to be studied for years on end with increasing pleasure. He thought of Howard Clark and his works.

Mirabel seemed to be taking an interminable time making two cups of coffee. He guessed that she was more moved by Andrew's condition than she cared to confess. George was uncertain how to proceed. Should he talk about the man, their relationship, or chat to Mirabel as if he had dropped in on an ordinary, eventless day? He did not know, did not like his difficulties.

At last the door was opened quietly and Mirabel appeared carrying a tray. Her progress across the room to a polished table was swift, efficient and yet stately. He could not see her face, but her bodily movements were beautiful. She was herself again.

'Sugar? Milk?' she enquired. He wanted neither and she served him with speed.

She carried her coffee and sat down opposite him. She lifted the cup to her lips. Her face shocked him. She had made some effort to suggest normality, with the use of face powder, but amateurishly, leaving an effect of careless roughness. Her lips trembled; her eyes were wet; tears had spoiled the effect of inattentively applied mascara. He caught his breath; the blotchiness, the uneven surface of her face, beautiful in shape as always, gave him the impression that he was looking at a middle-aged, overworked woman. It hardly seemed believable. Was her make-up usually so skilfully applied, so delicately, that faults, wrinkles, blemishes, were all hidden? He could not believe it. He dropped his eyes. She began to talk.

'What did you make of Andy?' she asked.

'He didn't look very well.' George spoke deliberately, each word divided from the rest of the sentence. 'But it's only the first days. Nobody looks too good so early after the accident. The nurses seemed to think he'd be all right.'

'I tell you what worried me. He was so quiet. Do you think he understood what we were saying or even recognised us? The first nurse we spoke to seemed to think he might.'

'I don't think so. He still seemed unconscious.' He answered her question truthfully, but wondered if he had spoken too crudely, cruelly. 'Not that I'm any expert.'

'It didn't seem like Andy. He'd always got something to say for himself. I'm not claiming that I always agreed with him, or approved of what he was saying, but to see him there absolutely wordless . . . it wasn't Andy. Perhaps next visit . . .'

'You want me to go along with you?'

'Why shouldn't I? It was good of you to accompany me this evening. I was terrified.'

George allowed a significant pause before he spoke again.

'I thought I might be in the way.'

'Why should that be?' she asked.

'I thought you loved him.'

The sentence seemed to have no effect on her. She tenderly touched her over-powdered cheek with delicate finger ends.

'No, no. Not at all.'

'I'm sorry.' His answer brought a small twisted smile to her lips.

'I've known him a long time. You know we were engaged once, at university, and for a time I did think we would marry. He was impressive, older, but not, I now think if I can put it this way, a sexual man. At any rate, by the time I reached the fourth year, the professional year when I took the solicitors' exams, I was madly in love with Charles Lockwood. I have no great deal of confidence in myself, so when a lecturer, an Oxford graduate, began to show favour towards me, I was swept off my feet.'

'Was that good or bad?'

'Oh, good. I worked like a dog at my books. You won't believe it but I won a prize and had my name in big letters in *The Times*. I took a job with Talbot and Watts to finish my clerkship. And Charles left the town to take a new fancy position in London. I thought that would be the last I'd hear of him. But, no. He began to write letters to me. They were brilliant, amusing and learned. He proposed to me by letter, just before he went off for a short spell at Geneva.'

'And you accepted him?'

'He could charm the leaves from the trees when he set about it.'

'And you went off to London? After you married him.'

'Yes. Charles got me a job in a solicitor's office, a big concern, well organised. It taught me how such an office should be run. But after a year or two I wasn't altogether satisfied. I would have liked a family. Charles was well settled in London, and earning a great deal of money. He knew how I felt about this, but he knew, or feared, that having a family had its drawbacks. He wanted no obstacles in the way of his rise in the world.'

'Was that the cause of your parting?'

'One of them, but by no means the greatest. He was the most inconsiderate person I've ever come across. Anything that stood in his way was dismissed as unreasonable. We rowed incessantly over that and other things, and in the end I left him. I think he was pleased. He thought I might cling to my position and status as his wife, and that if I couldn't I'd be as awkward as I could about the divorce. In the end he was generous, much more than ever I expected.'

'Why was that?'

'He'd found Wife Number Two.'

'One who'd do as she was told?'

'I don't know about that. She was a pretty girl. I could easily see that, though I only met her a time or two. She was the only daughter of titled parents. Not that I think that would influence Charles unduly.'

'Rich?'

'So they say. As Croesus. And influential. And a great admirer of Charley-boy.'

'Do you ever hear from him?'

'Rarely. He's put profitable bits of business in the hands of my firm. They're pleased. And when I think about it, I've decided he considers he's in my debt. I'm surprised that he felt any compunction about me. I'd served my purpose, and that was that. But no, he put bits of legal work my way, or my bosses', in return for any hurt I felt. Anything that made money appealed to him. I don't suppose he'd spend much time on it, but he made the effort and I was surprised.'

'You didn't refuse such jobs?'

'No. He wouldn't notice such small amounts so it might as well be me as anyone else he extended his patronage to.'

'Do you see him?'

'I've seen him once since we divorced. He was all charm. I thought he'd just acknowledge me, and then go off to talk to somebody more interesting. But no. He spent time being pleasant to me, as if he was about to woo me all over again.'

'Where did this meeting take place?'

'The annual lecture and dinner party of local lawyers.'

'Was his lecture worth hearing?'

'Brilliant. That's what I expected. Old Gervase Watts, the senior partner then, was a bit disinclined to include me in the five of us who were going. He thought I'd be embarrassed or even distressed to see Charles again. He didn't understand me at all.'

'Was he married? Your old boss?'

'Yes. Thirty-odd years. She's a nice old dear. He wouldn't think of dropping her.'

'No.'

'I suppose we judge everyone else by ourselves. You remember the man we took you to meet, Howard Clark? Now what sort of man do you think he is? I know you've only met him the once, but you'll have ideas about him. He's that sort of man.'

'He seemed successful, proud of himself and the position he's achieved.'

'A hard man? Knows what he's about? Goes bald-headed to get it? Yes, that's what I would have said, too. But . . .' Mirabel paused, screwing up her eyes.

'Some little time ago, two years ago perhaps, he said he wanted to talk to me. I was surprised. I even thought he might be about to propose marriage. He said he'd thought I was rather down in the mouth, that the break-up of my marriage and my return to this place had made me feel I'd failed in life. He said he'd more than once suffered from depression himself; from a feeling that, however hard he worked, he made no impression on the people he wanted to admire or praise his work. I asked him if that was so in any serious sense, and he said it was.'

She paused as if uncertain about continuing. George assumed a look of humility, or one willing to be instructed. She breathed deeply, and started.

'Howard Clark said he had been deeply depressed. This was before he came back home. He was living in Cornwall, in good health and working away every day. Yet, he said, he could not rid his mind of the certainty that he was getting nowhere. For the last year or two he had sold next to nothing. He'd had an exhibition that brought little reward. The critics who had praised his early work, overpraised it even, now were lukewarm, non-committal. His subject matter was dull, they said. He lacked vision. He repeated himself. There was no development. His skill as a sculptor was still there, but it was employed on the same old subject matter.

'He was at the time living with a woman who had connections with the art world. She wrote articles for the right magazines. He hadn't thought highly of her as a judge of art, his or anyone else's, but he loved her. She spent most of her time with him in Cornwall, writing a book on Rodin. She helped him over his wife's desertion. When the critics' condemnation of his last exhibition appeared she was back in London, engaged on bringing out a special edition of a magazine of modern art, and this seemed to run into every possible snag so that she hadn't the time to come back to Cornwall. When this had happened once before, she had sent him two or three witty, loving, brilliant post-cards every week, reporting on her progress. This time, in spite of the letters he wrote, he heard nothing from her. At the end of a month he was sure she had given him up, without bothering to offer him any explanation.

'When the special edition of the magazine appeared, it contained two short articles about Howard, without illustrations, written by two men he had never heard of, which were thoroughly condescending. Both agreed that he had started with a talent of sorts, but he had allowed it, by unimaginative choice of subject matter, to gutter out. Now he was a provincial with no hope who had squandered such gifts as he had once possessed, let them melt into mediocrity.

'He enquired about the qualifications of these two critics and found they were young, barely out of university, nothing to write home about, who had done or said not a word to suggest future greatness themselves. This angered him because he guessed that Ursula, his lover, had chosen these two self-regarding mediocrities to write him off. That must be the accepted opinion of him amongst the London intelligentsia, and Ursula had become convinced by this view. Here he was, written off, a poor hopeless case, a nobody, and she had now added her condemnation to theirs.

'Back in his house in Cornwall there were two wardrobes full of clothes which she had not collected. She must have been making a fair living by her pen to abandon all these, he thought. She'd barely earned enough to put butter on her bread when they had first met. Often he had paid her train-fare back to London, to keep her career intact. For several days on end he sorted through these flimsy bits she had worn with such panache. He recalled . . . and his forehead wrinkled and reddened, as he told me about it . . . that he opened one of the wardrobes and took out a beautiful white dress, delicately trimmed with lace, and stood shaking with fury in the middle of the room, holding this up, preparing himself to tear it to rags. In the end, he said, he came to his senses, and bundled the dress back on to its hanger. There he swore at it and stumbled away, his anger now equalled by his shame.

'He was a nonetity. It was hardly worth continuing with his work. He had just started this new phase of small watercolours, and he sat at his table before a village scene: a row of cottages, a church tower behind, and on the tree-lined road a man and woman cycling together. What could be more unoriginal? He was about, he told himself, to paint a cliché, and a plagiarism at that. Parrot-fashion . . . that was his contribution to art. His paint-box open, brushes ready, clean from yesterday, he rested his arms across the drawing board, a failure; a baffled, enfeebled, inferior, worthless caricature of an artist who'd done nothing to add to the beauty of the world.

'He sat thus, quite still, all the power, the will, drained out of him. He had done nothing so far, and the future would be blanker, bleaker.

'As he hunched powerless over the table his depression left him, not quickly but leaving him empty. This was no better than

100

his dejection. Or so he felt until slowly, almost against his better judgement, his emptiness of spirit seemed to change. It was emptiness, vacancy, but changing; now it became creative. This was no sudden flash of pleasure, but a slowly grasped certainty that he had not wasted his life.

'He had started from nowhere. There had been no art of any kind in his boyhood home. The opposite was true; his father had mocked his pretensions, had opposed his wish to attend art college. They, he and his wife, had made enough sacrifices to keep him at the grammar school, beggaring their holidays to a week in boring Skegness when but for him they could be on a fortnight's luxury and rest and culture in some foreign city, Nice, Grenoble, Prague, Budapest. Even at the time, he puzzled from where his father had trawled in these names. He'd prepared the list, it might be changed in a fortnight, to fling at his son's conscience next time the boy had come up with another of his preposterous, hideous, idiot schemes for himself.

'Yet with the fearful support of his mother he achieved his ambition. He'd done well at both his art colleges, won prizes, and three times been allowed to send his work to real exhibitions. The Royal Academy had displayed two of his student pictures. The local museum had purchased a small statue of an athlete in motion. He recalled a visit to the Castle Museum to see this.

'His father had reluctantly agreed to join the others and the three of them had stood at the end of a great chamber, by the statuette, in a place of honour. They said nothing. His mother was grimly silent. She dared not praise her son's statuette for fear of his father's anger, and a public quarrel.

'A well-dressed man and woman stopped by the work and the man confidently turned to his wife and said, out loud, "That's brilliant. You can see the power, the athleticism, the will to win." "Beautiful," the lady agreed, "beautiful."

'Father Clark had looked at them, face aghast. Howard was afraid he'd contradict these opinions, but no, the other man was physically too big, his voice too upper-class. Who they were God knows, but they were not, from mere appearance, the sort of people you'd choose to pick a quarrel with. Howard expected sarcasm when they reached home, but his father said not a word. Somebody of presence had praised his son; perhaps the boy really had talent.

He recalled all this for Mirabel, how he had begun to believe in himself again. It was not a sudden revelation; this new confidence spread like ink through blotting-paper, easily, confidently. He found himself after perhaps five minutes thinking in this slightly optimistic way that if he never carved another stone, handled another piece of clay or put a brush to paper, he had already made a success of his art. He could barely believe it, tried to dismiss it, but the conviction grew, that he was somebody that if he dropped dead that minute, he had left works which would be admired, would keep his name alive with art-lovers, for generations to come.

This confidence in his success did not last at strength in the next few days, but he could recall it to cheer himself, keep pessimism at bay. He wondered if he was a victim from that bipolar disease, manic-depression. A friend of his had suffered from it, a talented young man, a pianist, who had been studying at the Royal Academy. In his manic phase, he would spend money like water, drive his car like a madman, chide his contemporaries for not appreciating the beauty of the earth. Then he would sink to a painful dullness when nothing went right. The medics had restored him to somewhere near normality by the use of lithium, but he did not complete his musical studies at the Academy. He helped his father at his furniture shop, played the church organ, married, had children but in Howard's eye never approached the brilliance of his early life. He played the piano better than most, as well as the violin, 'cello and organ. There had been, it appeared, traces of the disease in his grandfather's family. In the shop he seemed a young version of his father who would sooner sell you a piano than play it to you. The son had died at the age of forty-one after an accident in his car.

Howard Clark was suspicious of this new optimism. A year or two later he had his first success with his small watercolours. When he returned to his home town he was making a good living. He took up his sculpture with élan and found himself praised in all the right places.

'And what happened to his girl-friend?' George asked Mirabel.

'I've no idea. I suppose she's still about. One thing only I know is that while he was still living in Cornwall he went to lecture in Paris, and she employed two men to break into his house, presumably to recover her clothes. He, crafty beggar, had changed all the locks on the outside of the house, and hidden the keys to the wardrobes. The men acted suspiciously and it so happened that the local policeman lived next-door and saw them in the garden. He had promised to keep an eye on Howard's property and so questioned them. It frightened them away, apparently.'

'So what happened to the clothes?'

'Howard's a funny fellow. I daren't ask him about them because I couldn't guarantee that he'd done something sensible with them, such as given them to a charity shop or even a church jumble-sale. You never know with him.'

'You mean, he might have given them to another woman?'

'Possibly.'

'You didn't get any?'

'No. I didn't know him at the time.'

They laughed together, gently. Soon after George made his way home. As he left her house Mirabel held up her face to be kissed. He hugged her, and went home happy.

VIII

George Taylor tramped the streets during the next few weeks, feeling pleased with his life and the onset of spring despite Andrew's condition. Mirabel had telephoned him several times on the slightest of pretexts and had spoken warmly to him. She, he noticed, never dawdled at the phone, but made the two or three minutes she gave him memorable. He began to believe that her interest in him was growing. He decided to test this out by inviting her to accompany him on a day-trip to the east coast.

'On a 'bus or a train?' she asked.

'In my car. I want you to myself.'

'Would it be to Skegness?'

'If that's what you'd like. All the amusements will be closed. They don't usually open until the Easter break.'

'So there'll be nothing to occupy us.'

'I go to the coast to stare at the sea.'

'And take your shoes and socks off and roll your trousers up and paddle?'

'The North Sea's not very welcoming at this time of the year.'

She could not go with him on the next Saturday but arranged to accompany him the following week.

'What if it rains?' she asked.

'We'll get wet, I expect, you pessimist. Since I've been able to please myself, I've made these little forays to the seaside about three times a year. I'm an islander, and I live just about as far from the sea as is possible, and so I go to the coast to see all's well.'

'And is it?'

'It's all well with me, not the ocean.'

She insisted that they use her car for the expedition.

'I like driving,' she said.

'Did Andrew allow you to take the wheel, then, in his car?'

'The number of times I've been out in Andrew's car could

be counted on the fingers of one hand.' She sounded cross, but George could not decide whether it was at his question or Andrew's reluctance to let her drive. There seemed something enigmatic about her even in the simplest conversations.

On the morning of their trip she rang George's front-door bell and walked straight back to her car.

'Are you in a hurry to get started?' he asked. He had stood back when he opened the front door, waiting for her to step inside. When she did not do so, he peered down the empty path. He walked down to the street and found her seated in her car.

'Are you ready then?' she asked.

'No. I expected you to give me some advice. About sandwiches and drinks.'

'There's no need. You go and get your coat on. And bring a brolly.'

When they were on the way she showed no signs of annoyane with him, but began in a normal voice to talk about Andrew's condition. She had after all, she said, visited him alone the previous evening.

'Does he seem more like himself?' George asked.

'No. He seems to find it difficult to put two or three words together.'

'Why is that?'

'He doesn't know. Neither do the doctors. His physical injuries, and they were serious, are now on the mend, but his character seems to have changed.'

'Did he damage his head?'

'It appears so. It must have been banged about.'

'Can he talk to you? Answer your questions?'

'Yes. Sometimes he answers me. His voice is much softer, less aggressive, but he speaks normally. But now and then he seems a different person, remembering nothing.'

'About the accident?'

'Yes, but also about other things. He couldn't remember his mother's surname. And one evening about six months ago we went to a recital by the Prague Quartet. They gave a marvellous interpretation of their first item, and were just about to start on the second, a Beethoven Razumovsky quartet, when a string broke on the leader's fiddle. He replaced it in no time, though he had to go off-stage to find the new string. It suited Andy to see that man putting the string on. He loves it when somebody who's a master of his craft finds himself at a loss, like any beginner. Well, I mentioned this incident and he hadn't the remotest notion what it was I was talking about. He'd recalled the incident several times since to me, and now it was gone. Odd.'

They made their way to Sutton-on-Sea. The rain held off, but the sky and the sea were uniformly grey. They stumbled along the beach, not cold but uncomfortable. George was happy, though, and sang 'Did you not hear my lady, Go down the garden singing?' Within a minute Mirabel joined him. As they reached the end of the verse, both laughed together.

'I could do with it in a higher key,' she said. 'I love Handel. Of all the great composers, he's the one I'd like to have met.'

'He was a funny old stick. Stood for no foolery from his women soloists.'

'He never married, you know.'

'He never met anyone quite like you. That's the reason.'

A little further on George found a bullet-shaped fossil. He wiped it clear of sand with his handkerchief.

'Here, look at this,' he shouted.

She took it from him.

'I don't know what it's called,' he said.

'A belemnite.'

'A what?'

She repeated the word for him.

'It's the internal shell of some sort of sea-creature.'

'And what does "belemnite" mean?' he asked.

'It's from the Greek word for a dart. That's what it looks like.'

'It's more like a rifle-bullet to me.'

'Yes. But perhaps bullets of your sort didn't exist when they first named the fossil.'

'How do you come to know all this?' he asked.

'We did it at school. They used to lead us out to parks and streams when we were in the first form, to show us the wonders of Nature.'

'And you liked that?'

'It seemed to give us a freedom we didn't get in other lessons. In our Latin exercise books we had to have the title and the exercise page and number, doubly underlined, thick and thin, and if we didn't the mistress would put "minus two" in a circle. We could score full marks for the sentences but only receive

106

eight out of ten because of the deadly "minus two" at the top by the title, and sometimes "minus one, untidy" at the bottom.'

'Did those marks mean anything?'

'With the Latin teacher, Miss Knighton, they did. They were entered into her mark-book and added up at the end of term, and a form-order established, and this was added on to our end-of-term report.'

'Is she still about, Miss Knighton?'

'No, she's been dead for donkey's years. She married a Mr Lamb and it's said, after my time, that one girl with a literary turn stuck a label on her celebrated mark-book, reading *The Lamb's Book of Life*.'

'What happened then?'

'That was another mystery. Apparently Miss Knighton, or Mrs Lamb, never attempted to remove the label from the book. It lay on her desk, for everybody to see. As if she was proud of it.'

'Did that seem a possibility?'

'When I think back I'd say no, but I may be wrong. Kids often make bad misjudgements. There wasn't an ounce of humour in old Knighton as far as I could see, and the fact that the writer seemed to be making her joke at the expense of Holy Scripture would have been judged awful, if not blasphemous, by the powers-that-were in girls' grammar schools of that period.'

George admired the upright way in which Mirabel walked. He had no doubt she was beautiful. While she related these not very interesting stories of her school life, he found himself entranced – that would have been his word. It made itself plain to him that he was in love with her.

At the end of the beach they turned to walk back, not quickly but at an easy narrator's pace. Mirabel came out, smiling, with some story of her first visit to France, as a small girl, and her surprise that quite ordinary-looking beings spoke in a language she did not understand. When she had finished the anecdote he glanced at his watch and said they'd try to get something to eat in the village.

'There won't be anything at this time of the year.'

'We'll see. If there's nothing open here Skegness will have something, if it's only a chip-shop.'

When they came off the beach he pointed in childish triumph at a notice over the door of the corner shop which advertised in fading paint 'Sandwiches', amongst other comestibles.

107

'There, look,' he crowed.

'That'll be only in season.'

They stepped inside. A friendly-faced woman who was re-arranging and dusting the shelves stepped down from her ladder, and enquired about their needs.

'Do you sell sandwiches?' George asked.

Her face showed surprise that anyone should make such a request but she looked them over a moment and smiled again.

'Just for the two of you?'

'Yes, please. If it's not asking too much.'

'With ham?'

'Yes, please.' She turned away, but as quickly back.

'I've just thought. Would you like home-made cobs instead of slices of bread? I was expecting visitors so I baked yesterday. This morning I heard, first thing, that they weren't coming.'

Hungry, they ate with pleasure. It grew warm inside the shop and they enjoyed their cobs in full view of the few passing strangers. The sky darkened, but it did not rain. When they had cleared their plates and coffee cups and had enjoyed the shopkeeper's anecdotes of people in the town and 'goings-on' in 'Skeggy', where even in winter there was a large-scale dance with a full band every Saturday night, they began to talk to her.

'Do you go?' George asked.

'I wouldn't miss it.'

'You go on your own?'

'No. At one time I went with my husband, but he died three years back. When he died, and he was fifteen years older than me, I was at a loose end. He left me nicely provided for, but I didn't want to try to settle amongst people I didn't know. So I kept on with the shop. He used to help me a bit with the serving, but I did all the ordering and so forth. He did his best for me but he had a job. He was married to somebody else when I first met him. I stole him away from her. And, do you know, I don't regret it or feel sorry for what I did to her. She didn't mind, I think. It seems awful when your husband leaves you. You feel you've failed. But once he's gone, if you're all right financially and are not dependent on his wages, you look round and see the advantages. He didn't really suit her.'

'He must have been an attractive man to have all you ladies chasing him,' Mirabel said.

'He wasn't bad-looking. And knew how to dress well. He was

108

still working when we first got together. He was a carpenter, and good at it. His first wife wanted someone from further up the social ladder. At any rate, he came in and lived with me until such time that we could get married. Some people knew about it, and talked. It did my reputation no good, I can tell you. Even when we married there were those who looked with, let's say, suspicion on us. But there was one curious thing about it all, that puzzles me to this day.

'Eve, his first wife, died two years before Harry did. And, do you know, in her will she left him ten thousand pounds. In the solicitor's letter with the cheque, it said it was in reward for the "many kindnesses" he did her. Harry couldn't believe his eyes. They'd been married about eight years when he left her, and had been at loggerheads for two or three before he went. What these "many kindnesses" were, Harry just couldn't guess.

'He made a joke of it. That was like him. He said she thought his greatest kindness was packing his bags, clearing off and living with me. But I could see he was troubled with it. Why she had left him so much, though it wasn't by any means the whole of her fortune, he could not make out. There was something there that he did not understand. Whether she tried to make him feel ashamed of deserting her, or whether there was something or things she was genuinely grateful for, he could not fathom, and it left him puzzled. On the wrong foot, as you might say. I said I thought she'd known how he'd react to the bequest. She was a crafty old bitch.'

'That's interesting,' George murmured.

'He never did anything with it, but let his bank invest it for him, and by the time he died it was there, bigger than ever, for me to do as I liked with.'

Outside, and in the car, Mirabel smiled, pleased with life.

'My word,' she said, 'she liked the sound of her own voice.'

'I was surprised she told us all that stuff about her marriage.'

'Yes. And confessed she had stolen him from the other woman. I wonder how near the truth that was.'

'I wondered if she wanted us to sort the puzzle out for her. Why the first wife, who should have felt aggrieved, had acted so generously when she was making her will.'

They drove along to Skegness where a few more people were to be seen, walking glumly along damp pavements. All the amusements and stalls were closed; one or two were being decorated.

The beach seemed to George flatter and the sea farther away than ever. He said as much to Mirabel. They didn't stay long, but walked a while.

'You remember it full of deck-chairs and children and noise.'

'I suppose so.'

How smart she looked, walking along the front. They reached the clock-tower a second time. He pointed a finger at it.

'That's the symbol to me of holidays and the sea-side.'

'It impressed you when you were small?'

'It didn't take much to impress me then.'

'You surprise me. I'd have thought you'd have been a sharp-eyed child, looking down your nose at these scenes of provincial pleasure.'

'No. I took my lead from my father. He'd dress up for the day out. He wore his best cloth-cap. His "nicky" . . . that's what we called his soft felt hat . . . he reserved for Sundays only. And on the Sabbath he wore starched collars. He sent them away to be stiffened.'

'Was this to go to church?'

'No. He'd nothing against religion, but never attended.'

They reached their car and began the journey home. Mirabel drove in a leisurely fashion and talked about her job.

'Are you comfortable in your work, then?' George asked her.

'What do you mean?'

'They say that nowadays people often change their careers in a way their grandfathers never did. If they started as a solicitor or a doctor, that is what they were still slaving at when they retired.'

'Except when they were no good at it.'

'And you're good at it?'

He saw that she turned her head sharply in his direction. Her driving was in no way erratic while she scanned his face.

'Yes, I think I could claim that.' She answered with neither boastfulness nor bashful modesty, only a smiling twist of the lips.

The journey ended in darkness with George at one stage falling asleep. He was wide awake when she drew up outside her house and invited him in.

She dug the key into the lock almost vindictively, then pushed the door wide.

'*Entrez donc*,' she shouted.

'You first,' he said, signalling her forward with a sweep of his hand. She stepped into the darkness of the hall, took a long step, and fell. It was almost perfect, like a circus act, a big stride which converted itself into a fall face-down. The hall was thickly carpeted, unlike George's which was terrazzo Venetian mosaic. Even so it would knock the wind out of her. She lay still, as if unconscious, before she jerked her head up and, as helpless, let it drop.

'Oh, fuck,' she said.

He darted forward, knelt, laid his hands lightly on her shoulders, shocked.

'Are you all right?' he asked.

She answered him with a kind of groan or sigh, but did not stir. He knelt on, not knowing his next move. 'Shall I lift you?' he asked.

'No, I'll stay here a moment or two, until I've got my breath back.'

He sat quietly on his heels, waiting. After a few long-drawn-out minutes she moved, put out a hand and pushed herself up to a seated position.

'Now,' she said, 'sit me up straight.' He managed this without too much difficulty. 'Then stand behind me, put your arms around me, and when I'm ready to be lifted, I'll tell you.'

He obeyed her and stood behind her, encircling her upper body with both arms. 'Are you ready?' he asked.

'No.' The answer came clear. He stood enjoying the strength and beauty of her perfume. Her chin was down on her chest, and twice she stretched her arms to touch the wall, and twice withdrew them, dissatisfied or reluctantly.

In the end she gave the word and he lifted her, awkward and heavy as she seemed.

'Put an arm round my neck,' he ventured. They stood together uncertainly. She murmured a direction, or that was how he interpreted the small, diffident sound. Obediently he entered the door of the drawing-room, where there was enough light from the street to see an armchair to which he guided her.

He lowered her into the seat; his right hand was round her right breast. Surprise struck him slowly; all sexual thoughts or signals should have been knocked out of her by the violence of her fall. He did not immediately remove his hand. She lolled; he straightened her legs, picked up a cushion from a settee, and placed it behind her head.

'Thank you,' she whispered, without opening her eyes, and

asked him to make a cup of tea with a spoonful of brandy in it. She issued instructions on how to find cups and ingredients in a quite ordinary voice though her eyes were shut tight. Before he left the room he turned on the lights and drew the curtains. She did not move her position in the chair.

George had no trouble finding his way about the kitchen. He located without any trouble a large cup and saucer, a tray, sugar and milk and one spoonful of brandy, and carried them back to the sitting-room. The expedition took, he thought, no longer than five minutes.

When he returned Mirabel was sitting straight in her chair, hands folded in her lap, eyes now wide open. In a strong voice she issued instructions about placing a small table by her side for the tray.

'Will you manage?' he asked.

'Yes. Of course I shall.' She glanced about. 'You haven't brought yourself a drink in. Go and make yourself what you like.'

Coming back carrying a cup of black coffee, he noticed that she had half-finished her tea.

'How do you feel?'

'Pretty normal.'

'No aches and pains?'

'Nothing out of the ordinary. I expect I shall be well bruised by tomorrow morning. Your cup of tea has brought me nearer robust health. God, it was a sharp fall. I went straight down. I thought I must have broken something. They say that if you break your arm or leg the bone strengthens itself when it heals, so that it's better than before the accident. I don't know whether that's true.'

'Nor I. Have you tried standing?'

'Not yet. I'm never in a hurry where my health's concerned.'

She tossed off her tea, and replaced her cup on the tray with a triumphant gesture. He watched as she relaxed back into her chair. 'Shall we try to see if you can stand?' he asked.

'We?'

'Yes. I'll come over and stand by you, to hold you if you fall.'

'"To hold me when I fall." The verse of a hymn.' Her tone was strongly ironical. 'Come on then. Take up your position.'

Barely giving him a moment to stand by her she placed her fingertips on the two arms of the chair and stood, straight.

'How's that?' she asked, head perkily to one side.

'What about moving?' he asked, taking a step forward. Perhaps she would collapse in his arms. She did not oblige, but stood holding herself ramrod straight.

'How's that?' she asked.

'Any pain?'

'No, not really.' She furrowed her brow as if puzzling it out. 'Not pain. A sort of stiffness, and a . . .' she searched for the words '. . . loss of confidence.' She took a pace forward, and another. 'There, you see.' Then, ruefully, 'I'll sit down again.'

'Are you sure you'll be all right?' he asked.

'I'm not sure of anything just at this minute. But I hope I'm on the way upward. To fall flat like that was a bit frightening.'

'Only a bit?' She made no answer.

They sat for the next half-hour exchanging conversation. At the end she said, 'Despite this, I've enjoyed today so much I'd like it to continue, but I've left myself a long hour or two's work to complete, if I can manage it. And I know you have to rise very early.'

George's pang of disappointment was soothed by her sincerity. She kissed him lightly on the cheek. 'Careful with the steps,' she warned. 'We want no more accidents.'

She closed the door quickly, not waiting to see if he reached the street safely. He took a few steps and, hiding himself from her view behind a large bush spent a minute staring at her dark house. He was rewarded as he saw a light switched on upstairs, and almost immediately by the sight of her energetically closing the curtains. She had managed to walk upstairs. He set off for home.

As he walked along the dark and almost deserted backstreets he mulled over the evening's happenings. After her fall, Mirabel had seemed disorientated, almost to the point of unconscious-ness, so that he'd feared he would need to call an ambulance. He had acted sensibly but touched her intimately. He wondered if she had noticed this or was too shocked by the accident to realise. By the time he had reappeared with her tea and brandy she was herself again.

So it had been, after all, a good day. Mirabel had acted and talked so modestly, had spoken so freely of her earlier life that he felt she had deliberately set out to think seriously about their friendship – perhaps even more. She had not referred to his occupation as a postman, either in deprecation or in jest. He certainly relished her conversation, and she showed by her behaviour that she liked him, and so talked freely to him. It was true, perhaps, that his attraction to her was not equally returned, but she was not a person who overdid matters where deeper feelings were involved.

Perhaps he had hoped that Mirabel would invite him to stay the night. He had not, he told himself, really believed this. Mirabel would not disclose her love so blatantly. It would be out of character. But then, so was the despairing swear-word she had gasped as she fell and lay winded on the hall floor.

In his state of optimistic enthusiasm, he almost immediately sat down and wrote her a letter. He was careful not to overstate matters, but let her know how much he had enjoyed her company, her driving, her appearance. He suggested another outing, similar perhaps, or shorter, an evening at a play or concert of her choice. He owed her a great deal for his day out on the east coast. He had, he wrote, once believed that these visits were not to be shared, only to be undertaken by himself in deference to his mood. She had proved him wrong, and he thanked her for it. He sent his love, feebly adding, 'if you want it'.

IX

Mirabel did not immediately answer this missive, but he did not expect it. She would take her time over her reply. If she thought anything about him, had even the faintest inclination towards him, she would consider her response all the more deeply. Whenever he thought of this, as he did often, George brightened, felt the better for it. He was uncertain sometimes; there seemed to be something almost superstitious about the raising of the spirits, as when a black cat crossed his path. He didn't believe it, really, but could not check the lifting of his heart. After returning from work he opened his front door so that he didn't disturb the pile of mail on the hall floor. It was mostly rubbish, but those advertisements and invitations to write back immediately to claim large sums of money might have rubbed outward surfaces with the one letter in the world he wanted to receive.

A few days later, he found a card amongst the bills, advertisements and other rubbish from his own postman, telling him that a parcel awaited his convenience at the local depot. George was partly annoyed by this, having carefully explained to his postman where to leave such matter, and yet quietly pleased. He was not expecting a parcel, could not think of any of his acquaintances who would as much as think of sending such a thing.

A bare ten minutes brought him to the Post Office depot, where he waved his card to the man who appeared at the counter.

'Hello, George. Have we lost something of yours?'

'Hello. I don't know yet.'

'Ah, you've come to the inefficient part of the Royal Mail.'

Another official straightened himself and came across with a neat, very square parcel in his hand.

'Here you are, sir,' he said. He looked at the parcel with a comical show of concern. 'It's from *The Times*. Looks like books.'

'Thank you.' He must have won one of their crossword prizes. He often submitted completed puzzles without ever winning, or even expecting, a prize. It occupied the time immediately after lunch.

At home he carefully unwrapped the package: a dictionary, a thesaurus, and a book of phrase and fable. He handled the brand new books with care, if not pride. He already had copies of all three, but felt the satisfaction of a winner. It was true the dictionary was an edition some few years more up-to-date than his own copy, so that he'd be able to find exact definitions of those words from IT which now forced their impudent way into the newspapers. And he realised that a new, unmarked copy of any book, of the slightest interest, would tempt him to open and read it and enjoy its still square newness, its unthumbed pages. He wondered whether the dictionary should replace the older version on his shelves. And what would he do with the two or three even older editions?

He did not know, nor care. Sitting at his table, the new book on his knee, he knew it did not matter. If *The Times* rang to tell him that he was not the winner of the competition, that a mistake had been made and asked him to return the prizes, he'd hardly be worse off in knowledge than he was at present. Moreover, he wouldn't send the books back. He'd never heard before of such circumstances, but he'd received, by luck, what he deserved, and he'd hang on to it. He'd lie, and bluster, accuse them of inefficiency before they'd get back one page, even one dot from an i, of their prize books.

He surprised himself.

There'd been no hint from the newspaper that they'd ask for a return of his prizes. The suggestion came from his own inadequacies, he decided. He had invariably counted himself amongst the non-prize-winners of this world; no Howard Clark he. His reward was solely the self-satisfaction he felt at completing the puzzle; now he'd actually done it, and in the lucky draw for the one or two persons to receive a reward for their skill, if that's how they decided who deserved the prize, he'd come up first. And yet he could not sit smilingly back and enjoy his good fortune. He wondered if he'd now give up his attempts at these puzzles; surely they would not award prizes to those who had already won. Even if his name appeared, they'd put it aside and search amongst the rest, some hundreds, he'd guess, for another

116

worthy to be rewarded with a mention in print and a neatly wrapped parcel of books which, like him, he or she already owned.

It did not take him long to turn his thoughts from prizes to Mirabel. That would be typical of him. He had attracted her sufficiently for her to spend time in his company, but he still thought to himself that he didn't deserve her. Even if in some sort of raffle he had won her, he would not take much advantage of the opportunity.

He half-heartedly cooked himself a meal: the rest of yesterday's beef casserole, potatoes and a packet of frozen broad beans. He concentrated but loosely on the preparation of his food, and this was rare since he was usually hungry after his morning's rounds and had been looking forward to the midday feast for an hour or two. He ate with his habitual appetite, but could not have said whether the meal was well-prepared and cooked, or not.

As he sat at the table he worked rapidly through *The Times* news stories. He took his last mouthful as he reached the two pages before the Register. Headed 'Encounters', these were full of small-print advertisements from men and women hoping to meet kindred partners. Each day he read one or two, from each sex, and wondered if he weren't a candidate to write one of the soul-baring appeals.

This morning's efforts were on the whole from people over forty and each carried a small headline in darker print. He wondered if the person in question or some young ... why young? ... employee of the paper provided these: *Attractive Slim Country Lady*; *Recently Retired*; *Voluptuous*; *Young, but Sophisticated-looking*. These were followed by half a dozen lines describing the virtues of the ladies concerned: intelligent, independent, looking younger than their years, shapely, warm, caring, cuddly, even sensational, many of whom WLTM professional, interesting, honest, n/s, successful, genuine gentlemen to enjoy the finer things of life, to share interests, GSOH, looking for LTR.

The men's requests and descriptions seemed rather simpler. One man said he preferred shopping to sport; another described himself as kind; another said what the lady should enjoy, be it fun or golf, art galleries or life's pleasures, not more closely described.

This early-afternoon George skimmed the packed columns with

117

more care than usual, and even began to sketch his own appeal for an encounter. 'Postman, graduate' it began. That damned him out of hand. He wouldn't be rich on a postman's pay and his degree must be poor, pathetically so, if carrying a couple of letters was all it qualified him for. Dampened in spirits, he decided he'd do his shopping. He searched pantry and refrigerator, made a list, concluding that he would have to take his car to carry the goods.

He parked amongst the many cars in Sainsbury's grounds, and stood, like an idiot he told himself, beside his locked vehicle to contemplate life. He managed that badly. His mind was alive with thoughts, yet seemed empty of anything of value. Rejected lover, winner of a crossword puzzle, he stood statue-straight.

He turned towards the shop, chose his trolley and wheeled it with cocky pride between the crowded shelves. He yielded right of way to elderly ladies, though one of them lost any claim to his consideration when she turned on her husband, who had returned from the shelves with the wrong commodity. At the top of her voice she chided him, called him a fool, said even his grandchildren would know that the rubbish he brought over had never been seen gracing their table at home.

The husband, a small man – though his wife was even more petite – paid no attention to her tirade, but stood one hand in his pocket, his over-large cloth cap pushed to the back of his head. He returned the offending packet to the shelves and shuffled back with whatever the correct comestible was. 'That's better,' the wife said, less belligerently. The husband nodded his contented agreement.

George tried to imagine the pair as young lovers, out of town at night in some near-rural waste making love to each other, when the husband-to-be proved himself masterful, putting up with no refusal from his future wife. The years had changed all that. Now she was in charge. He had presumably returned from his day-to-day work, whatever that was, and had resumed a subsidiary position to that of his wife. If she helped him, rarely, to build a shelf or replace a lock and key, she would temporarily assume a secondary rôle, passing hammer or screwdriver, only risking a word of criticism if he made more mess than she thought the job merited.

He compared the old man with himself. If George ever pushed his luck so far as to ask for Mirabel's hand in marriage, and she accepted his proposal, he had no doubt she would assume

118

a position of superiority. She would have had enough of playing second fiddle to Charles Lockwood; would not wish to be anything but the superior partner unless she were carried off madly in love with the new husband. If he were, oh, subjunctive, that husband, he did not for a moment imagine that she would be so bowled over with love or sexual passion for him. She had had one bad experience and now she was older, wiser, more experienced, would not marry him as a young girl, swept off her feet by his attractions. In his view he had none. He would consider that the only qualification he had to be her husband was that he was a quiet man, not strutting or boastful. He would be rather like a superior servant, seem as useful, judged for his virtues, amongst which modesty would hold a high place. In his present state of mind, even that seemed unlikely. He fell into a despondency out of which he could not argue himself.

He collected his groceries, not without errors which demanded returns and replacements. He could usually manage this chore, especially when, as today, there was nothing out of the ordinary on his list. He felt relief when he wheeled his groceries out to the car. It was almost pleasurable to empty his trolley and replace it alongside the dozens of others.

He did not know what the matter was with him. It was as if his judgement had been torn away from him so that now the simplest task seemed beyond his power. He sat behind the wheel of his car, tapping a foolish rhythm on it and staring out. He watched other people, mainly housewives better organised than he, load their purchases into their cars, and then drive smartly off without hesitation.

He remembered one of his senior colleagues when he was a schoolmaster, who used to sit every day without fail at the wheel of his car for ten minutes at least before he turned on the ignition and cautiously drove from the grounds and on to the street. The younger members of staff would laugh at these lengthy preparations but not to the face of the driver, who was well known for his short temper and sharp tongue. George wondered if the man still valued that interval of gathering his wits before he set off for home and subservient spouse, who had none the less nagged him into buying a new car.

He cursed his own nervy feebleness.

* * *

119

The letter from Mirabel arrived over a fortnight later when he was beginning to despair. She apologised for her dilatoriness in replying, but she really had been very busy. No ill effects from her fall, but every Tom, Dick and Harry in the town had been consulting his or her solicitor. The result was that she worked all day and had to take unfinished tasks home each night. This was not altogether bad in that she had learned a great deal from one of the cases, and in another had brought in some very lucrative business for the firm. Her bosses, 'the boys' as she called them, had told her that they were impressed, and felt that they were nearing the time when they could begin to discuss a partnership with her.

Having disposed thus of her work she turned to her other excuse for not writing to him. Andrew was still in hospital, and seemed not to be making much improvement. He had twice been dispatched to an excellent convalescent home, and twice returned.

He had never been himself since his accident; the outspoken, aggressive, never-to-be satisfied autocrat was now a quiet ghost, sitting or lying in bed, hardly speaking to her, sometimes not recognising her. She had questioned the medical staff, from consultant to the most junior nurse, and all seemed equally puzzled – or else unwilling to reply to her questions. They did not know: he should be better or at least improving, but there were no good signs. They must wait. Patience was required. Usually time would bring a cure, partial if not complete. Occasionally he spoke sensibly to her, answered her questions, but in a subdued voice. Sometimes, though, he barely knew her, but lay supine, asleep but uncomfortable, not resting.

It terrified her to think that a heavy blow on the head could have such an effect on a living person. She did not like making these visits, nor stay long. At first she'd expected him to surprise her by suddenly appearing as his normal, larger-than-life self, but now she had no such expectation. The nurses had suggested that she should speak to him. A voice he recognised might have the effect of handling him back to what he was. She had wanted to believe this and at first it had seemed possible. She now thought he would not recover.

Mirabel concluded her letter with a request that the pair of them should walk the streets together for an hour or so one evening. 'We can walk and talk,' she wrote. 'I don't get enough exercise, though I know you do. It will do me a power of good to try to keep up with a professional. Phone me.'

He did so, waiting until late-evening. She'd be home by now unless some unlikely happening had kept her back in the office. George put on his jacket, went to the telephone.

He dialled, the phone rang at her end, but no one answered. Deflated, he waited for a recorded instruction to speak his message after the signal. Nothing. She had forgotten to set her machine. That was unlike her. He kicked the floor in anger, but that altered nothing. He'd try again, he decided, after half an hour when she'd perhaps be in after her shopping.

He tramped back to his armchair and the morning's newspaper, still in its unblemished state. He unrolled and straightened it and, with a slight shock, saw that it was the *Beechall Post*, the city's popular newspaper. He scanned the first page, found nothing of interest, and began to wonder why he had received it. At the top of the first page 'No. 19, Flat 2' was pencilled, the address of the neighbour above him. He leaped from his chair, and carried the paper upstairs where he leaned heavily on the bell. He was rewarded after a second longer peal by the sound of shuffling. The door slightly opened and the hoarse whisper of his neighbour demanded, 'What is it?'

'It's Taylor, George Taylor, Mr Braithwaite. This is your evening paper, isn't it? The boy must have pushed it through the wrong letter-box.'

The door opened wider, and a claw-like hand was thrust out.

'That boy. He can't read or write. Or he's too idle to climb up a few stairs to deliver it. Typical. Anyway, thanks, Mr Taylor. I like my tea-time hour with my *Post*. Perhaps this signals change. Maybe I'll find it more pleasant or instructive to read at this hour of the evening. You're most kind, Mr Taylor.'

George made his way down, tripped, nearly fell headlong. Only frantic clinging to the banister saved him. Breathing hard he hung on, straightened himself, recovered his balance, then managed the remaining steps one at a time. By the time he had squatted in his chair for a quarter of an hour he was himself again. He sucked air into his lungs, found he could do so without pain, and swore out loud. He glanced at his watch, compared it with the hands of the wall-clock, and found that he'd wasted half an hour since he had replaced his phone. Stroking his face, he lifted the instrument from its cradle. Mirabel answered his call almost at once.

'George Taylor,' he said.

'I recognised the voice.'

'I rang half an hour ago but there was nobody in.'

'No. I called in to see a client on the way home. An old lady who can't get about very easily. Her bank is overcharging her, she thinks, and she thought a solicitor's threatening voice would set things right.'

'And did it?'

'Do you live in this world? The banks aren't open at this time at night. I'll chase 'em up tomorrow morning.'

'And you're all right? You're sure? No more falls?'

'Yes, I'm fine. I've said so.' She sounded miffed. 'We were to talk about walks, not falls.'

'I've been blaming myself about your fall.'

'That's ridiculous. I can manage to fall over for myself, without outside help.'

'You don't take me seriously. Ever.'

'I don't know what you mean by that. Explain yourself.' She sounded amused, if anything.

'It's difficult. What I'm trying to tell you is that I love you. I think you know that, don't you?'

'Not really.'

'And you never encourage me in any way?'

'I didn't know until a minute or two ago that you needed encouragement. You haven't exactly made it plain. That doesn't mean I think you're not serious now, or that I am teasing you by acting as if I don't realise that you mean what you say.'

George paused, brushed his mouth with the back of his hand.

'Mirabel Lockwood, I love you. I'll say it again. I love you. Now what do you say to that? How do you answer me?'

'I've heard you. And understood you. And I'm grateful to you for what you've said. But I can't make my mind up, one way or another, as easily as all that. Perhaps you think that if I could, you'd know immediately I'd spoken.'

'I don't understand that. It's mere babble.'

'I like you. I enjoyed our day out together. It was different, and interesting. But at present I am not looking for a serious partner, somebody to get married to, or to live with. My last attempt at marriage was a failure, an utter catastrophe.

'I admired Charles for his knowledge, his verve and wit, and I suppose his money and his manners, but that soon dissipated itself. After a year or two I knew I had to leave him.

There I was in a house with a man who thought nothing of me, did nothing for me. He didn't in any way care for me, that I could see. He hadn't fallen out of love with me; I was perfectly satisfactory to him as a wife in the same way that a piece of furniture would be. I was there, useful, looked the part, but didn't have any share in the important crises in his life, his work, his committees.

'I wasn't a nuisance to him; I didn't demand more than he could give. I'd attend social events with him, make a good impression, but that was all. I kept asking myself what would happen if we ever had children. They would mean nothing to him until they were older, and then only if they were male could they hope to be part of the important things in his life.'

'Did you try for a family?'

'Not seriously, not by agreement. We suited one another in bed. But if ever I mentioned children, he'd say we had plenty of time. When I confessed I'd given up contraception he was displeased, I could tell he was, though he tried not to show it. After a few months I found nothing happening, that I had not become pregnant, and suggested that we should both see an expert to find out why this was. Charles obviously saw it as a stroke of good fortune. "Let's wait for a couple of years," he said, "when I can truly support you."

'"You'll perhaps be even busier then with your own concerns," I told him.

'"Very likely," he said, and smiled as if I had come round to agreeing with him.'

'I see,' George said, not doing so.

'I felt utterly deserted. I expected so much from that marriage. I admired Charles so strongly, I could easily say I loved him. And he had chosen me out of all the women he knew. I fulfilled his every expectation of a wife. Or so he said.'

'He was a very successful man. You preferred him over Andy,' George said. 'I suppose I know now how you feel about me. You won't want to see me any more.'

'I didn't say that.'

'You implied it.'

'All I said was that I had not seriously thought about marrying you. I like you. The times we've been out together, I've thoroughly enjoyed. But bitter experience has made it plain to me that perhaps I'm not the marrying sort. In a way it was my fault

123

the marriage broke up. The more I think about it, the more certain I am that Charles would have stuck by me. It was only when I started talking about a family that I saw he didn't want it. And that made me suspicious. All he wanted was a pretty doll of a woman to complete the picture, the presentable public figures of himself and wife. As soon as I began to understand that, I could not bear it. I wanted him to love me as somebody worth his while. Perhaps all men are like that. I don't think you quite grasp that idea.'

'Listen,' George answered, 'to me. How do you think I feel when you tell me outright you won't marry me, or even think seriously about it? And though you may consider you're being honest, open with me, isn't it more likely that the thought of being very soon a partner in your firm, and then marrying a postman, begins to seem unlikely? I'd be on a postman's wage and that's all we'd have to live on if we had children, and you wanted time out. I can see that wouldn't appeal. The former wife of a high-flier, once a university lecturer in law, now a partner in a firm that really does coin money, stoops to wed a man who walks the streets in the nasty morning, poking cards and letters through the letter-boxes of every Tom, Dick and Harry in town. It doesn't seem acceptable, reasonable, sensible.'

'You've made all that up. Not one word of it came from me.'

'You implied it.'

'No, I didn't. Not for a moment. I never once dismissed you as a husband in my mind on account of your work.'

'Well, that's something,' he said ruefully.

They talked like this for perhaps another ten minutes, both claiming reason until they tired of the endless round and sound of the topic.

'I'd better ring off then,' George said. 'We both know now where we stand.'

'Right. Goodnight. Thanks for ringing.'

'Shall I hear from you?' he asked.

'We'll see.'

There seemed a hard certainty about this reply, so that he stood silently while she cut the conversation off by returning the phone to its cradle. Despondent, he crept away from the offensive silence, and rested in the armchair, where he lay with legs stretched out in front of him. He'd done himself no good by the exchange. He told himself he had at last, if not at least, confessed that he loved Mirabel. She had seemed by no means shocked at his confession, but excused her barren reply by attributing her lack of feeling to the desert dryness of her first marriage. There was perhaps some truth in what she claimed. She had appeared to her husband as no better than a superior servant who had dined with her master, shared his bed, but without any feeling of equality of love, regard, even gratefulness towards her from the one male she had truly admired, yielding herself over to his pleasure. She had found hell in what she had judged to be heaven, and, George guessed, ruined herself as a full woman.

He mulled over this conversation as he lounged in his chair.

He could not rid himself of the conviction that, for all she said, the basis of her decision to declare that she did not, could not, love him was that his status was below hers. He was a postman, a nobody; his progress in life had not seemed plain to her. She wanted somebody of her own level as a suitor. All those other excuses, and that was the word for them, might have an element of truth in them, but were not the whole reason. He had thought of her, since their first meeting, as a woman who knew her own mind; someone who could run comfortably contrary to convention. Having convinced himself that this was so, he could not rid his mind of the notion. She had said that they might meet again. It had been a miserly admission on her part, even rude politeness, offered to this presumptuous man out of the kindness of her heart. George swore softly to himself as he made for bed, but he could not sleep.

He rose on time, the tinny power of his alarm-clock battering the air of his room so relentlessly that he feared that more than one neighbour would complain. But he walked with a sprightlier step, head held high in the morning darkness. He wouldn't give up on Mirabel, whatever the omens.

X

George decided that he would give Mirabel a week to ring him. If she had not done so by that time he would get in touch with her. Whether this was a sensible decision he did not know, but it at least kept the connection between them open. This might not do any good, but it was better than doing nothing.

One evening he walked along the Boulevard. He hoped that if he went into the Tom Bowling, that odd man Francis Smith might be there with some snippet of information, or history even, which would lift George from the sad apathy that darkened every day of the week.

He was rewarded by the sight of Smith sprawled before his barely touched pint in an almost empty room. Public houses did not seem to be doing well in these parts. Perhaps it was the ban on smoking indoors which had kept customers away.

Smith looked up, languidly, then suddenly recognised George. He sprang to his feet and held his arms wide.

'My friend,' he shouted. 'Come and join me. I thought I'd not see you again. Do you never come in here?'

'Rarely.'

'I've been in most nights, hoping to see you.'

'You surprise me.'

'None of your sarcasm now. The last time I met you here, I felt so happy that I went out and bought some raffle tickets. Now I'm so unlucky that I never win anything on such things, but I felt so uplifted by our little chat that next day I bought five pounds' worth.'

'And?' George drowned his questioning mouth in his beer.

'And, yes, I won a prize. I felt certain I would. As soon as I bought them, from the landlord here, I called myself a fool. I knew I might as well have thrown my tickets down the nearest drain. I had felt so confident, yet as soon as he handed me them,

126

my spirits fell. But first thing the next Saturday morning the landlord's wife rang to tell me I'd won a prize.'

'Good.'

'Two hundred pounds.' He slapped the table. 'Two hundred smackers.' George said nothing. 'It's never happened before. I somehow connect it with you.'

'And there were no snags?'

'No. I called in early at the pub, and they handed it over. I bought a drink for the landlord and his lady, and then I went to catch the coach.'

'The coach?'

'Yes. I was booked in for a trip to Coventry for the cup tie. Beavor Buses run these trips, and I occasionally go with them. This time with my pockets unusually stuffed with money.'

'And did your team win?' George asked.

'Two-nil. They weren't the better team either. They had two decent shots at goal and they both went in. I had a fiver on them. At four to one. Nobody expected that result.'

'Your lucky day.'

'I've never known anything like it.'

'Have you tried again since that day?'

'No.' The other man's face crumpled as if he were about to cry. 'I've more sense. I'm not one of the lucky ones. I'm not daft, and I'm not inclined to throw my money away regardless. But I've been waiting since that day to buy you a drink.'

'That's very kind of you.'

'You were somehow responsible.'

'I don't think so. I'm not interested in football and know little about it.'

'It's not your knowledge that won me the prize.'

'I don't suppose it was.'

'It was more like magic.'

'Or superstition.'

'Don't be like that,' Smith begged. 'I wouldn't say I was a super-stitious person. But I thought of you just as I bought the tickets. I felt grateful towards you, and I hope you'll let me buy you a drink.'

'I've hardly started this one.' George did not sound enthusi-astic. 'I can't remember doing or saying anything out of the ordinary when we first met. We chatted, if I remember rightly, about the Lockwoods, young and old.'

127

'Yes. You were a friend of young Mrs Lockwood, the son's wife, didn't you say?'

'I did. Not that I had any luck with her. But now,' George went on, 'I hope you don't mind my asking, but has the sight of me this evening raised any unusual, elevating impressions in your mind?'

'No.' The word was dull, despairing.

'I'm sorry that I'm not on form tonight. Or perhaps it's you?'

'You can mock, but I remember how I felt when I first put my fiver down. You don't begrudge me my belief, now, do you?'

'No. Why should I?'

'Because it's wrong in your view.'

George Taylor felt sorry for the man. Smith had somehow brightened his life by attributing magic powers to a stranger. Good luck to him, then. The old man sat staring blankly at the pub wall, sullen if not angry.

'Well, you won two hundred pounds,' George said pacifically. 'And whenever you see me, you'll remember winning money.'

Smith's face fell, perhaps in disappointment at this flippancy. He shook his head, sighing noisily.

'Can I get you a drink now?' he asked humbly.

George raised his glass in a silent toast, then drained it in readiness.

'Why did you come in here this evening?' asked Smith.

'I was walking round. I go to bed early when I'm working, and I thought that I could just manage a drink before bed.'

Smith seemed delighted with the explanation, and asked if any thought of him had been in George's mind.

'No. I was pleased to see you here, when I came through the door, but I didn't attribute it to my magical, out-of-this-world powers.'

Smith took a smiling sip of his beer.

'"There are more things, Horatio . . ."' he said solemnly.

They left it there; talked, or Smith did, of football and of concerts.

George finished his beer and said it was time to be going.

'Would you mind if I walked back with you?' Smith asked.

'As long as it's not right out of your way. I live in the Park. Marlborough Road.'

'I don't mind that. My legs could do with a good stretching.'

'Do you know where Marlborough Road is?'

'I'm sorry, I don't.'

'It's the city side of the Park. We turn off this road and come across the Park gates eventually.'

'And then?'

'Only a few minutes' march from there.'

'I'll accompany you as far as the Park gates; that's if you don't mind.'

'Not at all.'

Out on the main Boulevard the pavements were unusually wide. Traffic rushed past noisily. Smith walked with considerable energy but erratically. George wondered if he were sober, but there were no other signs of inebriation. Smith talked, hoping to catch his companion's interest.

'Young Mr Lockwood, Charles, lived somewhere in this part of the globe, didn't he?'

'Yes, when he taught at the Trent.'

'And his wife?'

'I don't know if they lived near here before they were married. She has a house here which I think belonged to her parents She married him, if I've got it right, after he'd decamped to London.'

'I've never seen her. She must be a very good-looking girl for Mr Charles to choose her for a wife.'

At that moment a youth, the hood of his sweatshirt up, rode past them, neither slowing down nor braking. A few yards past them his arrow-like speed seemed to leave him as he parted company from his bike, awkward arms and legs flailing. The bicycle toppled and lay near the gutter, wheels still spinning. Not immediately George realised that Smith must have pushed hard at the cyclist as he drilled past them. Both pedestrians stood still. The cyclist had painfully pulled himself into a sitting position, which he held fairly still, groaning heavily.

'Are you all right?' George asked.

A mouthful of obscenities lashed him. The cyclist pushed himself upwards, not without difficulty, and stood, mouth wide open. Silently, his face working into lines of rage. He looked them over, swaying, and accused one of them of causing the accident.

'Yes, I did,' Smith said. 'You aren't supposed to ride on the causeway.'

The cyclist, recovering his breath, began to swear again at Smith, who looked at him with some curiosity, and then, without hurry, took a step or two to his right. Carefully, as if dealing with a precious object, he dragged up the bike, examined it, then stood holding the handlebars so that the frame was arranged like a fence between himself and his opponent who whirled his fists and jerked the bicycle away.

'And what are we doing now?' Smith enquired, as if to a child.

The youth wrestled his bicycle from his opponent's grasp, or attempted to do so. He failed. It resisted as if glued to the pavement. He swore at it, finally regained possession, and leaned it against the low wall in front of a short row of terraced houses.

'Now what have you got to say to yourself?' he gritted towards Smith.

'Goodbye,' Smith said. 'I hope.'

'Put your fists up. And shut your mouth.'

'I wouldn't threaten,' Smith said, 'or you'll get hurt.' His voice sounded peaceable, without menace.

The cyclist lashed out with his left hand which Smith seized by the wrist and pulled viciously towards him. The young man fell awkwardly to his knees, and then sprawled face down.

'Right, yo' bogger!'

He stood up, stiffly enough, breathing heavily until with his right fist, he struck out violently at Smith and Smith stepped back, but the blow was quick enough to catch and skid away from the slippery waterproof material of his garment.

The old man took another step, not aggressive but unexpectedly meaningful. He moved forward, and shoved a boot behind his opponent's legs. The man went down backward this time, and sprawled, ungainly, across the pavement. Smith watched him, threateningly silent.

The other man sat up, and immediately swore with a feeble note that expressed his hurt, his surprisingly revealed weakness. He had mainly injured his back. His attempts to stand roused pity, not fear.

'On your way,' said Smith, 'before you do yourself some more damage.'

The cyclist stood, mouth sagging open, trying to give the impression of strength, but failing.

'I'll get yo',' he said, his voice as feeble as a little girl's. He breathed deeply to recover his manhood, then tottered away, clutching his handlebars.

A few yards safely away he mounted his bike, but hesitantly.

'Get off the pavement,' Smith said. 'If you want to ride that thing, get on the road.' An expletive delivered at half volume, and an accelerando on the wheels of the cycle, were the only answers.

'Cheeky-daft,' Smith said, but did not attempt pursuit.

The youth did not look back.

'He didn't get much change out of you,' George ventured.

'Not the line you'd have taken with him?'

'No. I'm afraid brawling in the street isn't my strongest point. I might get a thick ear.'

'I looked him over. Wasn't in good shape physically.'

'But he's young enough to be your son.'

'Grandson, even,' Smith amended, with a smile, proudly. 'But I looked him over. And I decided that I could hurt him before he damaged me.'

'Do you often resort to physical violence?' George asked.

'Not these days. But I did seven years in the army, and they taught us. I was in a commando unit; we did unarmed combat. I was good at it. And when I came out, and I was in two minds about that, I went to jiu-jitsu classes. And I've kept it up whenever I've had the time. I enjoyed it, and got quite smart at it.'

George puzzled over the ambiguity of this.

'So you threw people twice your size over your shoulder?'

'I'm not claiming that. But certainly it puts you at a real advantage. Of course, you have to weigh your opponent up. If he's very strong and can get a heavy blow in first, then you'd be a fool to take him on. But certainly it's put me in a position to defend myself. I always did a bit of boxing in my earlier years. They taught me to punch my weight.'

'And this yobbo with the bike?'

'He wasn't very muscular, nor very fit.'

'Could you make a mistake?'

'Yes. With that as with anything. I still do exercises, both at the gym and regularly at home. And I don't go about the streets at night picking fights. Not at my age. There were two of us tonight.'

They walked on.

'I've often found myself weighing up some ruffian in the street,' Smith said. 'Mostly they were as innocent as the summer day is long, and were up to no mischief. That lad this evening, I don't think he meant to rob us. He brushed past on his bike, and his elbow caught me in the ribs, and that's why I hit him.

131

I don't suppose he meant to jostle me, and if he did, too bad for the old geezer tottering along the pavement. But he'd made a mistake, picked a wrong 'un. There he was, playing the bad-hat for all he was worth, and next minute he was flat on his back, and the old cripple standing over him ready to give him another dose of punishment.'

'He'd not learn his lesson?'

'No. If you pick victims who seem vulnerable, you won't usually come to much harm.'

They had by now reached the low, stone wall across the road which divided the Park from the plebeian street where they stood. A narrow iron gate allowed access to the well-to-do.

'I'll have to leave you here,' Smith said. 'I've enjoyed every minute of our conversation.'

'So have I,' George agreed. 'You're not off to buy some more raffle tickets then?'

'"Oh, ye of little faith." No, I've felt no such confidence today. Only pleasure, pure unadulterated pleasure, in your company. And I hope it won't be too long before we meet again. Would you favour me with your address?'

George fiddled for his wallet, extracted a card from it, and handed it over to Smith.

'There you are,' he said. 'In print.'

Smith moved a few steps into the light of a street lamp to peer at the card.

'Ho, there,' he said. 'You're an MA.'

''Fraid so.'

'I knew you were out of the ordinary. When my wife asks me who I've been drinking with, as she usually does, I shall tell her with a Master of Arts. That'll stop her criticism.'

'Doesn't she accompany you on these drinking bouts?'

'Only occasionally, on Saturday nights.'

'We must arrange to meet then.'

'Would you? What about this weekend?'

'I'm afraid not. I'm engaged. Tell you what, drop me a note of suitable Saturdays. I can't answer without my diary. I'm a slave to it.'

'To what? Your diary, do you mean?'

'Exactly.'

'Look out for a note from me. My wife might well have an arrangement with some orchestra on the radio or television.'

132

'That raises her in my estimation.'

'I'll tell her what you say. You'll soar in hers.'

Smith held out one large hand towards his companion. George shook it, swung round quickly, took three steps and went through the little gate. As he turned to replace the latch he waved his hand to Smith, who had not moved. His own hand was still held forward from shaving George's, in a position that seemed unnatural and yet at the same time welcoming.

'Bye,' he shouted.

Smith straightened himself, whirled his right arm into a salute, then held it vertically above his head, and turned proudly away.

But George Taylor turned into the Park road humming to himself. He smiled at his memories of Smith, which this last hour together had changed completely. If he had been asked to describe his companion at the beginning of the evening, he would have written him off as a relatively intelligent man whose chances of making a name or a fortune for himself had been dispersed by his parents' lack of interest in education. They had not seen the opportunities a grammar school would have offered their son. He could well imagine that they had never once attended parents' evenings and that their son's teachers had thus been denied the chance to praise the boy. Quite probably the Smith parents would have ignored such commendation. Their son was quick, they knew that, and the sooner he was put out to work, the better for all concerned. His subsequent life served to support this view. He had done well, and but for the unfortunate arrival of Gilbert might well have reached managerial status at one of the Lockwood factories.

But today had revealed a new, steelier Smith. The gently spoken elderly man had acted like a fighter, a physical defender of his old body, and a closer examination had suggested a strong, active, well-maintained physique with behind it a mind intent on combating any adversary, physical or mental. That he should have been so mistaken in his judgement of his new friend both shocked and worried George Taylor. He had enjoyed his passages of conversation with 'Trilby' Smith, but now he began to feel that he had begun to lose his judgement, and even to become uncertain about his razor rough-edge argument against his new friend's claims. The apparently simple theory that he, George Taylor, was in some way responsible for Smith's winnings had

133

been strongly contested and Smith had not held it against him. But the physical overthrow of the young man, unexpected as it was, had altered everything. Smith's fighting movements against his opponent had been smooth, quiet, restrained though their results had been violent enough, without much, if any effort on Smith's part. It was as incredible as Smith's belief that a meeting with him had made the older man lucky again.

XI

When the alarm clock jolted him into wakefulness George staggered about the bedroom, and in the bathroom forced the electric shaver almost thoughtlessly across his face. He scratched his cheeks and to his surprise found they were smooth.

He pulled his bicycle out from the shed in the far corner of the garden and into the street behind his house. He did this without noise, as he did most mornings when he was wide awake and ready for this early start to the day. Now his brain reeled, but he was safely out in the avenue, both lamps on and riding steadily towards the postal headquarters. There he propped his bicycle in the cycle shelters and clicked it safe with the huge padlock which flashed with gold. He staggered against the door, jarring his shoulder, the sharp pain wringing cautious observation and thought back to his swimming head.

After a ten-minutes interval of half-lively comprehension he was back to work, sorting out this morning's round in good time. He and two companions sipped boiling coffee together to prepare them to face the ice-cold day the other side of the door. George's round was heavy that morning so that he wished that he had brought his car, which would have saved him the zig-zag return. None the less he completed it in not more than half an hour over his usual time, and was home and cooking his lunch in readiness to burst out, full of life, for his usual unfashionable entertainment of a Wednesday afternoon: the bowls club.

The members were, on the whole, retired working-class artisans, intelligent and expert at their game. He was known well enough as a player to be taken up by one of the more skilful teams which had been let down by one of their members who had been dispatched to hospital that very morning with a heart-attack. George once more was left pondering the vagaries of human nature. The invalid was the youngest of this team; had played, they said, a stormer the Saturday before and led the singing in a Baptist Church Choir with all his customary vigour the next Sabbath morning, including performing the tenor solo. His team-mates had not expected the catastrophe, were shaken by the news of the severity of their comrade's illness, but played with all their customary care and energy this afternoon.

'Shall we send 'im some flowers?' the captain suggested.

'Flowers? He's not bleddy dead yet, is he?' the invalid's partner snarled as if he were the victim of the ordeal.

Halfway through the match they rang the sick man's wife, who was not to be reached, and then the hospital. 'Seriously ill but stable,' the answer came back from the stone-faced messenger, who immediately picked up his wood, and took his usual nerveless, well-balanced stance. An opponent commented on this. 'Well, it's a good job he's not dead. Horace wouldn't have left us an eighth of an inch to work with.' George did not match his partner for skill, but fortunately they won the game.

'You're not quite Phillip's class, but you did me well enough. More practice, twice a week extra, and you'll do me . . . be worth wittling about.'

A spectator would have judged that the players concentrated entirely on the game, but George guessed that they could not easily dismiss their colleague's misfortune from their minds. They did not imagine that they would be struck down as unexpectedly as he was, but they harboured the thought that they might well be suddenly afflicted, probably not with a heart attack but by some unexpected happening, accident, or misjudgement which, if allowed to play on their senses, their attention, might well ruin their game.

On the way off the green this afternoon his partner turned to George.

'In three weeks' time it's the first Spring Challenge. I doubt if Phil will be fit to play, and if he isn't, would you join me?'

'I'd have to look at my diary when I get home. If I'm free, I'll be delighted. Do you play all the year round?'

'Yes. Not on grass. The game'll be on their grounds, in Hucknall. It's composition. You'd have to practise on it a bit. But you seem serious and keen on the game, so I guess you'll be willing to put a bit of time and effort in.'

'I wouldn't fix it up yet,' another member of the group intervened. 'If Phillip can't play he'll want that nephew of his to replace him. He's good. Only in his twenties, but his eye and arm and wrist and judgement are damn' near international standard.'

'You just let me know,' George said, 'if you want me.'

'It's not so much for ourselves. It's Phillip we're thinking about. James here is right that he'd be very upset if we didn't call in this relative. And he's got plenty to put up with without our adding to it.'

'Just let me know,' George said, impressed. 'And fairly soon, if I'm to practise on artificial grass. No last-minute calls.'

'We can't guarantee that,' his partner said. 'But we're reasonable men.'

'Except when it comes to a cup match at bowls,' his companion grinned.

'Oh, yo' go and tittle.'

George handed over his address.

'Remember,' he said, 'I've never played on an artificial green.'

'We've only done it for two years. If you know what you're about on natural ground, real grass, you won't go far wrong wi' a bit of practice.'

George was pleased, flattered even, that he had been thus invited. Over the phone later that week, the new partner offered him practice-dates in which he patiently coached his raw team-mate. In due course, within fewer days than he would have liked, George played and they won; best of all, they were watched and congratulated by a rapidly recovering Phillip who said he hoped he'd be well enough to play the next round himself. He did so; they won; three of the team phoned George with the news. It was a time the newcomer could look back on with pride. He'd not let these serious players down in an emergency. He'd never be short of partners while these men were around.

But he had gone home later that afternoon of the first great victory, humming 'O, what can you see/By the dawn's early light?' He often sang the first line or two of that American national anthem; proud writing, he felt, before its composer ran out of inspiration and used quotations from other home-land-praising ditties. He wondered if his accusation of plagia-rism was just. Perhaps there were other musical celebrants of their ruler, heroes and country who had lifted their lines from an American original. He shook his head militaristically, in the opening of his chosen song.

137

At home he sat at the table, drank two cups of tea. He scratched around in his head for a suitable adjective to describe these univiting grey cups and their contents. 'Bland' might do, 'commonplace', 'flat'. After his performance on the bowling green he should be treating himself to unlikely champagne. He washed his plates and cups after the tea and sandwiches and settled down for the television news. He had convinced himself that this evening procedure brought him up to date with world events.

Slumped in his easy chair, he followed a bulletin from two newsreaders of whom he approved. Their pleasant facial expressions and easy voices would not upset him, he considered. If the news was, as today, a mere repetition of earlier events about which he had read, he watched the newscasters, though they word annoyed him, and measured their methods of delivery. He approved of the way they seemed to pay careful attention to their partner at points of high interest. If the cameraman or editors allowed one of them to be seen neither reading the news nor obviously waiting to begin the first line of the second paragraph of this important item, she, let's say, would put on an expression of approval or appreciation of her fellow-reader's skilful performance.

This evening, what with the afternoon's game, the further tea ritual and finally the darkness of the skies blackening the windows, George drowsed comfortably to sleep. This was not usual, and he vaguely suspected that he would not immediately drop off when he retired to bed a couple of hours later, but would lie churning his bed-clothes as he tried to sleep but could not. A man of habit, he hated changing his important guide-posts to the day: his arrival at work, the length of his round, the shopping he managed on Wednesdays or Fridays, his sleep, his exercise, the preparation for meals. He found if he did play Ducks and Drakes with the trivial round, he paid for it. If he and Mirabel ever decided . . . Ugh. It couldn't; they wouldn't.

He was jerked from shallow dreams by the phone. He staggered to his feet, crossed the room and stood, slightly trembling, by the phone.

'Hello,' he said gruffly in answer to a woman's voice on the telephone. Usually he spoke his number in an official manner, as if he were at the office.

'May I speak to George?' the woman asked in a choked voice which he did not recognise.

'Speaking.'

'Is that you, George?' she asked.

'Yes.' Why didn't she tell him her name?

'This is Mirabel.' He could barely believe it. This was the woman he imagined he loved, and yet he could not recognise her voice.

'Oh, George.' She broke off.

'Yes? Are you still there? Are you all right?' Long pause . . .

'I've some bad news for you.'

'I'm sorry about that. What is it?' His voice sounded level, controlled. Uncaring, for all his concern.

'It's Andy. Andrew Barron.' Her voice had not regained normality.

'Is he still in hospital?'

'He was.'

George waited. He could hear Mirabel's breathing.

'He's dead. He died this morning.'

'I *am* sorry. It wasn't expected, was it?'

'I didn't expect it. I knew he was very badly injured after the accident, but I had tried to hope he was recovering. I always saw him as a very healthy man.'

'And so he was. What happened then?'

'I'm not quite sure, as far as I can make out he had something like a stroke. It was soon after the doctors had finished their morning round.'

'And he'd seemed all right then?'

'He answered all their questions and never mentioned anything out of the ordinary, good or bad. Soon after they'd disappeared, though, Andrew suddenly seemed unable to breathe. And he'd lost the power in one of his arms. They sent out after the doctors who were still in the building. By the time somebody, the Registrar I think it was, came dashing in, Andy seemed to have lost his power of speech.

'The Registrar, a clever young man, examined him and started working on him and sent out for the consultant, but they seemed by that time to have lost him. They worked away like devils; I don't know what they do, but it made no difference. One of the nurses, not a young woman like most of 'em, talked to Mrs Barron when they knew it was all over; they had let his mother sit with him for a short time, though they plainly told her he was dead. Then this nurse . . . I know her . . . took Janet Barron out, to a side room, for a cup of tea and to fill in some forms, and it was there she said how sorry and shocked she was. The nurse suggested that it might be for the best. She told me by phone much of what she said she'd told the mother.

"For all we know if he'd recovered he might not have been the Andrew we knew. There'd been badly injured parts of his brain that perhaps would never have been normal again." I had said how well he was supposed to have been doing these last few days. "I know," the nurse said. "You can't believe it any more than I can, but the brain's a delicate part of you, and what seems to be minor injuries have serious permanent effects. People can't talk properly, or see; some even change their character completely. And I wouldn't like to have seen Andrew like that. Once he'd begun to come round he was such a fine man. He put up with all his pains, and inconvenience and weaknesses. He always thanked us for doing something for him. It might well have been unpleasant, and shaming for a strong, grown man, but he thanked us as if we had given him a lovely chocolate or something like that.'"

This picture of a saintly man of stoical patience did not tally with George's memories of Andrew, but he said nothing.

'I'd like to see his body,' Mirabel said. 'It's morbid, I know, but it's the least I can do.'

'Do you, would you like me to go with you? If it's possible?'

'I don't know when that will be, but I would. I would. Thank you. It will be sometime next week. I don't know who the undertakers are. Thank you for offering. You're a good man, George.'

'I know that.'

'I'm not joking.'

'Nor am I.'

Her silence showed him she thought he'd said the wrong thing. They stood unspeaking, embarrassed, hurt, at either end of the line. From her he heard a curious, subdued, rather sing-song sound. He listened, then realised that Mirabel was crying, but doing her best to stifle it. As he stood in silence he felt a tear squeezed from his right eye roll down his cheek. He dabbed smally furious at his face.

'Are you all right, Mirabel?' he asked.

'Yes, thank you.' The sound of her weeping had stopped. Her voice seemed normal. Mirabel the lawyer who could hear and bear any tragedy.

'What are you doing?' he asked.

'I'm standing at the phone in my hall. What are you doing?'

He looked into the mirror on the wall above the phone. He'd told her about it, and she'd said she would bet a man had put it there, so that he could study his expression as he talked. George was not very clear under the overhead light in his hall. He stared harder, if one could do that, standing before the darkened rectangle. Under each eye a large tear-drop hung, unmoving. With the back of his right forefinger he fiercely brushed both away; took in a huge breath she would surely hear.

'Much the same as you. Standing at the phone table, wondering what to do next.'

'Is that difficult? To decide?'

'No, I'm making final preparations to get to bed.'

'I was going to ask you to drive round, if you could, and give me half-an-hour. I'd forgotten that you have to be up at the crack of dawn and your tomorrow's already started.'

'I'm not well dressed for visiting,' he said.

'I wouldn't care if you were stark naked.'

He laughed slightly.

'I'll be round in ten minutes. My car's in the drive nose forward and ready for moving. I shan't be long.'

'No, you'll make yourself late for work tomorrow. I'd forgotten your day starts halfway through everyone else's night-before.'

'You'd be surprised how many people are about then.'

'Only, don't run over them. One tragedy a night is enough for me.'

She was herself again.

He donned an anorak, opened the gates, drove out. There was surprisingly little traffic and this did not delay him. Mirabel's gates stood open; he backed in with skill, then ran up the front steps, touched the bell. Almost immediately the front door was quietly opened.

'Come in,' she called, opened her arms, hugged him, closing the door with her foot. He squeezed the breath from her body with his embrace and plastered her face with kisses.

'Cup of coffee?' she enquired.

'No, thank you.'

She pushed him away, sat, then patted the sofa by her side.

141

He obeyed. Hesitating, he put his lowered arm round her shoulders. He felt her tension under his embrace. They sat in silence. He, hoping she was not disappointed by his presence, sat quietly beside her.

'It's so terrible,' she said. 'I've barely been home this week. We've been so busy in the office, and I had to spend yesterday in Manchester.'

'Have you been visiting Andrew regularly?' he asked. 'I wish I'd gone with you more.'

'Twice a week. Easier on my own, when I got used to it.'

'And did he seem to be improving?'

'Yes, in a slow way. But I came in last Saturday and he could hardly move. I don't know if they had drugged him with pain-killers. He said a few sentences but I couldn't understand him. There was one word I could recognise. It was Mirabel. But he spoke as if he was choking as he opened his mouth; it was quite unlike his voice. Not Andy. Somebody smashed.'

She broke off, as if unable to bear the horror of the last memory.

'I saw the Registrar once. I was there on my own again and that was sometimes unusual on that ward. This young doctor had come in to see some new patient. He came across when he'd finished and looked at Andrew. I asked him how he thought Andy was doing. He said there was no doubt he was improving. He said they had pretty well despaired for his life when they had first begun patching him up. His wounds were tremendous, and all in the places where it was most dangerous. "Any one of them would have meant the end for any other man."

'When I first questioned him he was cautious, reticent, not giving me the whole truth. I said as much to him. He asked me if I was a relative. I said I was Andy's closest friend. "Would you tell me what work you do?" he asked. When I said I was a solicitor, he looked me over, as if he was making up his mind about me. I asked him to be frank, and he said he wouldn't want his opinions made public at this stage. I said I'd be as careful as a judge. He then dropped his voice, and said, "It's our job as doctors to bring badly injured patients back to life, but in this case I am not convinced that it would be the best option for him. That's a dreadful opinion for me to hold, and I shouldn't mention it to a patient's close friend or relative. We shall do everything we can to keep him alive, whatever the consequences."

'"I don't know why I'm telling you this," he said, just before he left the ward. "When . . . if . . . we let him out, you will not be unaware of the change in the man, and you may help him and those close to him to come to terms with his state. But say nothing yet," he told me. "We don't know what will happen." He seemed a fine young man, this doctor, honest with himself. And he talked to me as if I were sixteen to his sixty, and he was nothing like my age.'

Mirabel fell silent, leaning on George. It was as if she had suddenly been deprived of the power of speech. Her eyes were sometimes open, sometimes closed, and yet seemed to focus on him. She breathed deeply sometimes, almost sighing, and at other moments drooped like a dead woman. He gently stroked her upper arms which were bare. She made no attempt, even slight, to respond. George found himself making humming noises of comfort which again she did not acknowledge. He was not altogether put out by her lack of acknowledgement; she had dispersed her bodily strength on her recital of her exchange with the doctor.

Finally she straightened herself, drawing away from him.

'And now,' she said, 'look what I've done.'

'What's that?' His voice spoke softly but good-humouredly, encouraging her.

'I've told you what he said. I swore I wouldn't let a word of our conversation out. Just what I swore I would not do, I've just done.'

George drew his breath in deeply, held her straighter.

'You did right,' he said, soft and strong.

'How can you say that? What good am I doing to Andy by breaking my word to the doctor?'

'You've told me, and I hope helped yourself by letting the pair of us know how ill Andy was.'

'But . . .'

'Just let me finish. You're a good, clever, discriminating woman. You praised the doctor as a good judge of character. He tells you what he thinks the exact medical position is. It clears it out of his system. He sees you all expecting Andy to recover, to be the man you knew before the accident. But if one of you knew the possible outcome – death or a half life, with Andy dependent on other people all the time; everything that he would not have wanted when he was himself and healthy – it might help him and his family and his other friends, and the doctors and nurses and carers who had to look after him, to accept gradually what his condition was.'

'But I came and let it all out to you.'

'Yes. Because Andy is gone and you think I'm a man who'll keep his mouth shut. As I will. I'm now standing by you at this terrible state of affairs.'

'I'm not standing,' she said. 'I'm lying on you.'

'And a good thing. I'm here to help you.' He felt cheered by her recovery. 'You sensibly looked for help. And such as there is, it's yours.'

'Thank you. But why should you bother yourself? You hardly knew Andy; the friendship never seemed to start.'

'It's you I'm trying to help. You should know by now, I'd do anything I could for you.'

'I don't think I deserve it.' Mirabel looked near tears again.

'That's not my opinion.'

She waved a hand before his face, as if to attract his complete attention.

'George,' she said, 'I don't want to mislead you. You speak as if you're in love with me.'

She paused as if expecting a reply from him. He did not answer. She continued, with quiet strength, 'I must make it clear that I'm not in love with you. I like you. You're a good man, an interesting man, but as things are I'm not in love with you. That may change. I don't know. My marriage to Charles has made me cautious. I would have said when he proposed to me that he was everything, had everything, I wanted as a husband. But it was all fool's gold. I'm on the rebound from that, and I don't wish to be hurt again, nor to damage you in the process.'

'I see,' he said. He did not, but he wanted to comfort her. He could not help thinking again that she did not see herself marrying a postman. He said nothing of that. The poor girl was in enough trouble already.

'Were you . . . are you in love with Andrew?' he asked. That was the wrong question, he knew, and he had asked it before, but the whole of their speech this evening had abounded in mistakes. They had put speeches grammatically together which collapsed in multiple error. They had not controlled their speech as would have been normal. Andy's condition and Mirabel's reaction to it had demonstrated the trouble in their minds. Mirabel had said something just now that he had not caught.

144

'I beg your pardon?'

'No, I'm not.'

'Not what?'

'I'm not in love with Andy Barron. Nor have I ever been.'

'Are you going to work tomorrow?' he asked, after silence.

'Yes. Why shouldn't I?'

He was pleased to hear it. 'What time do you finish?'

'Usually I'm home by five-thirty or six.'

'Then I'll provide your evening meal, about six-thirty at my place. Then we can talk again. Or we can go round to the under-taker's chapel of rest to see Andy, if that's possible . . . Is there anything you particularly like to eat?'

'It'll be Wednesday. I usually have simple fish and chips, which I pick up on my way home.'

'I'll do that for you. There's a good shop on the Boulevard.'

She stood, thanked him for his invitation, and became imme-diately business-like, politely ordering him to go back home to bed. She might have been ushering a long-winded client from her office. At the door she kissed him lightly, on the cheek; it meant nothing. She closed the door immediately he was outside. The cold air of the street struck him as exactly suitable for his exit.

At home George set the morning clock, undressed and was almost immediately away. As soon as the alarm shattered the quietness of sleep he was up and out of bed. His day went unre-markably but at speed; from nine a.m. onward he had forgotten his short night's rest and legged it up and down his round with élan if not abandon. A thick corned-beef sandwich passed for lunch, together with a cup of tea and an apple, a pear and an underripe banana.

He then washed his hands and commenced to cook apples, pears and plums together with sugar, and set them out to cool. He made sure that the large tub of vanilla ice-cream was in excellent order, as were the two caskets of fresh cream in the refrigerator. This occupied less of his time than he'd expected. He had soon searched out a beautiful red table-cloth which he laid ceremoniously on the table for them, and then lifted out from their expensive case fish-knives, forks, spoon, serving-spoons. These did not satisfy his inspection and were taken to the kitchen for cleaning. This accomplished, he laid the table, and decorated it with a bunch of flowers: red, white and yellow chrysanthemums he had bought on the way home.

Pleased with himself, he polished and dusted the furniture before slumping into his armchair where he fell asleep, more than satisfied with his efforts. He woke past four o'clock, baffled as to where he was. He stared about him, pulled himself together, stood up and looked over his domestic possessions. In less than two and a half hours Mirabel would be with him. He rang the fish and chip 'emporium', was surprised to find them there, ordered two portions of chips, one piece of bread-crumbed cod, one of plaice, and a double serving of peas, said to be a speciality of the house. They promised they would be ready if he called in to collect them at 6.15. He judged it would be colder with the end of daylight, and turned up the central heating. He put a bottle of expensive Australian white wine in the refrigerator.

Now for his own preparations. He washed himself thoroughly, denying himself a bath. Solemnly he donned his sole white shirt and a rather characteristically old-fashioned dark grey suit, light, patterned socks and a pair of his highly polished black shoes. He spent some time in front of a large mirror, not exactly admiring himself, but wondering why clothes could so much alter a man's appearance. The deodorant made him smell different, he noted; too much so. He didn't want to appear before his love reeking as if having just dropped a scent bottle. He laughed at his qualms: he had to venture out in the night air, and that would soon calm the ferocity of the perfume. He set out exactly at the time planned.

He must have walked more quickly than he'd intended for when he arrived the shop-doors were locked, though two young men in white caps and coats could be seen behind the light-less windows. At two minutes past six, one of the men noisily opened up.

They invited George to sit down while they repeated his order and assured him that it would be cooked and ready by 6.15. When his full parcel of food arrived, it was wrapped in large rectangles of greaseproof paper. He glanced at the clock above the counter: 6.28.

He made speed out in the street, hoping he had not kept Mirabel too long. Arriving at his front door breathless, he found she was nowhere to be seen. Was this lateness habitual to her?

He had just closed the stove door when the front-door bell pealed. It seemed loud but melodious.

She stood at his door, her face pale, thoughtful.

'I'm sorry I'm late. I couldn't find the cleaner whose job it is to lock up, to let her know I was away.'

'Where was she?'

'Heaven knows. Having a quiet fag in a partner's office.'

He took Mirabel's coat and hung it in the hall.

'Are you ready to eat now?' he asked.

'Give me five minutes.' He nodded and pointed out the cloak-room into which she disappeared.

Back in the living-room he awaited her return. He had already laid out supper on the large dining plates. Mirabel, entering, looked round the room, standing behind her chair before settling to the table.

'This looks good,' she said. 'I'm hungry.'

'Fine. I've given you the choice of cod or plaice.'

'Splendid.' She forked up a small chip and chewed with pleasure.

They did not exchange much by way of conversation over the first few mouthfuls until she laid down her knife and fork.

'This is lovely,' she said. 'Just what was needed.' She waved a hand over her plate and commented, 'They know how to fry, your fish shop. Aristocratic, I'd call it.'

'Hardly the word for such plebeian fare,' he said. 'Though they wouldn't thank you for calling their premises a "shop". They like to be known as the "emporium".'

'Meaning "a banqueting hall" originally.'

'A big shop, these days.'

They settled again to eat with vigour. Both were ravenous. George spoke more than she did, though Mirabel always capped his effort with some succinct quotation or anecdote. The pace of eating slackened until she said, 'I'm sorry, but you've beaten me.'

'Leave what you can't manage.' That was what his mother used to tell him when she thought he'd really done justice to her cooking. 'Would you like a drink? Water, wine, fruit juice?' She chose water. He fetched it in a glass that had belonged to his mother. Mirabel held it up to the light.

'This is a beautiful glass,' she said.

George returned to empty his plate. He felt he had won a

147

small victory over Mirabel. He dismissed that as ridiculous. This, whatever it was, was not a competition in gluttony. A little left on the plate, 'for Lord John Manners', another of his mother's expressions.

He cleared the plates away and returned with the stewed fruit, custard and cream.

'Cooked by me,' he said, 'only today.'

'What is it?'

'Apples, pears and plums from the garden.'

'Surely you didn't gather them from the trees.'

'No. Picked last autumn and kept in the drawers in a side-board in the garage. They last until Easter.'

'I'll try some, but only a little.'

'Help yourself.' He pushed the fruit, cream and custard towards her. Mirabel took a small portion of fruit and, on his encour-agement, an even more minute spoonful of custard and cream. This she ate daintily but cleared her dish.

She helped him clear the table, but found him stubborn in his refusal to let her assist in the dish-washing.

'No, thank you,' he said. 'You've worked hard all day.'

'You've only my word for it.'

He put on the kettle and she accepted his offer of coffee. Black, please. No milk or sugar. He fetched out his mother's coffee-cups, her Sunday pride and joy. He led Mirabel to the drawing-room and seated her before an efficient electric fire. When he returned with the drinks, she again admired the cups.

'My mother's,' he said. 'She always kept them in the china-cabinet, and they were there only for admiration, not as drinking vessels.'

'A woman of taste,' she said.

'It didn't altogether please my father. "What's the use of cups we never drink from?" he said. The pronoun begged his son's support.

'"They're things of beauty," my mother said.

'"If you blindfolded me, I wouldn't know what sort of cup I was drinking from."

'"All the more reason not to trust them to the hands of a pair of butterfingers like you and our George."'

This account seemed to please Mirabel; she sat smiling broadly.

'I feel honoured,' she said. 'Butterfingers is a good word.'

148

'Cricketers used it for players who dropped their catches. She came from a cricketing family.'

'She'll be dead by now, I expect?' ventured Mirabel.

'Yes. I've very few close relatives. Both my parents died in their early-seventies. That's why I have so many of my mother's possessions.'

'You've brothers and sisters?'

'No. Spoiled when in my childhood.'

Mirabel rolled slightly in her chair.

'This is a comfortable one,' she said. 'Are these your parents' chairs?'

'They are.' George now brought in a dish which he placed on the low table by her chair. 'Fruit?'

'Oh, thank you. I'm absolutely full, but I might just manage a grape. They look tempting.'

She seemed to wake up. 'It's lovely sitting all warm and cosy in front of this fire. And I'm learning more about you than I knew before.' This seemed to make much of little.

'You chose to eat fish and chips, I feared, to let me off the hook.'

'No. Pure coincidence. It's what I have on this night every week. And, like your mother, you have taste. Your emporium,' she giggled at the word, 'fries much better than my shop. I've been thinking about it. I don't see why I shouldn't call in on your man on my way home. I usually work later on Wednesday so they'll be open. It's really no more out of my way than my place.'

George blushed in the heat. This, he thought, is what it would be like if ever I married Mirabel. Both having done a good day's graft; both tired, but receptive. Would his pleasure be as great at the end of every day of the week? Would this preliminary joy appear humdrum as they thought of their sensual delight in just an hour or two's time? That was typical of him. Never take pleasure to the full. Always look ahead. Such decisions puzzled and delighted him. Oddly he kept at the other side of the hearth, made no attempt to touch, stroke, fondle her. Once he found that he had almost dropped off to sleep.

At nine o'clock, as the old family clock chimed its long-drawn out signal for the hour, Mirabel said, suddenly standing, 'I must go now. This is the most pleasant evening I've spent for months.'

'Could you say what the second most pleasurable one was?'

'Yes. A concert of Baroque music. I heard it at the Queen's Hall right at the beginning of the season. I was so delighted, I decided I'd attend a concert at least once a month.'

'And have you done so?'

'I'm afraid not. I find myself too busy when it's time for my concert. Or I don't like the programmes, and I won't put myself about to listen to music that doesn't appeal. But next month's concert is good. Bach, Mozart, Rossini, Beethoven's Seventh Symphony. May I take you to that?' She whipped a small diary from her handbag, consulted it, and announced a date. 'Are you free on that day? It's an orchestra I'd never even heard of.' George pulled out a diary of his own and marked it, thanking her.

'But . . . There's one more request, if you don't mind. Not quite so pleasant. On Saturday morning I'm going to a chapel of rest to pay my last respects to Andy. Will you go with me?'

'Surely,' he said as he helped her into her coat.

'I'm uncertain about it. I'm afraid I might make a fool of myself. I'll let you know the time.'

XII

On Saturday morning George again put on his dark suit, white shirt and a black tie. He spent at least twenty minutes polishing his shoes. He glanced in his hall mirror. A different man again stared back.

Rather earlier than they had arranged, Mirabel appeared.

'I'm a bit ahead of myself,' she began.

'Come inside,' he invited her. She looked him up and down, as if both surprised and not displeased by his appearance. She made no comment.

'How are you?' he asked.

'A bit uncertain. I don't know if it's because I shall be doing something unusual. I know he can't hurt me. Not that he would if he were alive. But I'm glad I have you going with me.'

'Yes,' he said. 'I understand that.'

He did not. Mirabel had always appeared to him as a woman who, at work or leisure, was able to assume a reasonable appearance of control. Now, she stood, but from time to time was afflicted with a huge shudder which ran through her body. George did his best not to notice.

'Let's have a turn round my estate,' he suggested. This expedition did not waste much of their time. 'Too cold for dawdling,' he said, taking her arm and wheeling her round his smallish back garden. Indoors again they sat down, neither knowing quite what to say. In the end she tapped her watch. George rushed for the loo; donned the heavy black overcoat which he had bought for his mother's funeral.

They travelled by Mirabel's car to the undertaker's premises where they parked in the ample yard. They were directed by a pleasant young woman at the reception desk. She appeared to be expecting them, and said she would tell Mr Inglewood they were there.

Mr Inglewood, the undertaker, a handsome man, decorously

dressed in a black coat and pin-stripe trousers, shook them by the hand and said that some few of Andrew's relatives had visited the body that morning. He expressed his sorrow, without exaggeration; led them first to his office, where they signed a kind of register.

His manner was friendly and yet solemn as he preceded them into the chapel. He switched on lights before they entered so that the room, not large, was dimly but cleanly lit, and faintly scented. He led them forward so that they stood in a small line of three by the corpse. Music quietly played. George recognised it as an orchestral version of the queen's lament, 'When I am Laid in Earth', from Purcell's *Dido and Aeneas*. They stood together for a short time until Mr Inglewood whispered to Mirabel that they would perhaps prefer a few minutes on their own with Andrew's body. Without a sound, he left.

George moved closer to Mirabel, but did not touch her. Both stared at Andrew's dead face.

Andy lay in his coffin as if he were asleep, with no sign of stress on his face. His hair was neatly parted and lay flat as it never did when he was alive. He was freshly shaved. George wondered what he should say to his companion who stood stiff and upright. Her black coat suited the formal pose she had adopted.

'He looks peaceful enough,' George said.

Mirabel moved away from his side and stood at the end of the bier as if to check on his observation. Then, speedily it seemed, was back in her first position.

'He seems too still,' she said. 'That never happened in his life. You could never get him to stop moving. He was always on the go. I wonder if I should recognise him if somebody took a photograph of him here.'

'Do his relatives live hereabouts?'

'No. They live in Durham.'

'And will he be buried there?'

'He's to be cremated. He left strict instructions about the funeral service and what was to be done with the ashes. I know little about his parents. He rarely spoke about them, and I had the impression that there wasn't much love lost between them.'

Mr Inglewood quietly came up behind them. 'He looks at peace,' he said.

'Can't you always say that?' George asked, and wished he had not spoken.

'Well, no, sir. We do our best, but in a few cases we cannot, we find, change the expressions on faces. Whereas this young man seems peaceful in a strong sort of way. He was, as you know, involved in a most horrific car accident, and must have been in great pain. He was afterwards, in some ways fortunately, often unconscious, and perhaps this saved him from the effects of the pain. We human beings are very various in our ways. But Mr Barron here seems to have thrown off trouble, if I may put it so, with death. His face is calm and strong as though all thoughts of his wounds have been discarded.'

George was surprised by this sermon, delivered in a hushed voice.

'Yes,' he said, not quite knowing what he meant to say, 'he was himself.' Speaking, he glanced at Mirabel who seemed to be weighing every one of his and the undertaker's words. The expression on her face was aloof, impassive.

At the door Inglewood shook their hands, saying he hoped to see them on Friday at St Peter's for the funeral service.

'Do we send flowers here?' Mirabel asked.

'Yes, madam.'

'I see there is a florist's next-door. Are they connected with you?'

'Yes, madam. They are. If you wish to buy flowers or wreaths, I can recommend them. You'll find them very helpful. I'll take you across.'

He did so, and introduced them as if they were royalty. They both bought wreaths and filled in the cards which were to accompany the flowers.

'Who is making the arrangements for the service? Is it Mr Barron's family?'

'No. It's a young man, a friend, Mr Barron's own solicitor. He left directions in his will.'

They moved out into the cold sunshine of the street.

'Well,' Mirabel asked. 'What did you think of all that?'

'When we were in the chapel of rest I didn't know what to say or do. It was my first such experience. I don't think, or I don't remember, either my father or mother lying in state. The undertaker took them away, and brought them back in the coffin for the funeral. It may seem a bit unfeeling on my part, but I didn't want any ceremony of that sort. They were both cremated. Simple service, all organised by the undertaker. That's what they wanted as far as I could gather from the wills.'

'I was surprised to hear that Andy had made one. Have you?'

'It doesn't seem proper to be arranging your will at this time of life.'

'Andy didn't think so.' Mirabel paused.

'What were we doing there? He wouldn't know. Nobody but the undertakers would know, I suppose – that's why we signed the book.'

'We paid our respects,' she answered.

'I didn't know exactly how to do that.'

'Didn't you think about things he did or said when he was alive?'

'I did my best. I didn't know him nearly as well as you did.'

'Yes. He gave me plenty to think about while he was alive. But he was kind to me when I came back up here from London, a divorced woman, not knowing which way to turn. Even though I had rejected him for Charles.'

'Would he have made you a good husband?'

'I don't think he was particularly interested in women. For all our engagement, in the end he seemed unbothered. It's odd that someone of such energy and drive, and so good-looking that the girls chased after him, should be so low on sexual drive. That's if he was.'

'What about men?'

'I never saw any signs. He was good friends with men and women alike.'

'That surprises me.'

'Everything about Andy surprised me. What he did for work, everything.'

They left the undertaker's premises and spent an hour over two cups of coffee each. They talked less than George had imagined, and such conversation as they had was about the vagaries of people passing in the street below. By the time they left, nearly eleven o'clock, they seemed almost cheerful.

Andrew's funeral service was held at two-thirty on Friday at St Peter's Church, on the outskirts of the town. The building had little to commend it, being drably late-Victorian, and in a district of two factories and three streets of terraced houses, a school, and a chapel. The weather was suitably dreary, and George, with Mirabel as passenger, had in spite of their early arrival some difficulty in parking. It took them seven minutes to walk back to the church, past a further clutter of streets, the battered iron railings of an ill-kept park, a row of shops, and a statue in an open space.

'Who's that?' he asked Mirabel.

'Andy's great-grandfather. He owned both factories and built the district up. Haven't you ever been round this part before?'

'Are the factories still in the family?'

'No. They're not factories as such now. They're divided into shops and workshops, and one was half burned out during the war. They were into munitions then. Old Mr Barron, the founder's son, had given both of them up in the early-twenties, and had retired into Derbyshire. Andy's father would have nothing to do with them. Another brother took over the family firm for a while.'

'What did he do then? Andy's father?'

'He was a universily lecturer in mathematics.'

'A scholar and a gentleman, eh?'

'I don't know about that. He could not get on with either his father, his brother, or his son. He married rather late in life, I believe, and Andy was a clever boy, just what he wanted, but with a bolshie temperament.'

Mirabel was pleased to chatter like this about Andy. It seemed to George as if she were trying to sum the man up for herself. She knew little about him; he'd kept his secrets to himself. Now she could hoard the bits and pieces she'd learned from his friends, who in all likelihood had been kept as much in the dark as she had been. She put guesses and hints together as best she could. George enjoyed listening to her. Andrew had puzzled him too, chiefly because he could not make out why the man had been interested in him.

'Have you ever been in St Peter's before?' Mirabel asked.

'No. It's not an old church.'

Inside the building – he'd dated it to just before the First World War – they sat, rather comfortably. The place was bare, more like a meeting hall than a church. It was well-kept; the woodwork shone with polish, and the original pews had been removed and replaced by metal chairs with leather cushions.

'I don't think much of it as architecture,' she said, after another intelligent inspection.

'No,' he whispered back.

'I wonder why they picked this place?'

'Pretty central, and plenty of parking space.'

'I came here,' she said, 'once before, for a lecture on an Antarctic expedition.'

'The temperature's suitable,' he answered. 'I'm glad I brought my overcoat.'

That made them smile and now they felt more at home, shuffling their feet on the concrete floor as they sat. They were startled by a loud, rather vulgar, shouting from the door.

"'I am the resurrection and the life, saith the Lord: he that believeth in me, though he were dead, yet shall he live, and who so ever liveth and believeth in me shall never die.'"

"'I know that my Redeemer liveth, and that he shall stand at the latter day upon the earth. And though after my skin worms destroy this body, yet in my flesh shall I see God; whom I shall see for myself, and mine eyes shall behold, and not another.'"

The chief mourners were shown to their seats at the front. George guessed that the two who came first, a stately lady and a big red-faced man, both with glasses and white hair, were Andrew's parents. Mirabel had been uncertain whether they would attend. The mutes retired and the loud-voiced parson, a young man, read a verse or two of a Psalm, and invited them to sing the first hymn: 'The Lord's My Shepherd' to the tune 'Crimond'.

'Not very original,' Mirabel said as the organist set about the first line.

That seemed to sum up the whole service for George: amateurish, without real feeling. The only piece well handled was the Nineteenth Psalm, 'Lord, Thou hast been our refuge from one generation to another', which was read, quite beautifully, by a woman parson, whether a curate in this church, or a relative or friend of Andrew's, no one knew on his later enquiries.

A middle-aged man paid tribute to his colleague Andrew. He seemed thoroughly uncomfortable, stumbling from one badly formed sentence to the next. He claimed that Andrew was gifted in his work, though without vocation. It felt, if at all, like the passing of an unknown man. The rest of the proceedings was read at the top of his voice by the vicar. He made sure that the empty back seats rattled with the echo, but there was little variation or understanding in his delivery.

Mirabel whispered to George,

'He must think God's deaf.' That put him in his place.

After the family and a few close mourners had moved out

156

elsewhere for the cremation, those who were invited to the refreshments at the Highbury Hotel, entrance by ticket only, hung about and then crossed the road, venturing up a steep stair-case to the second floor of the public house. A bouncer at the door examined their tickets. The room was well-lit and, as Mirabel remarked, no more suitable for the final obsequies than the church. After perhaps fifteen minutes the mourners proper returned, a small party, in adequate black, led by a young man.

'Who's that?' George asked Mirabel.

'No idea.'

A man sitting on a chair next to theirs overheard the question and answered it for them. 'That's John Mount, Andrew's solicitor. He was designated by Andrew's will to organise this morning's going on.'

They were invited towards the counter where sandwiches appeared in great variety. People walked across, filled plates with the food, and were told that coffee or tea or white wine would be brought to their tables. The atmosphere became both noisier and more cheerful. John Mount, the solicitor who had arranged the service and reception, came across and exchanged a few words. He asked their names and how long they had known Andrew. He seemed to take his duties more than seriously. They had already signed a register at the door; he apparently wanted to put faces to names. He drew an anecdote or two from Mirabel, seemed delighted, said it was a pity he had not asked her to speak at the service.

'Andrew was a curious chap,' he confided. 'He said he wanted a service that was commonplace but lively. Of course, at that time, about five years ago, neither of us had the slightest idea that he would die so soon.'

But Andrew had seemed unwilling to offer any detail about his private life. He had only named the colleague who was to give the funeral address. He had been at school with Andrew and had worked with him, and Andrew had left him a small sum in his will for delivering the tribute. It was a pity the man was not a better speaker. He'd had no idea how to catch the congregation's interest. Still, he'd done his best.

He was a man who knew his mind, was Andrew Barron. He'd warned Mount that his parents probably wouldn't turn up; had given him the impression that they were too elderly or infirm to risk the journey down from Durham.

'They were always at loggerheads with him, he said. That was five years ago, so when, after a little persuasion on my part, I didn't have much trouble getting them to attend, I was surprised.'

When Mount met them, their energy and comparative youth were also unexpected. 'They seem to be barely in their sixties, if that, though must be ten years more.'

Thomas Barron had retired from his job at Newcastle University where he had been Reader in some sort of abstruse mathematics.

'I believe he'd made quite a name for himself but had refused to apply for mathematical chairs in other universities or even to receive a belated professorship of sorts that the University of Newcastle offered him. He must have enjoyed being awkward, like his son. He retired to Durham where he lives in some style. There must be some money about, from what I could make out. The mother, Mrs Barron, is an Honourable.'

'She insists on the title?' George asked.

'In no way, so far as I can gather. We lawyers come across some rum characters in the course of our work.'

'Careful,' George warned. 'Mrs Lockwood here is a solicitor.'

This pleased Mr Mount, who shook her hand heartily.

'We've never met in the course of our work. Not that that's surprising,' he explained to George. 'I'm one who makes his living from the law, not my social life. Are you a relative of the Lockwoods of Lockwood & Son? If you don't mind my asking.'

'Not really. I was married to Charles, their son, at one time. He was a lawyer.'

'I've heard of him. Did he not lecture at the Trent?'

'That's right.'

'He made a name for himself. And a fortune, I believe, in insurance in London. He's a clever man. In his fashion.'

'He's that all right. You don't need to tell me.' Mount seemed put out by the knowledge. From Mirabel's answer the man judged he'd perhaps gone too far, and blushed heavily. He stood up, nobody speaking, made some sort of apology with his hands, and slipped away.

'That shut him up,' George congratulated Mirabel.

'I can't say I liked him.'

'No. At least he came and talked to us.'

'Not out of the goodness of his heart. Somebody would have

noticed us and asked him as the founder of the feast who we were. He didn't know but said he'd find out.'

'It's you they notice, not me.'

'I don't take it to heart. Look who's coming now, Andy's father.'

Mr, or properly Dr, Barron now stood at the end of their small table: broad of shoulder, red of face, the very picture of a farmer.

'Good afternoon,' he said, his voice courteously low. 'My name is Barron, Thomas Barron.' He put out his hand, which they shook in turn. 'I am, or rather was, should I say?' he broke off as if he had committed some social faux-pas, 'Andrew's father. I thought I would come across and thank you for coming. My wife is up in these social matters, and she said I should find out who you were, and how you came to know Andrew. I, like a good husband, did as I was told.'

'My name's George Taylor.'

'And mine is Mirabel Lockwood.'

'Taylor,' Dr Barron murmured. 'Lockwood, yes. I think my wife would like to meet you.' He turned and signalled towards his wife, who paid not a blind bit of attention. 'Excuse me one moment,' he said to Mirabel, and strode off. The two of them watched as he started his explanations; his wife, who had lingered, without much interest, suddenly stood and motioned her husband to lead the way. He did so, and she followed stately as a queen. He waited until she stood by him, looking disdainfully down.

'May I introduce my wife? Miss Lockwood, Mr Taylor.'

'Mrs,' Mirabel corrected him.

'Mrs,' Barron repeated. 'Oh, I didn't realise.'

George looked at Mirabel's left hand. She was not wearing a wedding ring.

'I was married for a time to Charles Lockwood,' she repeated. 'I retain the name, though the marriage came to nothing.'

'That's often the case these days,' Barron said. 'Not that I'm blaming you, or anybody else.'

'Unusual,' said Mrs Barron, so quietly that Mirabel did not know whether she was meant to hear.

There was a slightly awkward pause at that before Barron, not apparently put out by the implied criticism, spoke.

'Your name was not unknown to us,' he began. 'You may not have any idea of the nature of the relationship between Andrew and ourselves. I wanted him to go to Oxford, to my college, but he was dead set against that even as a schoolboy. It wasn't clear why. I thought I was doing my best for him, but he seemed to think that I was patronising him because he hadn't the brains to get to Oxford on his own account. I must declare I had no such consideration in my mind, but it caused us to break off relations.

'He went to Cambridge to study English at first, then Nottingham Trent for law. I don't know why he decided on Trent, particularly. Nobody in the family had any connection with the place. Perhaps that was the attraction. But he cleared his wardrobes and never returned home, not even for a single day.'

'Did you not find him like that?' Mrs Barron asked Mirabel.

'No, I don't think so. He knew his mind, and spoke it. But without rancour. Not as if I or his friends were to blame.'

There was another long pause, rather as if Mr Barron expected his wife to continue with the story. She did not, but sat straight in her chair, lips pursed.

'We heard and saw nothing of him. He sent, or somebody sent us, the official list containing his degree result. A piece of printed paper in an envelope. That's all. We wrote a congratulatory letter to him, and sent a cheque, but we heard nothing. He never cashed the cheque or paid it into his bank. It hurt us. He told us nothing of his career. If we heard anything, it was from a second-hand source. This did not change until something like eighteen months ago when my wife was taken seriously ill with cancer, and was in hospital for some months, on and off. Out of the blue he sent her flowers. No visit or anything like that.'

'How did he find out about your illness?' George asked Mrs Barron, without response.

'We were very friendly with a family here. The Groves. They used to live next-door to us in Newcastle and their son used to play with Andrew. My wife has kept up a fairly regular correspondence with them. I think I can say that their sympathies lie with us. Nigel, their son, passes on information about Andrew. And tells him how we're shaping.'

'I see.'

'About a year ago, at the time my wife left hospital, apparently cured, Andrew learned of this from Nigel and sent his mother a letter, congratulating her. There was no mention of me at all, so presumably he still felt antagonistic towards me.'

'I'm sorry,' Mirabel murmured.

'Don't worry about that. I would willingly have made up the quarrel. I didn't approve of his behaviour, but so long as he kept in touch with his mother, that had to be to my satisfaction. When he died we had a letter from a solicitor, Mount by name, giving us details, and telling us he had been instructed to make the funeral arrangements.'

'You didn't hear anything about Andrew's accident?'

'No. The Groves were in Africa, visiting another son who worked out there. They moved about and Nigel's letter with the bad news never reached them, so we knew nothing of Andrew's accident until near the end. My wife went to the bedside. Then, after that, the solicitor, Mr Mount, told us when the funeral was.'

'I see,' Mirabel said. 'He seems a very efficient man.'

'Yes. He's been helpful. Now when I heard your name, Mrs Lockwood, I was reminded that in the few letters Andrew wrote more lately to his mother, it was mentioned more than any other. That intrigued us.'

'Andrew had never made any mention of matrimony to us. And the frequency of the appearance of your name made us wonder if perhaps he was thinking of marrying you.' Mrs Barron spoke now, with a slow insistence on each word, as if she were speaking to a child or a foreigner with only a feeble grasp of English. She paused. 'Perhaps you'd allow me, as Andrew's mother, to ask you if there was any talk of this?' Again a gap, almost a stoppage of breath. 'We had never heard of any such thing before. I know my correspondence with him was not lengthy. But Thomas and I, perhaps unwisely, talked about it. I always shared Andrew's letters with his father. We're a conventional couple, and would have been delighted to hear that he was contemplating this step. So . . .'

Mirabel shifted uncomfortably in her chair.

'No,' she said. 'Not recently. Though I should tell you we were once engaged. I broke it off – I don't think Andy was broken-hearted. This was before my failed marriage. We were friends after.'

The women talked then about Andrew and his friendship with Mirabel. It all seemed very banal to George, but they enjoyed themselves and Dr Barron listened intently, nodding as some point of interest was reached and dwelt on. In the end, after nearly half an hour, the Barrons said they must say hello to a few other acquaintances; they'd then have plenty of time to catch a train to Durham.

'We're getting old now,' Barron said, 'and don't like to be out too late. But it's made it worth our while, coming down and having this talk with you.'

161

Mrs Barron seized both of Mirabel's hands in her own and kissed her.

'I wonder if I could ask a favour of you. I've enjoyed our chat so much. Would you come up and see us sometime? We don't have too many visitors these days on account of my illness, but I'd love to meet you again.' She conveyed the admiration, the attraction, she felt, though always with a stiffness of movement and an accent that would have exactly suited, Mirabel thought, a judge seated in the High Court.

Soon afterwards Mirabel and George left the wake. They bade goodbye to Mr Mount, and one or two people they knew, and made their way across the room to say their farewells to Mr and Mrs Barron.

'We'll write to you,' Mrs Barron said, 'when we get back. I have your card.' She searched her handbag to produce it and held it, almost formally, in the air for inspection. 'Is any time of the week convenient for you to visit? I'll let you know if there's anything interesting happening in Durham.' She kissed Mirabel hungrily and shook hands stiffly with George.

Outside they stood in cold sunshine.

'You made a conquest there,' he said.

'She seemed nice. Not the sort I usually fall for.'

'And what about father?'

'Yes. He was my sort. Tough. I'd guess he has to do as he's told at home.'

'From what we hear, Andy couldn't stand him.'

'It's possible that he tried to lay down the law with his son. Perhaps bossed him about to recover something of his own manhood.' Mirabel laughed. 'I don't know. I'm only making this up.'

'Mrs Barron didn't seem to blame him, and he didn't seem to care that his son was so antagonistic to him. Both of them took it as utterly natural.'

'I wonder if it was always so. If Andy, even as a little boy, didn't get on with his father. I wonder if the pair of them quarrelled over him. Andy'd spot that straight away and play on it. We're right friends, making all this up about them after half an hour's talk,' Mirabel said. 'Neither of them seemed particularly grieved about their son's death. I suppose that's because they had so little to do with their son.'

'He seemed to be moving towards a reconciliation with his mother.'

'I don't quite make them out.' Mirabel smiled. 'Andy was an unusual sort of fellow. That's what I liked about him. And he tried no sort of sexual approach towards me, after his first half-hearted attempt.'

'Weren't you disappointed about that?'

'Not really. He made up for it in other ways. Most boy-friends, if I can use such a word at my age, show signs of sexual attraction. You do, for instance.'

'I'm sorry.'

'Don't get apologising. I'm flattered when men show or say they're attracted to me. But, as I've told you, I'm on my guard, suspicious of all of them. That's on account of my experience with Charles. I let myself go there, and I paid for it.'

She broke off, and stopped, touching him in the crook of his arm and bringing him to a halt.

'Listen,' she said.

They were standing outside a music shop, the door of which in spite of the cold weather somebody had left open. Inside, music was playing. It must be extremely loud, George thought, as they could hear it quite clearly from the pavement. Mirabel held up a finger to warn him not to speak. This went on for a minute or two before someone inside closed the door from within and brought it noisily creaking shut.

'What a pity,' he said. Now they could barely hear the sound from inside the shop. She moved him on.

'That's a favourite of mine. Do you know it?'

'Schubert?' he hazarded.

'Well done. Right first time. It's his Fifth Symphony. He was only nineteen when he composed it.'

'He'd have been cheered if he'd known then that nearly two hundred years later, in a town hundreds of miles away from Vienna, people would be standing in a cold inhospitable street, rapt at the masterpiece he had just written.'

'Yes.'

'Especially a beautiful, intelligent woman.'

She smiled but said nothing.

'Most of us can't do anything worth remembering twenty minutes later,' he said.

They walked the street in silence after that.

'That's what I like about my acquaintanceship with you. Something interesting always comes out of it,' Mirabel said eventually.

'That doesn't come from me, but from yourself. You'd have been just as moved by the Schubert if you'd been coming away from Andy's funeral on your own. I didn't arrange to have that music played. It's mere coincidence.'

'It may be, but such things only happen when I'm with you. As they did when I was with Andy.'

'And I guess when you were with your husband, years ago. At first.'

'That's true.'

'I'm pleased such things happen when you are with me, and that you can connect me with them.'

'And do you know what I think you're thinking?' She said these words with a kind of mock solemnity.

'Perhaps not thinking but hoping that you are falling in love with me, as an unusual person. Not like Schubert, perhaps, or even your Howard Clark, but somebody a bit out of the way.'

'Exactly. But I'm not in love with you, George. I'm sorry, but I'm not.'

'Don't worry yourself. You don't perhaps, in this case, recognise the early stages of being in love.'

'You have a good opinion of yourself, my man.'

'No. We have curious ways. Schubert went to the house where the dead Beethoven lay to beg a hair of his head.'

'Did he get it?'

'He did. I don't know what he did with it.'

'I wonder. It makes the imagination work, doesn't it?'

'Imagination's often the beginning of love,' George said.

'You must be satisfied with that for the present.'

Within a few minutes they reached the car. He offered her a lift but she said she preferred to walk.

'Please yourself,' he said. 'I shan't be able to interrupt your imaginative bouts.'

He climbed reluctantly into his car, without touching her, and drove off at speed.

He drove quickly. He wished sometimes that she was less outspoken. He wished for her love, but would not, as he was, he knew, win it.

XIII

George heard nothing from Mirabel for a fortnight, and after some mental conflict, his exact word, decided to telephone her.

'Oh, hello,' she said. 'Where have you been? I've heard nothing from you these last weeks, and I thought you'd given me up.'

'Why should I have done that?'

'Or you might have been ill. There's a lot of 'flu about.'

'No, I'm fit. I've not annoyed you, have I?'

'No more than usual.'

After more of this not altogether pleasant banter, she invited him to walk with her on Saturday afternoon.

'Where?' He was surprised by the snappiness of his question.

'I did think of taking a stroll by the Trent. The paths won't be too muddy, and the days are really beginning to draw out now. It's pretty peaceful therapy. I went there last Saturday when you didn't ring me.'

'Were you expecting me to?'

'It's always good to hear from you. You've usually seen or listened to something worth talking about.'

'I can't think of anything outstanding now,' he said, rather sullenly.

'I've heard from Andy's mother.' She did not continue.

'And what had she to say for herself?'

'Janet Barron's not been well since she got back to Durham.'

'Not anything serious, I hope.'

'She didn't go into detail. By the way she spoke she's often off-colour, and has two or three days in bed. She said that she hoped I would go up there for a day or two when she was feeling more like herself and the weather was warmer. She did just mention that the nice man I had with me at the funeral would be welcome to join us. She said she liked you because you knew when to talk and when to be silent. Most men hadn't this gift. Half of them tried to impress with high talk, and the others were so shy they were liplocked at an unexpected meeting.'

'She's obviously a woman of discrimination.'

'Yes. I said as much to her.'

'And she said?'

'She asked, over the phone, whether we were thinking of getting married?'

'And you said?'

'My usual, damnable, hesitating answer.' Mirabel paused at length. 'On that walk beside the Trent, I thought long and hard about the same old story: how I had once fallen head over heels in love with a man, and married him, and it all disappeared into thin air. Then I wrote her a long letter, quite out of my usual style, explaining how my marriage to Charles went haywire after a clear, dazzling start. At the end of it, I was pretty sure I was as much at fault as he was.'

'Didn't you think that before you wrote your letter?'

'No. He was at fault. He didn't take marriage seriously. He never tried to make it work. His concerns would always be given first place. I don't think he was exactly disappointed in me as a wife. I don't think he wanted us to break up, but when I realised how low I ranked in his table of valuables, I began to show him I could be awkward, to get in the way of his schemes, even deliberately to find I couldn't be free to go to some important function he had to attend. I hadn't much to do at such affairs, merely sit and silently shine. And that wasn't too difficult: they looked after me, those important lawyers, City big-wigs, because they felt Charles was a rising man, would be able to do them good.

'It took a little time for him to see what I was up to, and then the balloon, as my father used to say, went up. Trent University here were giving Charles an honorary LlD and I said I had an earlier engagement. I won't forget what happened then. He ripped the diary from my hand and held it open at the date we were discussing.

'"What the bloody hell do you think you're doing?" He held the diary out, with his forefinger down on the empty page.

'"I'm expecting Helen Moore to . . ."

'"You tell her you're coming to Beechnall with me. Go on. Write it in. It'll be no trouble. You can buy new clothes for the event, expensive as you like. I shan't complain. I never do. Now, you lying bitch, write it in your diary. I don't demand much of you, and the little I've asked you to do so far you've done well, but when I ask a favour of you, I expect you to do it for me."

'"I don't want to go," I said.

'"You realise, you're a smart enough woman, that attending these affairs, boring as they may be, is as much of an advantage to you as it is to me."

'His eyes were standing out in his head. That was unusual. Whenever he asked me to do something for him, or was arguing some point with me, he kept his face calm, not dark red as beetroot as it was then, and he usually spoke quietly, reasonably, to me. Now he looked violent, insane, unlike himself.' Mirabel drew in her breath.

'"I don't want to go." I spoke it plainly, provocatively.

'"Would you be kind enough to explain why?" he asked me.

'"No. I just don't want to be at your beck and call every time you make a public appearance."

'"When you go out to one of your important events, you expect me to accompany you. You invite me . . ."

'"That's the difference. I invite you, not order you."

'"Fill that diary in. Now. I mean it. This is important to me."

'His voice menaced. I wrote with the attached pencil. He watched me, then lifted the diary almost delicately from my fingers. I had written, "*Not* going with C. to his honorary degree ceremony". He stood stock still. We faced each other. He breathed heavily. I was shaking all over.

'Suddenly he moved, drew his hand back, and hit me across the face with the diary. The blow was so violent, it rang inside my skull, and knocked me off my feet. I staggered and strained to keep upright, but could not do so. My legs gave way under me, they crumpled, and I fell to the floor. He flipped the diary in my direction on to the ground beside me, and stormed out of the room. I lay stunned. I could not move, but lay listening to the sounds he made elsewhere in the house.

'How long I sat crouched there on the floor I don't know. It seemed an eternity before I could pull myself upright and collect the breakfast-pots. I carried them out to the kitchen, and lined them up in the dishwasher. I straightened things out, and walked up to our bedroom. He had vacated it. I heard the front door close, his car start, and made my way to the bathroom to wipe the tears from my face; I had been crying all the time since he'd hit me.

'I knew he wouldn't be back that evening as he was out at another of those schoolboy get-togethers that he and his high-flying fellow lawyers, bankers, investment advisers, organised – where they'd sit and boast about their achievements. Well, maybe not Charles. He never made a fuss. He kept it all to himself, and when the news of another triumph came out, they were all the more envious. But he'd sit here with a glass of red wine and talk to them wittily and confess to doing nothing interesting in the last few months, enjoying a mock-confession of idleness that they all knew to be false.' Her voice stopped.

'And that was the end of the marriage?' George asked.

'As far as I was concerned. Charles realised he'd gone too far. As I say, I saw nothing more of him that evening. The next day I laid breakfast out for him as usual, and he didn't say much, but then he never did. He thanked me and was pleasant when he came home for dinner. I cooked it but it was nothing much, frozen stuff. I answered him when I had to, but that was all. I began looking round for work elsewhere. I got my present job some three or four months later. As soon as I had made the arrangements, I told Charles. He seemed really shaken. I think he saw himself as a charmer who'd win a way through any difficulty. And that the ill feeling between us was over and done with.

'"I thought we were getting on so much better," he said to me.

'"We weren't. You had no more consideration for me than you'll have for a pet cat or rabbit."

'"I'm sorry. Mayn't we have another try? I went a bit over the top about that LID." That's the nearest I got to an apology from him. I just let him try to talk his way out of it, but I'd already made arrangements to stay with Marjorie Banks, an old college friend, until I had worked my time out in London and was ready to move up here. My parents had a home which they made over to me. It all proved easy enough. And do you know what Marjorie Banks, the woman I went to lodge with, said? "I didn't think it would last long. You and Charles Lockwood are too much alike."' Again Mirabel stopped talking for a while.

'Now you see what sort of woman I am,' she said to George across the distance of the phone.

'What sort is that?'

'One who can stand up for herself. And doesn't forget slights. There's nothing magnanimous about me.'

'I see, and I'll bear it all in mind.'

'You'd better.'

On this note the long telephone conversation ended. He took the exchange seriously, knew depression but was just as determined not to abandon his courting, fruitless as it appeared.

Their subsequent meetings were polite, almost loving; walks, a concert; but as soon as he raised the matter of love in plain words she rebuffed him just as clearly. She had obviously given up any idea of marriage or at least marriage to him.

About this time the Professor of Adult Education sent a card, asking him to call in to talk to him as soon as possible.

He'd always looked on Professor Myers as a man who could never be hurried. His lectures were dull but full of facts. He seemed impressed by no one, even the writers he lectured on: Woolf, Forster, Lawrence and Bernard Shaw. George had attended some public lectures of his, and had not been attracted by the account the professor offered, though he knew when and where the authors' works first appeared, what critics regarded as their strengths, who was in fashion, or not, and why. Whether this was deliberate or not George could never decide. Myers gave an outline of a writer's life and work, but never showed his own enthusiasm or lack of it for any of them. Now, at sixty, he looked eighty and was preparing in his slow way to retire. Why the professor wished to see him, George could not guess.

Three days later he knocked on the office door. A weary voice bade him enter.

Myers rose from his desk as soon as George opened the door.

'Ah, Taylor,' he said. 'Please sit down.'

Myers now went through the usual pantomime he enacted before answering a question or approaching a new topic. He ruffled his short, grey hair with a delicate hand, took a deep breath, and knitted his brows as if considering what he was to say.

'Ah,' he breathed out. 'I'm glad you could come so promptly to see me.'

George lowered his head.

'Within the next six days this department will be advertising for a lecturer in Adult Education. Did you know that?'

'No, sir.'

'Well, it is so. Now, I was talking this over with Dr Whitton and he said he hoped you'd apply. He also indicated that you'd probably, on account of your modesty, not put your name forward.'

Myers rolled his head as if he were inviting an answer to this.

'He'd probably be right,' George said. 'Not that I had heard anything.'

'Whitton said you were at present working as a postman. I told him that I did not hold that in any way against you. I understand you do this on account of your health. This may prevent you from even considering the lecturer's position. Does it?'

'No, sir. There's improvement. I've had no difficulties.'

'Good. Now you will understand I cannot in any way offer you the post. It will be advertised. I have here a copy of the advertisement to appear in next week's *THES*.' He waved his piece of paper vaguely in George's direction, but made no attempt to hand it over. 'There'll be a couple of heads of department and perhaps even the Vice-chancellor himself on the appointments committee so I can easily be outvoted. They favour out-reach these days. But I'll see if I can't get Whitton on to the committee too. That will be unusual, but I can argue that he represents the future, not that I believe that. In many ways he's as old-fashioned, if not more so, than I am.

'We'll be looking for someone who's read widely in literature, and can argue a point of view as we know you can. Anyhow, think about it. And then get your application in quickly. If we can capture someone like you, it'll settle my mind before I retire. The last two appointments we made were poor. Both of them had good PhDs but their reading was narrow. Doug Whitton and I want a candidate who reads for pleasure. We're not looking for somebody who'll drill students for examinations. When I started here people came to our sort of classes for enjoyment. Now, the university wants "students", i.e. those who are working their way towards degrees, never mind the length of time it takes.'

Professor Myers dismissed him, still chuntering. George could hear him after he'd closed the door and was out in the corridor. He wondered about Myers, who seemed so worried about his department. Perhaps he had got across someone in the university and thought that he was writing his own valediction: 'I am the man who appointed a postman to save my department.'

George had another talk, with Whitton, who encouraged him and picked up the forms he had to fill in.

'Myers will support me in what I want,' he said. 'He doesn't know whether he's done well or whether they mock him behind his back for allowing his department to go to pot.'

'Do you?' George said.

'No. He's done quite well. He comes from the grand old days of amateurism, when people would join our sort of classes out of interest, not to gain qualifications.' Whitton jerked his head up. 'The pay won't be great. You realise that, don't you? They start you at the bottom of the scale, despite your age.'

'I'll look into it.'

'I'd like to have you as a colleague, but I don't want to entice you here at the risk of reducing you to poverty.'

'I'll look into it, as I said.'

'Good. You know, I think we might collaborate on a book. I've been working on late-seventeenth-century poets for months now, and getting nowhere. A colleague's help might well spur me to start writing. Does that appeal?'

George was by no means sure. Whitton was an idle brute, and if they completed the book George knew that he would have been responsible for the bulk of the work. He did not say as much to his colleague who thanked him a day or two later for the application forms, and, in fact, went out of his way to do so.

George had read them through carefully, and found he had to write a short essay of not more than five hundred words on what he would offer the department. He enjoyed writing this, and this surprised him because he was certain he would not get near the interview, never mind the job. Myers would support him as he had promised, for he was no liar, but would withdraw if anything like opposition was observed in the Vice-chancellor or his fellow professors. The Professor of Chemistry was one of the two on the appointments committee, and he was a man who liked the sound of his own voice and certainly regarded a PhD as a superior qualification to any amount of teaching classes. Moreover, he had shown active dislike, if not contempt, for the work Myers had put into his department. Whitton wanted George, would write a splendid testimonial, but he would probably not get near the appointments committee at the vital time, despite Myers's efforts.

His two former headmasters would both offer excellent reports

171

of the high standard of George's teaching, but that would cut no ice with the rest of the panel. He could imagine the chemistry king's northern voice dismissing him.

'Look, here's a man of forty. He's done well enough as a teacher in two grammar schools, but that's hardly the same as a university lecturer. He has done little or no research of any depth, and then within the last few years he has left his school teaching behind him to become a postman. Oh, yes, I know it was on grounds of ill-health, but, off the record, that doesn't recommend him to me in any way. I'd want a man in any of my departments to be fit, fighting fit, even. Lecturing is in no way a soft option, a cushy job for those who can't or won't put in a full six days a week of hard graft.'

Who'd stand up against that show of strength in this place?

George completed the forms within a week and posted them on to the university. He felt relief that this attempt to alter his future was now in the hands of fellow postmen. The Department of Adult Education was henceforth silent as the grave.

With some diffidence, he mentioned his application to Mirabel. She, walking alongside him, greeted his news with enthusiasm. Her step seemed to quicken as he explained the nature of the work.

'Isn't it unusual to appoint another full-time lecturer in that department? I thought they looked round the district, amongst other lecturers at the university, schoolmasters, professional people, to deliver casual lectures for them? As they did with you and your Victorians. Why have they changed their practice?'

'I've no idea.'

'Where did you find out about the new position?'

'Professor Myers sent for me and invited me to apply.'

'Doesn't that mean you're as good as home and dry?'

'It does not.'

'Explain, my man. Explicate.'

'Whitton, his second-in-command, bullied him into it. He sees himself in Myers's chair when the prof retires in a year or two. And he knows if he has me as his assistant I'll work, not only on departmental duties, but on his private concerns. He's said, and it's been on every tongue in the department, that he's writing on seventeenth-century poetry. And he thinks I'll help him write a book that will bring kudos on the university.'

'Doesn't he know anything about the subject then?'

'A great deal. Enough to write two books.'

'Why doesn't he do so?'

'He's lost his grip, his nerve. And he's idle, bone idle. And he thinks I'll be able to shake him out of it. The fact that the book has both our names on it won't matter.'

'This seems odd to me,' Mirabel said. 'I've heard him lecture once or twice and he seemed to me to be right on top of his subject, and interesting with it.'

'Yes. He did his PhD twenty-five years ago and I suspect his supervisor pressed him into completing it. Then he got the job here, and dropped into the comfortable life. He's been here ever since.'

'And hasn't written anything?'

'Short articles. Reviews. Yes. All sensible and learnèd enough. But Myers didn't harry him enough to write a big book. Some profs would have made his life hell, even threatened to get rid of him.'

'Does Myers himself publish good research?'

'He brings out books. He's read plenty and wasn't averse to working hard on research at one time. His productions are useful. Primers, if you like. But without new ideas. Useful, but not original. And I think, from what I've heard, the new Vice-chancellor and his like want a high-flier as the next out-reach Professor of Adult Education. This university is going up in the world. The scientists are making a name for it. One of them has won part of a Nobel Prize, no less. So they want some original research from the English brigade, at all levels.'

'And doesn't Whitton know this?'

'Yes, more than most.'

'Do you think you could help him complete his book?'

'It's not my subject, but it would be a challenge.'

'Won't the Vice-chancellor and his ambitious clever-dick friends realise what the pair of you are up to?'

'I expect so. And even if they didn't, they wouldn't be too eager in any case to appoint a middle-aged postman. There'll be plenty of bright young people keen to get a job here.'

'You won't get the lectureship, then?'

'Not a dog's chance.'

'Then why are you applying?'

'Something interesting to do. To keep my soul from rusting. To give them something to think about, if ever we get as far as an interview.'

173

Mirabel stopped. Standing to attention, she slapped the back of her left hand, quite hard, with the flat fingers of her right.

'George Taylor,' she said. 'You astound me.'

After a minute she walked on. He spoke first after a dozen or so silent strides.

'And what have you been doing?' he asked.

'Nothing in the same league as your Machiavellian goings-on. Well, well. And I thought you were an honest man.'

She giggled to herself as she pressed forward, almost as if she were trying to escape from him.

'I've visited Andy Barron's mother for three days in Durham.'

'And was it interesting?'

'Yes. More than I expected. She's a remarkable woman.'

Mirabel paused, making him wait.

'Once she realised I was friendly she began to talk about herself, and from then on she hardly stopped. She's not a happy woman.'

'Why's that?'

'Well, for one thing she doesn't think very highly of her husband. She met Thomas at university. He was some years older than she and a lecturer in the maths department.'

'Is that what she read?'

'No. I think she did history. But she met him at some sort of social affair. He was very handsome, she said, and she agreed with herself that she still thought so, forty-odd years later.'

'Had they much in common?'

'That's the odd thing. I don't think they had. But he was a bit of a mystery. Not only to her, but to other students in other departments. He was researching some sort of very out-of-the-way mathematics. Only he, and two or three other people in the world, could understand it. Or so it was reputed. You know how students exaggerate. He tried once or twice to explain what he was doing, but she hadn't a notion what he was talking about. He wasn't a great explicator in any case.'

'But he made it plain to her that he loved her.'

'He must have. She would have been a catch. Her father had been made a peer just before she went to university, and she had letters addressed to her as "The Honourable", which made her seem different. She'd have cut quite a figure at what was a comparatively small provincial place. Her father was a Conservative politician and held one or two positions in the government of his day. He was a consultant surgeon previously and came to politics late in life.'

'Did her parents approve of Thomas?' George asked.

'Yes. He was very quiet, and dressed well, and was obviously not short of money. He was presentable. And his reputation for being something of a mathematical genius impressed them.'

'Did this mathematical stuff he did ever come to anything? He isn't exactly a household name.'

'No. It didn't. I think that's why he stayed at Newcastle, and even refused the chair they offered him there near the end. He can be awkward, apparently. But I think he was disappointed too. He added little bits to his theories, but it didn't make him famous. A mathematician, a professor at Durham, did once predict to her, apparently, that somebody might take it up and use it and make Thomas's name. "It happens in mathematics," he said. She told her husband, ages ago, but he wasn't exactly pleased.

'"And how did you enjoy married life?" I asked her'. Mirabel recalled it for him.

'"The first three years were fine. It was very different from what I'd known before. But I expected that. I found myself a job teaching History in a girls' grammar school. I didn't expect much difficulty there. I had a good degree."'

'"And how long did that last?"'

'"Not long. Andrew was born about fifteen months after we were married."'

'"And how did your husband take to that?"'

'"He seemed pleased. But Andy didn't do anything to endear himself to his father. Not while he was lying in his pram, anyhow. I made him do things for the child. Wheel him out in his pushchair or take him for a walk.' She adopted a waddling duck gait, presumably the young father's method of perambulation."'

'"And Thomas did his best there?"'

'"I suppose he did. He was always thinking of something else. If I asked him to lay the table – and that wasn't often, I can tell you – he couldn't get it right. For two people we need two knives and forks, I'd say. He'd look at me as if I had gone mad. But two boys, in two years, both strong and lively filled my time up. By the time they'd started school my marriage seemed sterile."'

George enjoyed the apt way Mirabel imitated the voices. She did it without apparent effort and though he was in no position to judge the accuracy, he felt thoroughly convinced. Mirabel said how much pleasure she found in the small satisfactions of conversation, the little details. She hadn't even known Andy had a brother.

After a time he asked, 'Why didn't Andy get on with his father?'

'Interesting, that. Thomas didn't pay much attention to the boys when they were very small. It was quite noticeable. He never played with them even when they were away on holiday. He was quite interested in them, I suppose, in a distant, disinterested, I beg your pardon, uninterested way. The only thing that seemed to concern him was his research. He seemed to be immersed in that all his waking hours.'

'Was he a good teacher?'

'Passable, as far as I can make out. She said he could always solve the problems they couldn't. And he'd bother to make it plain. One of the students told her that he wasn't like some of their teachers, who couldn't understand what was puzzling them.'

'Were both sons good at maths?'

'Yes. Both of them. They took after their father. They occasionally asked for his assistance. And he would just mutter a sentence or two that put them on the right path. Later on, as he told us, he wanted Andy to go to his old college in Oxford, but he wouldn't. He wanted to do literature, and his schoolteachers told him that Combridge would be the place for him. His father tried to argue with him. But Andy had made his mind up. And once he went to university, they saw little of him.'

'Didn't he come home in the holidays?'

'No. Rarely. His last vac he had got himself a job, and they heard nothing, his mother told me. "For me, the worst thing was not hearing from him, finding out what he was up to. Not a phone-call, letter, not even a post-card . . ."'

'"His father and he had words the last time Andy called in to see us," Mrs Barron said. "Before he went to Trent. He never came back. I never saw him again. He wrote me once or twice in the last year or two, when I was so ill, but he said little about our absence or silence. I often thought about him and blamed myself for not trying to get in touch. When I did receive a letter or note from him, I wrote back at length giving him some idea of how things were at home."'

176

Mirabel recalled the conversation, even as she tried to outline it to George.

'And your other son?' she had asked Janet Barron.

'He wasn't so touchy as Andy. He followed his own way, though, about which university he was to attend. And he went off to Australia where he still is. We exchanged odd letters or phone calls, but he was not much of a writer.'

'Did your husband never mention them? The boys, I mean.'

'I showed him Alisdair's letters. He'd nod and grunt or mutter some banal remark to the effect that he seemed to be making a way in the world.'

'Did Alisdair not marry?'

'No. He was like Andy in that.' She had sighed. 'I was disappointed. I think I would have liked grandchildren. It seemed singular to have lost both sons, like that. Four other people I know have very little contact with their children. As long as they thought their offspring were well, that seemed enough. Our absence and silence seemed different, more official. I blamed my husband. I don't know how he felt all those years. I'd always mention their birthdays.

'And what did he say?'

'Nothing much. "I wonder how he's spending it?" Something of the sort. As if we were mentioning an old neighbour with whom we'd not kept in touch. He'd show no anger or resentment. Or interest.'

'But he came with you to Andy's funeral.'

'Yes. I was surprised. I'd been called to the hospital at the end, returned, told him Mr Mount's arrangements, and he said straight out that he'd attend. I didn't say anything but I wondered if his retirement had made more of a human being of him.'

'Did he still carry on with his research now he'd retired and moved to Durham?' Mirabel had asked.

'His main work was complete and published. But all through his life, he had done little bits of research.'

'Were they published?'

'Yes. One or two made something of a stir, in the small circles of university mathematicians. I read somewhere that they have usually done their best work by the time they're thirty. I can't say whether that was so with Thomas. If he had, he didn't know it. He seemed just as absorbed with it. He is to this day. Newcastle wanted to make a professor emeritus of him, you know, but he wouldn't allow it. He was just like Andy. If he'd once made his mind up he wouldn't change it.'

'Did it worry him? That he wouldn't let them honour him.'

'I suppose that was it. He felt that he had not got as far with his research as he would have liked. When he was younger he was disappointed with himself, and as he grew older he withdrew into himself.'

'Do you think that was why he didn't seem to miss his sons?'

'That's a possibility, I suppose. Actually some years ago, a German and two Americans finally took up one of his "bits and pieces", as he called them, and applied it to some conclusion about chemical research of their own, nothing that Thomas seemed to be interested in or even knew anything about. Anyhow, the story found its way into the press and made something of a stir. Thomas was invited to go to America to receive some sort of prize.'

'And he wouldn't go?'

'He did go, but he didn't take me.'

'Were you cross about that?'

'I was at first, but he didn't mention it until it was too late. He never showed me any of the paperwork connected with the prize. When it came out that I could have gone with him, I set about him. He said I'd have been bored with the whole proceedings, and I told him it would have been nice to have been asked. That seemed to penetrate his skin somehow, and he apologised several times. In fact, I had to tell him to stop it. I still can remember the look on his face as I told him I wanted to hear no more of it from him. He was like a little boy.'

'Were you sorry then?' Mirabel had asked her.

'No. No longer angry. That's all. In some ways I was as bad as he was.'

'You never thought of leaving him?'

Mrs Barron said she often felt like leaving her husband. 'I could have done it more than once. I'd plenty of money to finance the move, but it seemed wrong, as if I'd be breaking my solemn word. I've often thought why I looked at it in this way. My parents weren't religious. Nor was I for that matter. Or, at least, not in that way?'

'In what way, if you don't mind my asking.'

'I believe there is a God, capital letter or not. And I would in some way like to live up to his standards.'

'You don't go to church?'

'Not regularly. I go sometimes if there's some special music. Or sometimes, and I can't claim it to be often, I just drop in on a Sunday evening. But their way of worship seems to have nothing to do with the God I vaguely imagine. It's perhaps the worst of all worlds, but that's typical of me, all over.'

'You're too hard on yourself,' Mirabel had comforted her.

'That's how I like to be. I don't want just to drift through life, looking after the house and seeing to it that my husband was properly dressed when he went to work or to some ceremony. In some ways he was, is like a child, and needs looking after. I wonder what he'd say if I told him that?'

'Would he be angry?'

'No, I don't think so. He'd give it careful consideration. But I ask myself if my reaction to him could be called love. It's certainly not what I felt for him when first he proposed marriage. But I suppose that is the same with everybody.'

'You read in the local papers about some old couple who've been married for seventy years. And the husband says, unless they put the words into his mouth, that he loves his ninety-year-old wife as much as he did when they walked down the aisle together.'

'And you believe everything you read in the papers?'

'No. But I wonder if it's right. Even in a very few rare cases. My husband and I,' Mirabel went on, 'fell out of love. Yet when he asked me to marry him, I thought he was an angel.'

'And did you suddenly think one day that you'd fallen out of love?'

'No. It was a gradual affair. Dreadful for a day, at the start, then next day bearable. But within a few weeks I knew it was the truth. He thought nothing of me, and I wasn't standing for that.'

'You left him then?' Mrs Barron sounded surprised.

'Yes. I think he was caught out. I don't think for a minute that it had crossed his mind I'd had enough of him. He was very clever. But he didn't know *that*.'

Mrs Barron thought that quite likely.

'I think,' she spoke rather lugubriously, 'I would only have left Thomas if I'd met a man who was really sexually attractive to me.'

'And you never came across such a paragon?'

'No. I thought there was such a one once, but it came to nothing.'

They talked in this frank way for the last full day of the short break.

179

'It was as I imagined one could talk to a sister,' Mirabel concluded to George, '– not that I knew what that was like, I was an only child – and Janet was old enough to be my mother. It was like being freed from shackles when I talked to her. I'm going to spend a whole week with her very soon.'

'Those Barrons are replacing the Lockwoods,' George suggested. 'Another old couple for you. But it will be interesting to learn something of Thomas's mind.'

'I said as much to her, but she wouldn't have it. He'd be very polite to me, she said, but he'd disappear to his study after each meal. When I asked if he'd be pursuing his mathematical studies, she said that's what he'd like her to think, but she guessed a good part of his time would be spent fast asleep. She'd caught him nodding off in there several times. He wasn't pleased, she said, and tried to make out that he was deep in thought. She didn't argue with him. He knew quite well that she'd caught him asleep. He wasn't altogether a fool.'

When they parted outside her house Mirabel suddenly said to George,

'Janet asked me how you were. She liked you. "That man who came to Andy's funeral, she said. I really took to your young man . . ."'

'"He's not that," I said.'

'"You could do worse." Janet noted. "And I was struck by the verse he put on the flowers on Andy's coffin. I learned it:

> Fall, winter, fall, for he,
> Prompt hand and headpiece clever,
> Has woven a winter robe,
> And made of earth and sea
> His overcoat for ever,
> And wears the turning globe.

'"Who wrote it?" she had asked.'

'"Housman. A. E. Housman. It's only two verses. The first is about a young man who hated the winter's cold. He died, as if on purpose, and was buried snug and warm in the earth."'

'"Did you know it?"'

'"No. George lent me a book. I read some of the other poems."'

'"Were they good?"'

"'I didn't complain. Sad. Pessimistic. Suited my mood at the time."

"'Yes,' Janet said. "He's the right person for you."

"'Are you something of a clairvoyant?'"

"'No. It's more common-sense. Or, at least, I like to think so.'"

Again Mirabel summarised all this to George on her door step.

'I take it,' said George, 'I'm not to give up hope?'

'It made me think,' Mirabel said. 'She's a clever woman. But don't read too much into it.'

She patted his arm, smiling, then kissed him. His spirits leaped. But with moderation.

XIV

When George rang Mirabel the next weekend the call went unanswered as did three more during the following six days. He concluded that she must be away from Beechnall, probably visiting Janet Barron. He hoped Mrs Barron still kept her good impression of him, and repeated it with conviction to Mirabel.

One afternoon he picked up, he did not know why, an early edition of the local *Beechnall Post*. As his eyelids drooped he was suddenly jerked into attention by a name: Francis James Smith (69), his acquaintance in the pub. George sat up, on the alert. It appeared that a young man named Frank Hall had broken into Smith's house, and had made such a noise forcing the window in the kitchen that it had woken Smith, who was fast asleep by his wife's side in the bedroom overhead.

He had jumped up, donned his dressing gown, and picked up a rolling-pin which he kept upstairs for such occasions. He crept silently down and found the intruder helping himself to a cased set of fish-knives and forks, and other valuables. Smith had challenged him, and the young man had snatched up a big carving knife which he waved threateningly about. He did not in any way reply to the house-owner's challenge except to hold the carver ferociously in front of him. Smith spoke again, but still received no answer. The burglar stepped towards him. 'Get back,' he growled, 'before you get hurt.' Smith took a pace forward and, with a swinging blow, knocked the knife from his hands. Before the man had time to recover either sense or position, Smith hit him hard on the top of his head with a rolling pin. The man dropped to the floor. Smith then called to his wife to come down.

He had taken a clothes line, which was hanging on his kitchen wall, and tied up the intruder while his wife phoned the police. Meanwhile the burglar had come round and lay groaning on the ground. Mrs Smith offered him a drink. Neither she nor her husband had ever seen the young man before. The time all this started was, Smith had carefully noted it from the kitchen clock, 12.25. Their neighbour, returning from work and seeing all the lights on in the home next-door, had come round. He was a journalist who had been to Birmingham to report on a visit there by the Chancellor of the Exchequer. Always on the look-out for the unusual, he had knocked on the Smiths' back-door. He then helped call the police who, in no hurry, sent a car round in about half an hour.

On the arrival of the police car its occupants, two constables, were given the full tale again. They expressed surprise that a person of Smith's age and build had managed to knock out the intruder, and tie him up. The intruder had carried a bag which held, by the journalist's guess, the profits of two other burglaries at least. Smith expressed surprise that a man, however young and strong, could carry about so heavy a haul at the same time as breaking into a locked house.

Over an hour later the policemen uncoiled the clothes-line from the burglar, clapped the handcuffs on him and bundled him out in to the street. They had made a list of the valuables in his bag, but left Smith's fish-knives in the house where they belonged. The three of them, Smith, his wife and the neighbour, then talked for another half-hour over fresh tea.

George learned all this detail when he looked out the Smiths' address and phoned them. Mrs Smith answered him; he'd often wondered what she looked or sounded like. Yes, Mr Smith was at home. Who was this calling? He told her and was rewarded by an answer he did not expect.

'You're that MA he's always boasting about?'

'Yes.'

'He's very fond of you, proud, y'know.'

'Good. I read about your burglar in the newspaper.'

'Oh, that would be Harold Leake, the man next-door. He writes for the papers, and made our incident into a story as if it was fiction. He said in his article about unusual violence, that he'd often tried to imagine what it would be like to face an intruder, what he'd do, and how he'd shape. Anyhow I'll go and get Jim. He'll wonder why I'm spending so long on the phone. He knows I don't like telephones, have never got used to them.'

George didn't make much of Mrs Smith's character from her voice. She spoke with a local accent, unlike her husband, and might have been one of a dozen housewives he'd seen choosing a cabbage or a packet of frozen peas at the greengrocer's.

'Oh, oh,' Smith called down the phone. 'Mr Taylor. I'm glad you've called.'

'I wondered how you were after all your excitement. I read it in the paper.'

'Yes, man next-door wrote that.'

'I'm surprised, not to say pleased, that you were able at your age to capture your burglar.'

'He's not my burglar. Anybody else can have him.'

'You know what I mean.'

'Can I call round for half an hour, to tell you all about it?'

'Now? Well, yes. But tell me first, did he put up much of a fight?'

'He didn't get a chance. I had a longer reach than he had, longer arms. That's one thing they laid stress on in the army. We had to judge our advantages over an opponent's. And these days, when I'm creeping further down this vale of tears, it's an absolute priority. I hit him and knocked him out before he had the chance to stab me. It was common-sense.'

'Yes, if you have time and judgement.'

'One of the policemen wasn't so sure, either. He said you shouldn't ever set about a trespasser until you could prove he attacked you. Nowadays, you have to be so careful. You could find yourself in the dock, defending yourself for injuring an intruder.'

Smith arrived and, talking in full spate, gave a second violent account of the whole incident. He was at his most fluent as he described the thief's knife, and the success of the opening single blow.

'You don't know about these things. I've hit a man with a heavier implement than that rolling-pin, and with a great deal more force, and nothing happened. No skin broken and the man still on his feet, looking just as fit as before I walloped him. You can't be sure. I was glad when this lad went down, I can tell you. I had him trussed up in no time. And you never know with the police. They may make you wait for hours before they turn up, or maybe not come at all.'

'Did he come round before the policemen appeared?'

'Yes. He was still shaken when my neighbour Harold appeared. I was glad to see him. He's very articulate. He doesn't speak well, he's no orator, but writes like an angel.'

'Have they tried the burglar yet?'

'Not as far as I know. He's appeared and pleaded guilty, so the case won't be transferred to a higher court. He could have asked for that, but he didn't. He'll get a lighter sentence with the magistrates and no jury. He knows that all right, he's got a black record as long as your arm. I wouldn't have thought they'd have allowed him to stay in a magistrates' court, but I suppose they know what they're about.'

'You didn't seriously injure him then?'

'No. And even if I'd killed him, they wouldn't touch me, they said, in view of the difference of age and health.'

George noted how this didn't quite square with his earlier account.

'Ah, well. Congratulations.'

'Thanks. But I'm not too pleased with myself. He looked so innocent and vulnerable just after I'd clobbered him.'

'Will you have to appear in court?'

'Not as a witness, I think, now that he's pleaded guilty. I asked the police to let me know when the trial was.'

'You didn't tell them about your history of unarmed combat or jiu-jitsu?'

'I did not.'

'Well done. You showed up to advantage again.'

'I hope so.'

'Never mind hope. Yours was action. Well done. I'll buy you a drink next time I see you.'

'When will that be?'

'I don't know. Now, steady there. How about coming round here again about eight one night? I'm free if you are, though I don't keep late hours. And I'll provide the booze. Would your wife like to come with you?'

'Don't suppose so. I'll ask her.'

At this the telephone rang.

'I wonder who that is at this time of the evening.' George was not left long in ignorance. It was Mrs Smith, enquiring where her husband was.

'He's sitting here, happy as a lark.'

'I thought from what he said he'd be back by this time. He told me he didn't want to waste your time.'

'No, he didn't do that.'

'He wasn't boasting, was he?'

185

'No. But he has something to crow about: knocking that young burglar out. You've recovered, I hope, from all the excitement? You could do without that, I expect.'

'Yes, I should think so. I was terrified. The burglar was threatening Jim with a knife.'

'That didn't put your husband off?'

'No, he stood there as cool as a cucumber. But the expression on Jim's face was horrible. I'd have been scared out of my wits to see him look at me like that. And then he hit the man, and the burglar went down like a pole-axed bull. I was amazed.'

'He goes to classes in self-defence at the gym, doesn't he?'

'I knew that, but I didn't expect him ever to make use of the knowledge. There's always a bit of cloud-cuckoo-land about Jim.'

George looked round at Smith. 'He's no bruiser at home then?' laughing.

'Gentle as a lamb.'

'Would you like to speak to him?'

'No. Just tell him it's after seven o'clock now, and it's time he started making tracks for home.'

'I don't think I dare,' George joked. 'He might set about me.'

'I don't think so. He admires you. Jim's done quite well for himself in life, but he's envious of those who are properly educated. I mean, you are an MA, aren't you? That's what he says. Is it right?'

'Yes.'

'You never know with Jim. He exaggerates. He likes to make a good story out of his tales. Tell him to come home. I don't want to be waiting all night before I serve supper.'

'Would you like to tell him yourself?'

'No. He understands English. And he knows the sort of things I'd say. He'll get my message. Recognise it, I mean.'

Smiling grimly to himself, George conveyed the instruction to Smith, who seemed in no way put out.

'She gets frightened,' he said, 'being left in the house on her own. She's nervous. Always hearing little noises, and jumping. She can't help it.'

Smith got to his feet and said he must go.

'Your wife must be more confident,' George said, helping him into his raincoat, 'now she's seen you in action.'

186

'It's my view women worry more about what they imagine than what they see. Pity I have to go, I was enjoying myself.'

He moved with some haste.

Two days later George was pleased to hear on the phone from Mirabel.

'I've been wondering,' he said, 'where you've been.'

'Couldn't you guess?'

'I thought you might be paying a visit to Andy Barron's mother.'

'Right in one.'

'And did you enjoy yourself? Was she in good health?'

'Yes. No.'

'Oh, thank you,' he said. 'Exquisitely clear.'

'She was quite ill. She has these bursts or bouts of illness and has to stay in bed.'

'What's wrong with her?'

'Several things, cancer among them.'

'Can't the doctors do anything for her?'

'She's had two operations this year. She spoke as if she might well have died without them. She's due to have another shortly. That's why I went up rather earlier than I, we, intended.'

'And she seems bad?'

'Yes. Weak. Tired. In pain. But lively. In control of her mind. And I could help them out by cooking lunch.'

'Cleaning the house?'

'No. She has a woman in to do that. If Janet doesn't improve, they'll have to employ a cook.'

'Didn't she like the idea?'

'Her husband complains, Janet says. The woman she occasionally employs is an excellent cook, miles above her standard, but Janet can't convince Thomas of it. He's mad, she says. Has out-of-the-way ideas on many subjects, and this is one of them.'

'And how did he judge you in the cooking stakes?'

'Neither of them said anything to me. But then I don't suppose he complained to the real cook. Anyway he knew it wouldn't last more than a week.'

Mirabel paused, as if the memory weighed heavily on her.

'She could talk, could she?' asked George.

'Oh, yes. Beautifully. She is a marvellous woman. She spoke about her childhood, her young womanhood, her meeting with her husband, their marriage.'

'She regretted that, I take it?'

'Her marriage vows mean something to her, but she's now becoming an invalid, unable to carry them out because of illness.' Mirabel paused. 'And what have you been doing?' she asked.

'Nothing much.' He then gave a short account of Smith's tussle with the burglar. Mirabel expressed interest.

'Two fights, to your knowledge,' she said. 'Does he look like a fighter?'

'Not at all. He's well-built, and muscled, I guess, but you don't see that under his raincoat. And he wears a pair of old-fashioned glasses, all twisted out of shape, which make him look aged and hopeless.'

'Is that deliberate?' she asked.

'I shouldn't think so for one minute. But then, you don't know with him. And his wife was terrified by the look on his face as he was about to attack the intruder.'

'I think I should like to talk to your Mr Smith. You pick up some interesting friends.'

'Easily managed. I've invited him, and his wife if she'll come, round to my house for a drink, and they can meet you.'

'Good. Janet Barron asked after you. And she spoke of you again in glowing terms, very confidently, as though she had known you for years.'

'What else did the pair of you find to talk about all of the week you were there?'

'Men. Marriage. Money. Health. Wealth. The life to come. She held her own with me, quite easily, even when we were talking about some legal point. She seemed mostly interested in the relationships between people. She spoke of her childhood when it seems she didn't get along too well with her mother.'

'She blamed her, did she?'

'Not really. Janet was a nuisance as a child, she said. That's the marvellous thing about her. She can put both sides of a case very strongly, almost with equal power, so you wonder which way she'll come down. Then she'll sort it out so beautifully that she carries your assent to her conclusion without any demur from you. She'd have made a marvellous lawyer, in that she'd have given clients good advice before they entangled themselves in complicated and expensive cases. She describes the struggles of people to you so clearly that you can almost hear the voice of the ones in trouble.'

'Do they always take her advice?'

'Oh, no. And she can always give good reasons why they haven't done as she said they should. She doesn't hold it against them. People who are wrong are often to be admired for what they think, she says. I didn't entirely agree with her there, but she always seems to have substantial reasons for what she says. And another thing: she sees that people don't always act according to reason, and that sometimes they are right not to do so. I felt it was a real privilege to be allowed to talk to her. I learned, or began to learn better, how to handle some of my clients.'

'Did she always listen to what you had to say?'

'Yes. And if I didn't altogether express it clearly, she'd rephrase it.'

'And Dr Barron, Thomas, what had he to say for himself?'

'He was out most of the time.'

'Where?'

'I mean out of our way. He'd be in his study, up on the third storey, working away at his mathematics. But he'd turn up for meals. She, Janet, would come down if she felt up to it. Towards the end of the week, she seemed weaker. I wondered if I hadn't overdone it, but when I mentioned this to Thomas, and asked if he thought I was overtiring her, he pooh-poohed the idea, said she was having the time of her life. She loved talking to clever people. I told him I wasn't all that intelligent, and he said she thought I was, and that was recommendation enough for him.'

'Good for him.'

'For days he left the house all day.' She paused, making a mystery of it before continuing, 'He went, so I gathered, one of the days to visit a friend, another mathematician. He was grateful to me for staying with Janet.'

'"They are a pair of oddities, Thomas and his pal," she summed them up for me, "though there are worse things than oddity. There are so many people about, perhaps it's my fault, that I find simply are not worth talking to. You're a jewel to me. As soon as I first spoke to you I knew that here was somebody I could confide in. I felt delighted," she told me, "as well as ashamed. One ought to be able to talk to anybody. I think I've grown out of patience. I can't wait for people to make themselves interesting to me. It's a bad fault."'

189

'I felt really sorry for her,' said Mirabel. 'She seemed so much in charge of herself, even of her diseases, that this surprised me.'

'She didn't seem over-pessimistic about her illnesses?'

'She described her chances as plainly as she would describe what she expected for the next meal.'

Mirabel spoke for nearly half an hour about her new friend. She talked with such delight, with an enthusiasm that seemed almost girlish. The same face, figure, movements he knew, were at the other end of the line, but she spoke with such power that her voice, her words, seemed new. She had become alive in an unaccustomed way during the few weeks she and Janet Barron had been in touch.

'Did she say much about Andy?' asked George.

'Yes. She often mentioned him. She was very proud of him. Apparently as a small boy he was outstandingly bright, with a marvellous memory and a logic that caught adults out.

'She hadn't seen anything of him in these last few years, after he'd quarrelled with his father, but she always spoke of him with pride.'

'But she managed to convince her husband to attend Andy's funeral.'

'Yes, though she told me again no one was more surprised than she. "I'd prepared for a long argument," she said. "I was all ready to blackmail him with 'What will people think?' and finally to tell him to come down here just on my behalf, to support me. But these weren't needed. I asked him, and immediately he agreed. He said, 'I know you want to go, and I shall support you.' She thought he'd changed. He sounded exactly like Andrew; so much so that she wondered if she had pressed him earlier he might not have agreed to invite Andy back home, even if it had meant his getting out of the way while the visit was on.

'She told me: "At that time they both seemed so convinced in their veins that nothing would change their mind. Death had pierced Thomas's defences. He finally remembered how delighted he was when the boy won mathematical prizes at school, and represented the county in a nationwide competition and won every stage."'

'Perhaps he hoped Andrew would join him at the university and help him to some notable conclusion that would make them both famous?'

'Perhaps so. But she didn't think Thomas wanted to be famous.

What he seemed to be searching for was some sort of mathematical answer, some big, useful conclusion that he could not reach so far, with all his puzzling and bits of answers. Andy would not study maths at university in spite of the A+ marks and national prizes he scored in his A-level exams. He wouldn't stick with it, and not entirely with anything after.'

Mirabel seemed pleased with their, or rather her, descriptions of the arguments between mother, father and son. She giggled with pure pleasure when she compared those complex arguments with the elder Barron's research; all sorts of small arguments settled but no crowing universal conclusion.

'Tell you what,' she said, 'I'll come round and see you tomorrow evening. We can come to our own, overwhelmingly convincing, final conclusions.'

'Are there such?'

'Oh, ye of little faith'. She laughed. 'I tell you what, see if your Mr Smith will come round here instead tomorrow evening and bring his wife with him, if he will.'

'To your house, do you mean?'

'Yes, here. To my house.'

Once off the phone to Mirabel, George rang Smith without much hope and put the invitation to him.

'Tomorrow?' Smith asked. 'That's very short notice.'

'Mirabel doesn't hang about. She makes up her mind in a flash.'

'Wait,' Smith said, 'while I ask my wife.'

George heard him put down the phone and speak to her. The invitation apparently needed some explanation: who Mirabel was, her relationship to George Taylor, where she lived, why she wanted to see them. Suddenly he heard a statement from her as clear as if she had spoken straight into the mouthpiece of the phone.

'Windsor Mansions?' Mrs Smith queried. 'They'll be those big houses at the top end of Mapperley Park. I'd like to go inside them. I used to go past them when we were first married and I worked for Mrs Latham.'

Smith mumbled something indistinct, came across the room and picked up the phone again.

'Thank you very much,' he said. 'We'd be delighted to come.'

Further enquiries about the exact situation of the house followed, multiplying.

'My wife says she knows it. But she often claims exact information when she hasn't really much idea. Typical.'

On the next day George received a letter from the university inviting him to attend an interview for a lectureship in the Department of Adult Education. It was in a fortnight's time at ten in the morning. He looked up his postman's duties and found himself free that morning. A good omen, though it did nothing to raise his hopes.

He put on a suit for the visit to Mirabel's. He thought long enough about this, and decided he'd do it in honour of Mrs Smith. He smiled at the half-comical explanation. Why should he wish to impress Mrs Smith, unknown to him except for one phone call? It should be Mirabel he wished to please. He arrived at her home twenty minutes before the allotted time, and gave her his news, asking what he should think about in preparation for the ordeal.

'Now why should I know that?'

'You lawyers know everything.'

She threw a stray cushion at him, and they laughed together.

'You look a picture,' she said. 'Is that the suit you'll wear for your interview?'

'No. That will be a darker, more sober version. I've only worn it about twice since I bought it two years ago.'

'Do you have a special shirt and tie to go with it?'

'Of course.'

The front-door bell rang loudly, vigorously, surprising them.

'You go. That'll be the Smiths. Show them in. I'll change and be with you in a few minutes.'

He had hung up their outdoors clothes in the cloakroom and settled the Smiths in armchairs when Mirabel appeared, brilliant in red. She had changed the less flamboyant frock she began with for this eye-catching confection; it needed some such word, to describe her clothes.

Perhaps it was Mirabel's striking appearance but they all seemed rather at a loss for words. Both Smith and George stumbled to their feet. She shook hands with both Smiths and signalled the husband back to his chair, the wrong one, not the one he had occupied before her arrival. The visitor toppled rather clumsily into it, attempting a broad smile to cover his embarrassment. Mrs Smith's forehead creased with worry. She was obviously afraid her husband would say something out of turn.

'I hope he's looking after you,' Mirabel said. 'I see he's not provided you with anything to drink.'

She pointed at George who stood by his chair.

'What would you like?' to Mrs Smith.

'I'm driving tonight,' she answered, 'so I'd like a soft drink, if that's possible.'

'Of course. That's very sensible.' She listed those available and Mrs Smith chose apple and blackcurrant.

'I can recommend that,' Mirabel said.

'I read in the paper,' Smith said, 'just recently, that if you regularly take soft drinks, you do your system more damage than if you regularly drank port.'

'In what way?' George enquired.

'Gout.'

'I don't think one glass of this will do you much harm,' Mirabel said. 'Mr Smith, now?' She again named the alcoholic drinks that were his for the choosing. He elected for whisky.

'Without an "e" in it.' George smiled at his own explanatory addition.

'What are you talking about?' Mirabel crossly snapped. 'You come along and help carry the drinks in.'

Mrs Smith seemed ill at ease with this correction of her husband's friend, her lips drawn tightly into a thin line. She wore a rather dark green two-piece which seemed to emphasise the pallor of her features. Her legs, which were rather fat, were held closely together over her heavy shoes.

George carried in the tray; Mrs Smith's soft drink, whisky for both men, and for Mirabel herself, surprisingly, a glass of lemonade. This pleased George. She'd chosen it to make Mrs Smith feel at home. Her usual preference was for gin and tonic.

They took their drinks, and all thought this the moment to begin the evening's conversation properly. Mrs Smith made the first effort.

'This is a beautiful room, really beautiful.'

'You like it?'

'Oh, yes. Do you have help in the house?'

'Yes, it is pretty large for one person. But I don't make a great deal of mess. I wouldn't have bought anything of this size if I'd had the choice, but my parents left it to me. I let it out to two families when I married.'

'Are they your ancestors?' Mrs Smith asked, pointing to two moderately large oil paintings.

'No. My father picked them up at some auction. Both he and my mother were fond of sales of house contents.'

'Did they patronise car-boot sales?' Smith asked.

'Not as far as I know. There weren't too many cars about then. I guess when they could afford to spend money, they'd dulled their appetite for antiques. I expect they took a walk round the car-boot sales in later years but were disappointed.'

'So your house is full of valuables?' Smith asked.

'Yes. But I daren't tell you what they've worth.'

'Don't you have to insure them?'

'Yes. But I don't do it seriously.'

'Do you not have burglaries in these parts?' Mrs Smith spoke almost eagerly. 'Jim here caught a burglar at it.'

She began on the long drawn-out tale, ending with Smith's question, first to her, then to the youth as he regained his senses. Should he send for the police, or let him off, or give him a good hiding, kick, and then throw him out?

'What will you think if I let you out now?' he'd asked their burglar. 'What an idiot? Or, I've been lucky with this man?' Then the neighbour arrived, urging action, and Mrs Smith phoned the police.

By the time Mirabel had provided coffee, triangular sandwiches and cream cakes, Smith had given them the benefit of his eloquence with two anecdotes of army life in which, to George's surprise, he did not play the hero. One concerned a PT Instructor, a sergeant, who had saved his wife from burglars; the other a corporal, a marvellous rifle shot, who'd won prizes every year at Bisley, but who had murdered his wife. She was, apparently, a pretty, complacent woman who saw to her husband's every need. Smith, with the permission of the colonel, was allowed to visit the corporal in detention.

'I was only a lance-jack myself at the time, but could never understand why the prisoner had killed his wife. She was, according to her husband, a decent woman who looked after him, never put a foot wrong. He talked about her,' Smith said, 'as if she were still alive at home, preparing his tea. I never knew how to get round to talking about why he had committed the murder.'

'Was he mentally deranged?' George asked.

'You wouldn't think so to talk to him. He was always pleased to see me. It was only for a day or two before the police took him away to a civilian prison and for trial.'

'Was he found guilty?'

'Yes, but they had a great string of doctors and psychiatrists and psychologists to examine him and speak for him. They were no more successful than I was at finding out why he'd done her in that day.'

'What happened to him?'

'I don't know. I made some enquiries and found out what prison he was in. I wrote to him once or twice, but got no answer. But that's just like the army. You get to know somebody and become real friends, or so you think, thick as thieves, and then one or the other is posted and you drop out of one another's lives.'

'You enjoyed every single day of it in the army,' his wife said. 'You know you did. And you're always talking about it.'

'There you are,' Smith said, smiling. His face took on a different shape when he was pleased. 'I have to watch what I say.'

They ate their sandwiches with evident relish. Mrs Smith almost purred with delight as she enquired about the fillings. Mirabel had put herself out in the preparation of the food. As Smith's face seemed to alter as he smiled, his wife became a different woman as she ate. Her body relaxed, her hands flew as she praised the food. The two guests had not expected this, and were prepared to take their pleasure without hurry, with a deliberate enjoyment.

Just before ten the plates were empty. As Mirabel's mantel-clock struck the hour, Mrs Smith looked at her husband and tapped her wristwatch. He noted the warning with a nod of the head and a closure of his eyes, but continued with his anec-dote. This was an account of some honey-tongued salesman behind the counter who had tried to sell Mrs Smith, Edna, a blanket, which she did not want. Failing with the lady, the shop assistant had turned to a second ploy, inviting her husband to feel the quality of the blanket and to admire its colours.

'What would you say, sir? Isn't this real value for money? You need fear no longer a cold bed in an icy bedroom.'

Smith had smiled politely and followed the salesman's instruc-tions, and then had given his judgement.

'I know little about blankets. But I see that my wife has taken against this one, and that means she will by no means buy it.' The shop assistant made as if to intervene but was stopped by a gesture from Smith. 'I know nothing of blankets until they're wrapped round me in bed, but I know my wife. We've been

195

married forty-odd years, so I'd be a fool if I didn't, and my advice to you, young man, is to wrap this up,' he slapped the blanket with his flat hand, 'and put it carefully away. My wife, who is an expert on such things, has decided against it, and you will make no sale of it today. Waste no more of your time, or hers, or mine, in trying.'

'You should have seen the man's face,' Mrs Smith said. 'And Jim here, Francis James Smith, might have been a judge pronouncing the death sentence.'

'And then what?' George asked.

'We left the shop. Jim took me by the arm and guided me out of the place. We left as if to music. It's a marvellous thing when you see your husband defending you like that. I felt so proud,' she said.

'I don't like bullying in any shape or form, whoever it's from,' Smith told them.

Mrs Smith turned to George then. 'I hope you'll speak up for your lady.' She swung round to face Mirabel. 'I can tell you one other thing. I have never spent such a friendly, comfortable, luxurious, luminous evening in the whole of my life. This is a beautiful home, and your entertainment has been beyond criticism. You've made us so welcome that I felt, if I can be slightly rude, as though I was sailing inside myself. The food was flawless, matchless, wasn't it, Jim?' She smiled at him, and then at George.

'"For we on honeydew have fed/And drunk the milk of Paradise,"' George exaggerated his diction.

'That sounds like poetry,' Smith said.

'Coleridge. "Kubla Khan",' George answered him. 'Slightly amended for the occasion.'

'And it brought the best of words out of these men. Jim spoke, told us his yarns, beautifully tonight, as he does when he has been well fed.'

'Thank you,' Mirabel said, bowing. 'Thank you, both. All three.'

'I feel twice the woman I was before we visited you,' Mrs Smith. 'I wouldn't have thought it possible.'

The Smiths buttoned outdoor coats, but slowly, and made their way to the front door, where they began their paeans of thanksgiving once more. Mirabel and George followed them down the front-garden path and stood at the gate to watch Mrs Smith take over at the wheel and drive carefully, confidently, away.

Back in the lounge Mirabel seemed silently jubilant, if the two words were not contradictory. She was not shouting for joy, but on her tiptoes with delight.

'They're a wonderful couple. I know: another of my old couples,' she said. 'And she wears the trousers without making too much fuss about it. Is she better educated than he?'

'Slightly. That's possible. She perhaps left school at sixteen, and he'd have been out in the world at fourteen.'

'He's a good talker.'

'And intelligent. And he's got on in the world.'

'What did he do?' she said.

'Partner in some property firm. But the important matter to him is his physical confidence. *Nemo me impune lacessit.* Nobody provokes me with impunity. I bet that blanket salesman wished he'd never dragged Smith into the transaction.'

'But he doesn't seem to have terrified his wife.'

'They really admire each other. I bet those anecdotes he comes out with, she will have heard dozens of times, but she never tires of them. So he must perhaps vary the tales with the tellings.'

'Yes, I noticed Mr Smith was nearly always the hero of his stories.'

'That's not surprising, though he had modest tales too. He's had to fight his way up the ladder of promotion. In his sort of life there are no rich uncles with power and influence, to put a word in for him at the right time. He's got where he has by his own efforts.'

They cleared away the cups, glasses and plates, but Mirabel would not allow George to wash them up.

'I've a machine out there for just such occasions as this. They'll be beautifully sweet and clean in no time.'

'In that case, I'd better get back home. It's twenty-past ten.'

'You're not at work early tomorrow.'

'No. But I've burdened you with my company long enough for one evening.'

'I'd hoped you'd spend the night here with me.'

This utterly surprised George, and he was not sure what she meant.

'I've got no sleeping clothes,' he said woodenly.

'You won't need any for what I have in mind.'

'I don't quite follow you,' he said.

'I'm inviting you to share my bed.' Mirabel stared him in the face. 'Does that shock you?'

197

'It indicates a certain change of mind on your part.'

'Yes. That's so.'

He walked across to her, pulled her fiercely into his body, kissed her with fervour. She returned his embrace. They broke apart and stood, breathing heavily. She rested her face on his chest.

'I love you,' he said.

She did not answer in words; merely tightened her hold on him. They kissed again. He could think of nothing outside her lips, and her body. He thrust a hand up her brilliant skirt. She made no demur.

'God,' he whispered. He did not know if she heard him.

In time Mirabel gently pushed him away.

'I'll lock up for the night,' she said, 'and then,' she giggled, 'we'll retire.' She stood back, offering a slightly ironic little bow before she left the room. He stood, mouth half-open, unwilling to believe his good fortune. When she returned he threw his arms about her again, as if to convince himself.

'Come on,' she said. 'Onwards and upwards.'

She pointed out the bathroom, and her bedroom.

'Get a move on,' she said, briskly. 'I can't wait all night.'

He used the bathroom, and then, while she was out of the room, undressed, hanging coat and trousers on the clothes-hanger she had passed to him. She came back to find him sitting naked on the bed.

'Don't sit there, shy boy,' she said. 'It's not warm enough to dawdle about.'

He clambered in, shivering on the cold sheets. She followed him almost immediately. He kissed her, gently. She too, stark naked, seemed now somewhat removed, more remote. Her body was warmer than his, but her stillness not quite intelligible to him. They kissed again, perhaps awkwardly.

'Is this what you want?' he asked, hoarsely.

'Don't be silly.'

'I haven't any means of contraception,' he excused himself.

'I've seen to that.'

She answered in her solicitor's voice, efficient and reassuring to a nervous client.

They fell to love-making, his fingers and lips learning her body with a wild freshness. When they reached climax he groaned with joy, and later, when she lay with her back to him in the darkness, both naked still, he stuttered out his love and its satisfaction. She didn't speak much, expressing her happiness with fingers and nuzzling body. She fell asleep very soon, in satiety, but he lay enjoying the warmth of her closeness. She had been satisfied, he was sure; had found with him the plenitude of shared pleasure.

He slept with breaks of wakefulness unusual for him but did not hear her get up, and so was surprised when she woke him with a cup of tea. Mirabel was dressed smartly but soberly for work. She put down his cup and kissed him on the mouth, then jovially along his forehead. This was not a long celebration. She told him she'd be ready with breakfast in fifteen minutes, asking what he'd like. He chose coffee, cereal and toast, with marmalade. She marched from the room, a woman ready for a day's work.

They ate together like man and wife, not saying much. She pushed across her *Guardian* for him to look at, but he did not need reading matter. They washed up together, without talk of machines, a five-minute job, before Mirabel disappeared upstairs.

'I'll be about ten minutes,' she said, 'then I'll be off to work. I'll take you back if you like, it's not far out of my way. Or you can stay and read the paper, as long as you drop the catch when you go.'

On her return she was wearing a well-cut, light overcoat. She stepped across the room towards George.

'I love you,' he said. They kissed. 'Will you marry me?'

'I'll think seriously about it,' she said. 'I don't believe in rushing these things.'

He did not feel too disappointed at what yesterday he would have considered a rebuff.

'Are you going or staying here for a bit?'

'I'm going. I need a shave.'

She stroked his face with her fingertips.

'You don't need to tell me.'

They walked out into the hall together, where he donned coat and scarf. Before she opened the front door, she held out her arms, to be kissed.

'Don't spoil my make-up,' she warned. 'I need to look respectable in the office.' She broke away, but smiling.

'I love you,' said George. 'For ever and ever.'

'Good,' in her solicitor's voice. 'And I feel as though I'm sixteen again.'

She didn't exactly hurry him down the path, but drove off with the briefest of goodbye gestures. He stood there as she waved the fingers of her beautiful left hand at him and was gone. He set off in the same direction but, after a few steps, turned about, deciding the other way was shorter.

The street seemed empty.

XV

For the next few days George saw little of Mirabel. That one evening at her house had to suffice. He spent his spare time preparing for the interview.

On the morning of the ordeal, Mirabel rang him early. He was still in his pyjamas.

'Are you all ready?' she asked. 'I'm ringing to wish you luck.'

'I don't think luck will count for much.'

'Why is that? Who is on the committee . . . a lot of old fogeys?'

'No, as expected the Vice-chancellor, Professor Myers, Professor Goodliffe, the head of chemistry, and Professor Vowles, economics and politics.'

'And what are they like? The Vice-chancellor's new, isn't he?'

'Yes. I've never met him. He'll be keen on making his name. Wants to be involved in out-reach. They say he's bright.'

'And the others?'

'Goodliffe doesn't like me much. I've crossed him, it appears. Vowles I know nothing about. He's been here these last three or four years. He'll be keen on impressing the new VC.'

'And Myers, your man?'

'He'll be a broken reed. If it were left entirely to him, he'd support me, but he won't oppose the rest of the panel.'

'Do you know anything about the other applicants?'

'Not really. They're all young men, all PhDs. I got that from Whitton.'

'Hasn't the professor said anything to you?'

'No. That's all he'd tell Whitton. He wouldn't show him their applications. Said it would not be professional.'

George quite enjoyed meeting the young candidates. They were pleasant and more nervous than he, since he had by now convinced himself that he stood little chance of winning the post. Whitton had told him that the Vice-chancellor had taken a special interest in this case, claiming that the Development of Adult Education must equal that of the other departments.

'I don't want it to be a social meeting of people who do not think of the topics their lecturer deals with from one meeting to the next. We must look for high standards. We want to produce graduates. I know I could put an argument just as strongly for the other side, but that will mostly profit only those who have already had the advantage of a university education. If this does not convince you, it's what the government wants, and they provide the money. In this world, he who pays the piper calls the tune.'

This from a man who, in his few months at Beechnall, had already shown such malevolent dislike of the government that the Mayor, himself an outspoken buffon, wanted him to moderate his language.

George went in second. The interview proved not unpleasant. Even his enemy, Professor Goodliffe, seemed not only friendly, but asked for enlightenment on some points that were well-worth answering. Myers put a couple of dull questions on the administration of the department and the necessity of homework. The Vice-chancellor stammered through a question about the Metaphysical Poets, so convoluted that it could scarcely be under-stood, never mind answered. George replied with whole sentences from Dr Johnson's famous essay, which had Myers nodding sagely at his learning. Vowles quizzed him vaguely about the advantages of poetry to a person who was already launched into the world of employment and making money and providing for his dependants. George answered rudely, at which the chemistry man laughed outright. He left the presences in their room, feeling that he had not disgraced himself.

When, at the end of the process, all the candidates were called back together before the panel, the Vice-chancellor congratulated them, saying they had done themselves credit. Nevertheless, he could choose but one, and that was Dr Summers from Hull. He asked them all to call in at the office at the far end of the corridor where their expenses would be reimbursed. Dr Summers might, he hoped, be good enough to give Professor Myers half an hour of his time, to make some preliminary suggestions about the subjects on which he would be prepared to lecture.

The other candidates shook hands in the corridor, congratulated Summers, and marched happily enough towards the office where they made their claims.

George, excluded from this last exercise, drifted away from the rest and over to the car-park. He was more disappointed than he had expected, and shuffled along the paths, his hands deep in his rain-coat pockets. At home, he lay rather than sat in an arm chair, middle-aged, with a cup of weak, reviving tea. He had done as well as he possibly could, but it had got him nowhere. He even doubted whether they'd offer him any work next year now they'd taken on a full-time jack-of-all-trades.

This did not quite account for the depths of his depression. He had not expected to be offered the job, as he'd told everybody. Now he admitted this was not the whole truth. He'd thought he could do better than either Myers or Whitton; could liven the department as they couldn't. That wasn't the whole answer either. Mirabel might have accepted him as a husband if he was a university lecturer, but never as a postman.

To his chagrin he discovered a tear rolling down one cheek. He pulled out one of the handkerchieves he had himself ironed to a kind of perfection for the interview, and wiped his eye. Sitting up straight to face the hostile world, he caught and upset the fragile table by his chair. The tea cup bounced awry and smashed by the fender. That was the sort of day it was. Nothing would go right. He picked up the pieces, noticing for the first time that it was one of his best cups, his mother's. He cursed as he threw the shards into the dustbin.

George made his way upstairs, changed out of his smart suit, and donned his old clothes. Jacket-and-tie-less he prowled about the flat, every room, doing nothing useful. He stood for nearly a quarter of an hour at one of the large drawing-room windows, but for all he saw and registered he might as well have kept his eyes shut in the coal-cellar. Pulling himself together, he came across the newspaper still folded from the letter-box, thrown abandoned on to a chair just before he had set out for his interview. He resumed his seat, opened it and read the ways of the world.

'Child Murdered in Frenzy'; 'Widow Accused', 'Tram fares Unfair'; 'New Styles of Interview'; 'Man 93 Marries his Secretary', 'Met on Valentine's Day'. The headlines wavered before his eyes; he made himself read columns of text, one as much as four times, so that he understood them. He momentarily forgot his disappointment and so ploughed on, page after page. The stories had their effect and in half an hour he was asleep.

When he woke half an hour later his head felt heavy, as if he had a cold. He brewed another cup of tea, and ate without relish a thick slice of currant cake. He felt the cold and turned up the heating.

He waited until 6.45, it seemed hours, before he judged Mirabel would be home from work. Three times he tried to ring her between then and ten o'clock, but all he heard was the phone sounding in her empty rooms. She must be out, and had turned off her answering machine. She had said nothing about being away this evening on which nothing would go right. At ten he turned in, but slept badly, waking at intervals expecting to hear the telephone.

It was a relief to be woken by the alarm clock, to stumble out of bed, to eat his breakfast toast and drive round to work, where everything at least seemed much the same. He had said nothing to his colleagues about his failure to get away from them; he was half-sorry now that he had not mentioned his attempt to change employment. They would have commiserated with him, but would no doubt have despised him for thinking he could escape their trivial lives and chat. Who did he think he was? Not one of those writers whose works he had taught and admired. Not an artist; a Howard Clark who could shift his troubles from sculpture to watercolour, and flourish; or a Thomas Barron whose work developed from an undeveloped man. Not even a middling lecturer on such figures of talent. Man of letters; postman. His minor sufferings made for nothing, only more suffering. Perhaps he would apply for a job as a school-master again. It did not appeal.

Just after he had dealt with the crockery he had used for his lunch, he seated himself in his armchair with his newspaper. He had barely turned from the front page when the phone rang. It was Mirabel. He waited for her to begin the conversation. He had not expected her to call at this time.

'This is Mirabel,' she said.

'Where are you?'

'Durham.'

Her voice seemed strange, on half power. She had gone to visit Andy's parents, he guessed, but that did not seem altogether possible. It was hardly any time since she had been up there last. He waited for her to explain. She seemed hesitant; it was apparent over the phone.

'Janet was taken ill two days ago.'

'Is she in hospital, then?' He tried to help her out.

'No.' Again an awkwardly long pause. 'She died. Yesterday evening.'

'Was it expected?'

'She's been very ill this last few days, weeks, even. The cancer had spread. She was in great pain and they were drugging her with diamorphine. She said she wanted to see me.

'They, my employers, said I should go at once. There was nothing at the office of any great importance, or at least that couldn't be put back for a few days. Ernest, one of the senior partners, drove me home to collect some clothes, and then back to the station in his car. He was marvellous. I'd always thought he was rather a cold-blooded, unsympathetic sort, but not this time. He treated me as if it were my mother who was ill.'

'Was Janet still alive when you reached her?'

'Yes, but only just. She opened her eyes, but wasn't capable of speech.' Again the silence, as if Mirabel could not bring herself to tell him the details. 'I don't know whether she knew me. I thought when I first arrived that there was a flicker of recognition in her eyes, but that was perhaps my imagination. Thomas said she had been constantly asking for me for the past two days, but by the time I arrived it was too late. Both a doctor and a nurse called in. They fiddled with the pump or whatever it was delivering the anaesthetics. They both said she'd only hours to live.'

'Were you there when she died?'

'Yes. Thomas and I were in the room with her.'

'How did he take it?'

'He didn't show much emotion. He rang the doctor and, when she'd called, the undertaker. He spoke very normally. I would have shown more upset if the newsagent had failed to deliver my *Sunday Times* and *Observer*. But that's just him. I searched about in the fridge and the pantry, and cooked us a meal. He ate heartily, whereas I could barely take a mouthful. He made up, with my help, a bed for me. I decided, he asked me, to stay for a day extra, to help him out with arrangements for the funeral. I'm glad he did. It gave me something to occupy myself with. You wouldn't believe how shaken I was with grief. I shall come back tomorrow. Thomas seems grateful.

'The doctors and the hospital and the funeral directors are all very helpful, but he can't seem to make his mind up on anything.

I chose the coffin and the flowers, and the university chaplain at Newcastle, the nearest they had to a friend there, will take the service. We talked it all over. Thomas really was useless. He hardly seemed to know what a hymn was, let alone suitable Bible readings.'

'You could tell him, could you? You knew?'

'You'd be surprised what solicitors are asked to arrange. It'll all be very ordinary, banal even. I don't think either of 'em was really religious. And then he asked me to make an address. I said I hardly knew Janet, that she must have had friends who knew much more about her than ever I did. He said not. So I had to get an outline of her life from him. You talk about blood from a stone. He seemed deliberately not to want to answer my questions. We often have clients like that. They don't want to tell you anything, even if it's to their advantage.'

'Why's that?'

'It's something that embarrasses them or they feel ashamed of.' Mirabel paused. He could imagine her wry smile. 'Often nothing of importance, but they don't want to talk about it, or start on a line that might lead to it.'

'But you got what you wanted from him?'

'Yes. I don't want to deliver the address, but if I must, I want to do it properly. There is just a chance Janet's sister will come down, and if she does I'll ask if she can speak instead. I told Thomas that if that happened, he should allow it. He said Janet had left instructions to ask me. I said we had to consider the living, not the dead, and I didn't want to cause family trouble.'

'I see.'

'And how are you?' Mirabel's voice seemed brighter as she introduced a new topic.

'Oh, down in the mouth.'

'Why's that?'

'I didn't get the job at the university, and I feel very disappointed.'

'Oh, I thought you were reconciled to that from the start. You said Myers wouldn't support you in an argument, and so you might as well not go to the interview.'

'That's what I thought. But when the Vice-chancellor announced who had got the post, I felt down, crushed. I'd had a good interview, and the person who seemed to be most strongly on my side was Goodliffe, the chemistry professor, who didn't like me, or so I thought.'

'And what about the others?'

'Oh, Myers asked a couple of dull questions about the organisation of the department, and the changes I'd make if I were in charge. If I'd said what I thought, it would have appeared I was saying he didn't do it right, and that would be my application down the drain. I just played it safe. I blamed the government a bit. That would appeal to them. But I didn't go there to talk about administration.' George broke off suddenly, sullen.

'And the others?' she pressed. 'The VC and the other man, an economist, wasn't he?'

'The Vice-chancellor asked me about the Metaphysical Poets. That was a bit of an insult, really. The other candidates were now PhDs but I was a postman, ignorant, not likely to know anything.'

'And how did you answer him?'

'As learnedly as I could, with Dr Johnson and pieces of Donne.'

'And how did that go down?'

'He nodded at what he considered valid points, but he nodded at the wrong times as far as I was concerned. As for Vowles, he asked what of importance I could add to the lives of busy or retired people by introducing them to poetry. And what sort of poetry would it be. I was fairly rude to him, and said that his question seemed to imply that he didn't have much use for poetry.'

'Was that fair?'

'No, but I'd had enough. The only questions that were sensible came from the chemistry king. He asked about the novel, and showed that he'd read quite widely in contemporary fiction. I enjoyed that. We argued a bit, but he didn't seem to mind. He reminded me of some of the best students in my classes.'

'Who got the job then?'

'A young man called Summers. He's just finished his PhD at Hull.'

'Was he a good choice?'

'His PhD was said to be good, and he seemed a lively young man. Why he wanted a job in Adult Education, I don't know. I'd have thought a lectureship in an Eng. Lit. department was nearer his line. But there. Perhaps there was none going.'

'So you were disappointed?'

'Yes, I don't know why. I hadn't expected to be. Perhaps I'm more fed up with being a postman than I realised.'

'And what are you going to do now?'

'I'm not sure. Look for a job in a school, I suppose. Or carry on with my round.'

'They'll still offer you an evening class again?'

'I expect so. If I have to go a long way off then they won't be able to offer me anything. But I've seen neither Myers nor Whitton since the interview.'

They paused, hardly able to continue the conversation.

'So we're both in a sad way with our worlds?' he asked.

'Yes.' The affirmative was delivered with so little enthusiasm that he did not expect to continue with the subject.

'Yes,' George said, 'yes.' Now he made a desperate lunge that he feared would do him more harm than good. 'One thing hasn't changed. I still love you.'

'Thanks,' she said, dully. He could easily imagine the look on her face.

'You haven't changed your mind about that, have you?' He'd started; he might as well continue.

A long, awkward pause. Each could hear the other's breathing.

'I don't think, George, you can imagine the effect of Janet Barron's death on me. There was such a spark between us. That's an odd word, but the feeling was electric. I admired her as I have no one else recently. It was how I felt about one of my school-mistresses when I was fifteen or so.

'She seemed to know so much, and was able to apply her knowledge or insight so brilliantly to any problem that came up, and I don't mean only academic problems. Whether it was personal, or political, or even scientific, she seemed able to throw light on it, and make people like me understand what was involved. I envied her as much as admired her. I once asked her what birthday present I should give my father. She said she didn't know him, and so her view was not likely to be very useful. Then she went through the list of proposed presents I had made and dealt with each one, and what sort of person would be pleased or helped or uplifted by them. I was amazed. Using her ideas, I chose a book for him.'

'Did he like it?'

'Yes. It was *Cranford* by Mrs Gaskell.'

208

'I should have thought that more a woman's book than a man's.'

'He said that it was the best present he'd ever had. He made my mother read it. I think she was as surprised as I was at his missionary zeal. But my teacher had done it again: made a choice that was near-perfect.'

'And what happened to this paragon?'

'She left the school to be married.'

'And was he her match?'

'I don't know. I only saw him once. He was a good-looking young man. Somebody told me he was outstanding at cricket and rugby. And he had fair, curly hair.'

'And what happened to them? Their story?'

'I don't know. I wrote to her once, but she never replied.'

'And she didn't make her name anyhow or where? Never got into the newspapers?'

'Not that I know of. I missed her, I can tell you. For two or three years. And I often think about her still. I tell myself I'm a fool in that I'm always on the look-out for these gifted people.'

'You could do worse,' he said. 'I can see why I'm ruled out.'

'I thought I'd picked such a one in my husband. But I found I'd made a bad mistake.'

'Don't be cynical,' he said. 'There aren't many perfect human beings.'

'Have you not found any?'

'No. There have been dozens of people I've admired, people who have managed things I could never approach. But I can't pick out just one or two who stand head and shoulders above the rest of us.'

'We're different. Is it that you won't admit that such people can exist?'

'If one such appeared, I'd recognise him or her, I'm sure. But so far, no luck.'

'Then why are you always pressing me to marry you?'

'I love you. You're on the same flat earth that I am. You're not a goddess, but you're still miles out of my class. I love you because I want to cherish you, to look after you. It's as if I've come across a jewel, and I don't want to lose it. I can see that I'm not much of a catch. Why should somebody with a life as interesting as yours, someone who found somebody as gifted as Charles Lockwood, with all his interests and talents and money, choose anyone as ordinary, as old-fashioned and banal as I am for a husband? Who'd marry the postman?'

'I don't promise to marry you, George, because I've been misled once. Remember, it was I who left Charles, not the other way round, because he didn't seem to notice I was there. Oh, he was always polite, gave me good presents at Christmas or on birthdays, but I had to fall in behind him in other things, even holidays. I could see he tried to incorporate the odd one or two of my ideas, but if he wanted a holiday, it had to be to some place he was madly interested in.'

'Were his choices interesting?'

'Yes. Better on the whole than I'd have chosen, I'll admit that.'

'Well, then.'

'Every time I talk to you, I seem to be complaining about something.'

'A good grouse gets it out of the system,' he said.

'Well, every time I talk to you, I feel the better for it.'

'Thank you. That's a compliment that'll keep me smiling for a day or two.'

She blew him a kiss over the phone, and rang off.

He tried to put himself in her place. She had found a friend whom she admired, and, he guessed, who admired her. When she was raised to enjoyment, typically, death intervened. She had no luck. If he married her, he would consult her, not beyond her expectation, but as an equal. Not that he saw her acceptance of him as a husband as a certainty, but she had, in her sorrow for Janet Barron, seemed to talk to him more openly. The question was not turned aside unanswered, but at least considered; certainly not brushed off as ridiculous.

George felt cheered and began to sing. He burst into the line of a hymn, in the manner of his father. There was no subject in the world that his father would or could not celebrate with a verse from Charles Wesley. 'Lo, to faith's enlightened sight, All the mountain flames with light.' Why he'd chosen that and its jaunty tune George did not know. It was a favourite of his father's, though. He'd not heard the old man's performances for over twenty years, but this couplet still rang in his head as if it were only yesterday he'd learned it.

He remembered how, once he was in the grammar school, he'd questioned his father about the author of the hymn, only to find that his father's interests were, in order of importance: the message in a hymn's words; its tune; the composer of the tune; the author of the hymn. 'Who wrote it?' George would persist. His father seemed not at all put out that he couldn't answer the question with any confidence, but smiled. 'Are the words any good?' he'd ask in return. 'Yes,' the boy answered, 'they're memorable.' 'Then they'll be by Charles Wesley.' 'Are you sure?' the boy demanded. 'Of course I'm not bloody sure!'

He'd come from a very religious family who'd sent him to church four times every Sunday, not counting week-days, and his good memory had harboured much of what he'd heard. Once the old man had reached eighteen he went to Sabbath services no more, but if one had plucked him up from his desk or fireside and dropped him, at the age of fifty in the middle of a Non-conformist act of worship, he would need neither hymn book nor even Bible to follow what was happening.

'All the mountain flames with light,' sang George. His father could probably have quoted the first line of the hymn, and the next two, as well as the name of the tune. Poor Charles Wesley, mused George sadly as he happily belted into the couplet: 'Faith's enlightened sight'.

XVI

Mirabel rang not at all in the next few days, just as George had expected.

She would have returned from her three days in Durham, and then rushed to the office to work like a dog, catching up with the tasks she had neglected, and would have managed them inside two days. Then, when all was straight, she would have returned to the North Country for the funeral. George had learned the date of that from the receptionist at her office who knew him and felt able to pass on the information.

He sang out loud like his father.

He felt happy, and knew the cause of his happiness. While he was away on his round that morning, his postman had delivered a letter which now lay on the table as he cleared his luncheon plates.

When he'd pushed in after his morning's work, the letter had caught his eye amongst other papers, advertisements and appeals. He'd picked it up and stared at the print on the envelope: University of Beechnal. His lip had curled in derision; his address was typed and so he did not know who had sent it. He guessed it was from Professor Myers; a hypocritical screed, telling him how well he had done at his interview, and commiserating with him that they could not offer him the post. Once he'd opened the letter, Heaven opened for him. It was from the Vice-chancellor himself, dated and written in his own hand.

Dear Mr Taylor,

I write to offer you the post of lecturer in the Department of Adult Education. Dr Summers, to whom we offered the lectureship in the first place, turned it down since he found, on arriving back in Hull, that his own university had appointed him to a lectureship in the English department there. At a hastily convened unofficial meeting of the panel we agreed *nem. con.* that the post should be yours, should you still be willing.

I feel that this has turned out for the best. We were divided all along between you and Summers, and I, as a newcomer, felt bound to yield to more established voices. Now my choice has been allowed me: 'What the gods themselves dared not promise, the rolling day has brought unasked'. I don't quite remember the exact quotation. Is it Virgil? I seem to remember it from my schooldays. You'll know. Anyhow, my congratulations. I look forward to having you as a colleague.

Perhaps you would write to me to accept our proposal, and get in touch with Professor Myers to make arrangements, at your convenience, for next year's work. Human Resources will be in touch, officially, as to salary and conditions.

Again, my congratulations.

Yours sincerely,

A. C. R. Hardwick-Wilson,

Vice-chancellor

George, while overjoyed, could not but mock the Vice-chancellor's style and pretensions. There seemed to be something hypocritical about the letter. He was sure that Wilson had not voted for him in the first place. That being so, Myers and Vowles would have opted for Summers too, and only the chemist, George's former enemy, would have spoken up for him. As for the alleged quotation from Virgil, he dismissed it. He did not recognise it nor see its relevance to the situation. If it were there to demonstrate Wilson's wide learning, it had failed with this reader. The man should stick to his science.

George tried to rid himself of these ungenerous thoughts. The VC had attempted to speak to him in his own language and should perhaps be praised for his attempt, however feeble. The claim to have been overruled by other members of the panel might be no more than the truth. George did not know the VC, had only spoken to him on the occasion of his interview.

These bits of sour thought did not spoil his delight, though he despised himself for allowing them. This must be his nature; nothing that happened to him, however good, but he could spoil it. He washed his lunch-time dishes, hurried back to the dining-room to re-read the precious letter, then wrote to the Vice-chancellor accepting the post. As he laboriously worked, breathing heavily, he tried to keep the style cool, polite, diminishing the excitement he felt. He remembered as he altered a word here and there that they had rejected him out of hand, and only because Dr Summers had turned them down did he get a look-in. The second-best as always he said to himself, but he felt he was somebody now, half-hating the thought even so.

Still, he looked forward in a new mood of optimism to phoning Mirabel with his news, but not at work. That would reveal a childish streak in his nature that he hoped she had so far missed. He sank into his chair, slept for ten minutes, felt glued to his cushion. He forced himself up and stood holding himself steady by the edge of the table. His mind moved but arrived nowhere useful until he decided to walk into the centre of the town. There was not much advantage in doing that, except that he'd made a decision, kept to it, and that pleased him. With his anorak collar turned up over a long, white, woollen scarf, he set out along the street.

The sun shone brightly over the freshly painted houses, but the weather was just as cold as when he'd done his morning round. The north-east wind bit more vigorously. George pushed on quickly. He passed a small elderly couple who greeted him by name. He replied when they were almost past him; they were the old folk who lived on the third floor. He stopped but they shuffled on.

'Too cold for standing about in the street,' he called after them.

They stopped, and the husband turned his head; his thin, white hair stood up against the wind in spikes. He was smiling.

'Ah, Mr Taylor,' he said, 'it *is* cold,' each word woodenly enunciated, before the two of them turned slowly away from him, dragging their small polished feet.

George pressed on at speed. Thank God the pavement was dry, with no signs of the morning's frost. He could step it out, leg it, without fear of slipping. At this pace he could have treated the world to a burst of song, but the cold wind on his cheekbones, on the crown of his head, inhibited him.

He reached the centre of town, marvelling how many people were about on a working day. A vulgar, cheerful call from across the road dragged him from his day-dream. 'Afternoon, Mr Taylor.'

The Smiths, arm in arm, but, oh, how changed. They were dressed for some grand occasion, he thought. Smith wore a long,

214

brand new, tweed overcoat with a matching, sporty hat. His wife, beside him, boasted a fire-red coat, with a white scarf and a basin-shaped scarlet felt hat with a prominent feather. These did not suit her, though George could not help inwardly applauding her efforts. She clung almost fiercely to her husband's arm, and smiled into the wind, teeth agleam.

'Isn't it beautiful?' she said, walking towards the sun.

'Do you know what it is?' Smith asked.

'Somebody's birthday?' George hazarded.

'Right,' Smith standing to attention. 'Mine.'

'How old is he?' Mrs Smith asked, coyly.

'Fifty-eight.'

Their laughter cackled. They swayed for joy.

'He's seventy.'

'Congratulations. It *is* an auspicious day,' George said, shaking them by the hand. Both wore brand-new kid gloves.

'What sort of day did you say it was?' Mrs Smith asked.

'Auspicious.'

'Is that good?'

'It means full of favourable omens. Prophesies good for the future. I don't know whether there is any difference between an auspice and a good omen. I think perhaps auspice is connected with the Latin "*avis*", a bird, but I wouldn't bet on it. And what have you done by way of celebration today?' he asked.

'We had lunch at the Mikado.'

'Was it good?'

'Nothing like as tasty or nourishing as what my wife serves at home.'

'Oh, thank you. That's because you haven't much experience of fine dinner.' Then to George, 'All their herbs and spices and wines are wasted on him. He's for plain cooking.'

'And now we're walking it off round the town, dressed in our Sunday best,' Smith said.

'You brighten the streets.'

They laughed their thanks.

'It's a good day for me,' George said. 'I've got myself a new job.'

'Can we guess?' Mrs Smith asked. 'I'll say,' she paused for extra thought or greater effect, 'Postmaster General?'

'Is there such an office today?' Smith asked. 'Wasn't he a cabinet minister?'

George stood, smiling.

'Not connected with the mail,' he said.

'Poet Laureate?' she tried again.

'No. Not bad. But this is a full-time, paid occupation. Lecturer in the Adult Education department at the university.'

'Perhaps if we find our retired life too empty we'll sign up to one of your evening classes.' Smith spoke solemnly. Mrs Smith hugged her husband's arm in support.

'Good idea. We can acquire that education you're always bemoaning.'

'There speaks a grammar-school girl. I'd like to learn Latin. I don't suppose you do that?'

All smiles, they parted after more trivia. George turned to look back at the beautifully dressed pair making their powerful way along the crowded pavement. He felt the better for these few minutes in their company.

At home he toyed with his newspaper, ate a leisurely tea, tidied his rooms in preparation for next morning's visit from his cleaning lady. He did not usually do this, but realised why he did so today; he was passing time until he could ring Mirabel at her home, and announce his new job. He did not know whether this would advance his chances as a prospective husband. He thought this was the case, but did not hold it against Mirabel.

He'd decided to ring her at 6.30. On an ordinary day she'd work until five o'clock, but there was no telling whether this was such a day. Sometimes she suddenly worked overtime and he could never decide why. It was her own choice, her seniors never seriously overloaded her with unexpected tasks. On the rare occasions they did so, she willingly stayed behind, because the work was usually interesting, and was seen by her as a test of her fitness for partnership.

The clock struck the half-hour. He compared it with the time on his wrist-watch, which was invariably accurate. He put down the pile of papers he was about to pack away, breathed deeply, straightened his jacket and then stared into the mirror. The reflection gave no encouragement, his face lacked colour, which time out of doors in more clement months would leave bronzed. His mouth drooped, his eyes seemed dark, without lustre, under his thick eyebrows which he had trimmed rather crudely. He turned away from the mirror, in no way comforted or encouraged. This would be the sort of day when Mirabel was not at home, had

216

chosen to take advantage of late-night shopping or gone to see some film with a woman-friend.

He went to the phone, looked sombrely at it, and dialled her number, expecting nothing.

'Hello.' Mirabel's voice sounded dull, giving nothing away.

'George here.'

'Oh, hello. Where have you been lately?'

'Hereabouts. I rang you one evening, but you weren't at home.'

'I've been about, since I came back from Durham.'

'Oh.' He had nothing to say.

'There was the funeral, then I helped Thomas begin to clear up. Janet had left me a keep-sake. It was a jewelled clock. A beautiful thing, with real diamonds; French, I think. And with that a small gold ring with a large, most beautifully green emerald.'

'That sounds expensive.'

'Nothing like the clock. Both of them belonged to her mother, and that's why she wanted me to have them.'

'Barron told you all this?'

'Yes. He spoke it all like a human being. Told me how Janet thought highly of me, claimed I had altered her life.' She drew in her breath. 'He surprised me. I had judged him as somebody so interested in his work he'd little or no time for ordinary observation and comment.

'By the way, some professor in America has now taken up some of his equations and, by using them, made a significant advance in astronomy. Don't ask me what. I learned this at the funeral from a colleague who had come down from Oxford, I think. It's as though the work keeps going on without him. And this latest development had made Thomas quite famous, inside their rather closed world. Only, next time somebody writes a book for the general public on what's new in the universe, he'll reap a considerable mention.'

'And this has made him into a human being?'

'That, and his wife's death.'

'Didn't Janet know all this about his theories?' George asked. 'She spoke of some developments – could she have imagined this?'

'She knew some of it and that increasingly his work was being justified. But she'd have been pleased, with this newly added application, that all his mathematics hadn't finally been wasted, despite disappointments throughout.'

217

'Did Barron himself not mention any of this to you?'

'He said it was pleasant to think that he had produced something that had proved so useful.'

'Good,' George agreed. 'Thank God he stuck at it, when nobody else paid any attention to what he was doing. It's a lesson to us all.'

'And he surprised me,' said Mirabel, 'in quite another way.'

'What was that?'

'He was telling me how much I had meant to Janet, and even said that I had made the last weeks of her life bearable for her.'

'That's true, isn't it?'

'I'd make no such claim for myself. But while he was explaining all this at length, he suddenly changed tack and said my visits had helped *him* along, while Janet was so ill.'

'Just by being there?'

'I don't know what he meant. I knew the two of them only for weeks rather than months. Just the short time between Andy's death and his mother's. And Thomas hardly had exchanged a word with me while I was there. I said as much to him.

'He agreed that he was not much of a sociable being, but said my effect on him had been tremendous; had kept him at his work while he saw Janet being taken away from him. I had changed his world, he said.'

'And this surprised you?'

'It did. But what came next surprised me more. He asked me if I would keep in touch with him, visit him occasionally. I said I would. He then turned to me, I nearly said on me, in a curious way. He asked me if I would seriously consider marrying him. He thought Janet would have approved. There was no great hurry for me to answer. I was to get to know him better.'

There was a pause. George felt his own news was insignificant after this. All this morning's younger optimism disappeared. His shoulders drooped.

'And what did you say?'

'I told him that I could make no such promise, that my thoughts in that direction were already elsewhere engaged.'

'To whom?'

She made him wait.

'Don't be silly. It's you.'

'You mean . . . ?' It had hit him like a catapulted pebble.

'That if you asked me again, I'd say yes.'

218

'I can't believe it.'

'Don't put the question now, then. Tomorrow will do. It will give you time to think the matter over.'

'I don't need that. My mind's made up. I love you.'

'Do as you're told. If you marry me, that's what you'll have to get used to. Come round tomorrow evening. Bring your things and stay the night.'

'I love you,' he said.

'I love you, if it comes to that. Now, what's your news?'

He explained, a little stiffly, about his appointment to the Adult Education department at the university. Mirabel congratulated him in a temperate way, using her best solicitor's tone. He thought she could have shown more enthusiasm, but suddenly it struck him that she had accepted him as a husband before she knew of his change of occupation.

'You hadn't heard?' he asked.

'No. Who would have told me?'

'I don't know. Word of anything spreads round this town like wild-fire.'

'Are you pleased?'

'I was. Until I heard what you had to tell me.'

'Oh?'

'I'm no Charles Lockwood. I'm nothing out of the ordinary.'

'If you were, I wouldn't be telling you this, nor would he want to hear it, or anything like it.'

'I can hardly believe it.'

'That's why I've given you twenty-four hours to let it sink in.'

'I don't need that. I feel like dancing like a madman round the room.'

'Be careful. Don't break anything. Are you at work tomorrow morning? And the day after?'

'Yes. Alas.'

'Don't worry. I've three alarm clocks. I'll see you're at work on time. Bring your bike round.'

'That's very banal advice.'

'That's what I do all day. Give dull and sensible advice. To keep people from acting rashly, against their own interests.'

'But they can't all have been as fortunate as I am. Why did you change your mind about me?'

'I didn't. I always found you attractive. But I wanted to avoid the trouble I found in marriage to Charles. Then I met Janet.'

'I'm not perfect, y'know.'

'I didn't say you were. I don't think you are. Or I shall get a surprise if you're anywhere near perfection.'

'I'm nowhere near your class either.'

'Do you mean social class?'

'You know I don't.'

Again a pause, so long he began to feel alarmed.

'Now, you. Just listen to me. If I am going to devote tomorrow evening to you, it means I have a couple of hours hard work to plough through tonight. I tell you what you can do. Go down to that fish shop of yours on the way here tomorrow, and bring us two great platefuls of plaice and chips. That'll free my mind.'

'Oh, thank you. I'm glad you've given me a little task that's not beyond my talent.'

'Well, then.'

'Well, then, what?'

'I'm going to close this conversation. We've said it all. And I have work to do. I'll repeat it again for you. George Taylor, I love you, and I want to marry you. All you have to do is to sit at home and think about it. Tomorrow evening you can go down on your knees and propose properly to me, if you're that kind of man. And I shall accept you and your proposal.'

'Is that what Charles did?'

'No. And while we're at it, I don't want his name dragged in at every verse-end. Understood?'

'Yes, ma'am,' he answered.

'Then, good night, young man. I love you.'

She replaced the phone in its cradle before he had time to reply, 'Young?' He stood breathless, the world's happiest man.

Or so he would have claimed.